STARSHIP
Librarians

STARSHIP
Librarians

EDITED BY
Shannon Allen and JR Campbell

TYCHE BOOKS LTD.

Starship Librarians
Copyright © 2025 Shannon Allen and JR Campbell

The publisher does not have any control over and does not assume any responsibility for author or third-party websites or their content.

This is a work of fiction. All of the characters, organizations, and events portrayed in this story are either the product of the authors' imagination or are used fictitiously.

Any resemblance to persons living or dead would be really cool, but is purely coincidental.

Published by Tyche Books Ltd.
Calgary, Alberta, Canada
www.TycheBooks.com

Cover Art by Lorna Antoniazzi
Cover Design by Indigo Chick Designs
Interior Layout by M.L.D. Curelas

Tyche Books Ltd Edition 2025
Print ISBN: 978-1-989407-86-8
Ebook ISBN: 978-1-989407-87-5

THE CARD CATALOGUE

010 : Table of Contents

INTRODUCTION

JR Campbell

A couple of points to begin with: First, I'd ask you to take a second and consider how you would define a library. Put a pin in that, shelve it for a moment; we'll come back to it in a minute. Got it? Thanks. My second point: As a long-time consumer of science fiction, literary and other media, it's incredibly rare to come across a science fiction universe that doesn't contain a library.

They seldom take the spotlight, but science fiction is rife with libraries. For a genre which spans such vast imaginative spaces, from utopias to dystopias, galaxy-spanning cultures to a dying civilization's last remnants, each vision goes to great lengths to name-drop their library. When Hari Seldon and his followers seek sanctuary in Trantor's Imperial Library, Doctor Zaius quotes from the lawgiver's scared scrolls, Captain Kirk and the crew of the *Enterprise* travel to Memory Alpha, the Doctor in THE Library, and Obi-Wan seeking a lost planet in the Jedi library, it's clear that, bleak or hopeful, a future without libraries is almost unimaginable.

At least, unimaginable to the science fiction consumer. There's a logic baked into this, science fiction is—in its pure form—based on science, which is based on reason. Without libraries and the history and knowledge they represent, how can reason persist?

It's time to take the pin from our first point, your definition of a library. Chances are you consider a library as a collection of books (or other media) accessible to (almost) anyone with an interest in that collection. Of course, as many of you are aware, borrowing and reading of material from a library by any interested individual is a historically recent notion, one which started in the late nineteenth century but took root in the twentieth. Before then, access to a library's information was tightly controlled by those who owned them. Previous libraries were open to the public for very, very narrow definitions of "the public". *Library* is one of those historically slippery words whose meaning has shifted subtly but significantly over time. At the time of this writing, it's almost certain your definition of a library means a collection of media accessible by those who need it. In other words, a public library, a concept which really did not exist a mere two hundred years ago.

A person from the eighteenth century could easily describe what a library was, but their description would not include the concept of public borrowing. That your definition includes the notion of public access is an example of how a new idea can quickly take root and change the world for the better. It is, in other words, amazing.

This is not to suggest the library revolution is over. There are still those who see no profit from such institutions, many who feel allowing the public to choose what they wish to read is somehow misguided, who feel that art should be limited to those who can afford it. They seek to rewind the calendar and return the concept of libraries to their ancient, privileged definition. For those who labour to ensure libraries remain public, you have our gratitude. More importantly, future generations will share our gratitude.

Of course, this anthology is not about libraries. It's about librarians, without whom the concept of the public library simply does not work.

While the definition of library has undergone a radical change, the same cannot be said of the concept of librarians. In literature and other media, the presentation of a librarian is usually accomplished with a number of unfortunate stereotypes. How many times have you seen a librarian recommending a book as opposed to telling someone why they cannot read it? How often is a librarian shown quieting the excitement of someone's discovery with an authoritative "shush" rather offering encouragement? These are clearly holdovers from a time when libraries were designed for the special few rather than the general public. As much as we've accepted a modern notion of libraries, many of our concepts regarding librarians remain firmly rooted in the distant past.

But not all of the librarian concepts are so negative. Among the cardigans, glasses, cats, and demands for silence, most of the librarians encountered in literature serve a particular function: A love interest. Again, the logic is straightforward. It's not unreasonable to expect someone surrounded by books to be well-read and, by extension, intelligent. Since the modern library is a public institution, offering assistance to those in need, a librarian is easy to present as kind and idealistic. Historically, since the public library revolution, most librarians have been women. As such, employing a librarian as a love interest is shorthand for so many positive traits, it's not surprising so they've captured the hearts of so many protagonists, time travelling or otherwise, even when the librarians were more interesting than those who fell in love with them.

In terms of narrative, nothing moves a story along like a librarian's info-dump or a shocking discovery within the pages of an all but forgotten book the protagonist was directed to by a kindly, knowing librarian.

Professionally, it is understood a librarian must be organized. This is likely why so many librarians in literature hold high positions in rebellions. Not only is it safe to assume they understand history, when pressed they are quite capable of organizing an uprising. Once I finish alphabetising these shelves, I need to smuggle weapons across the border. I must admit I find this juxtaposition of a quiet public life in the library with a private life of wild, extreme danger utterly delightful.

The genesis of this anthology lies in the rant of a family member complaining about the negative librarian tropes, an event kicked off by a deleted scene from *Star Trek: Insurrection* discovered on the internet. It's a scene full of outdated librarian tropes gathered together for a one-note joke which falls flat. Shannon and I, knowing the librarians in in these pages were unlikely to escape the librarian topes completely, were determined to be more respectful than that clip. We were seeking more thoughtful librarian stories, to give the librarians of science fiction a moment in the spotlight while showing our support for the current generation of librarians fighting the good fight on our behalf. Our hope is that you'll enjoy the following stories as much as we did. Tropes are played with, a variety of futures explored, there's love interests and rebel leaders, bright futures and dark, and through them all, the librarians and the library communities they serve.

Enjoy!

JR Campbell
May 2025

As a rule, themed Science Fiction anthologies rarely have an opportunity to speak with someone whose job description matches their titles. Astronauts are thin on the ground, aliens even more so; however, this anthology is delighted to include a short reflection from Sephora Henderson, current head librarian of the Merril Collection of Science Fiction & Fantasy at the Toronto Public Library. This collection, recognized as one of the finest Science Fiction and Fantasy collections in the world, was first established in 1970 when author and editor Judith Merril donated five thousand books to the Toronto Public Library. The Collection continues to grow, now containing more than eighty-five thousand items in its temperature-, humidity-, and light-controlled stacks. Open to the public, the Collection's holdings are reference-only, but can be requested and viewed in the reading room. If you can't make the journey, hundreds of items are accessible through the library's digital archives. The Merril collection is a treasure to all those afflicted with a love of speculative fiction. Sephora Henderson became Senior Department Head of the collection in 2017 and has graciously provided us with the following notes of her journey. The editors want to thank Sephora for indulging our interest in speaking with an actual science fiction—or should we say Starship— Librarian.

LIBRARIAN'S NOTE: MAKE YOUR OWN SHOES

Sephora Henderson

y friend, Peter Halasz, recommended a visit to the
Merril Collection to his friend, Nalo Hopkinson. She
sent me an email, introducing herself and telling me
that although she had a tight schedule, she was willing to come
by for a visit and sign a few of her books, as suggested by Peter.
Now, a quick search of the Merril Collection catalogue will tell
you that there are ninety-one items attributed to Nalo
Hopkinson—novels, short stories, anthologies, and graphic
novels. Her signature graces some of these items, but there were
yet a few full-length novels that were unsigned. She certainly
needed no introduction, and her presence would be an honour. I
was thrilled.

On the day of her visit, she arrived at the Collection early in
the day. She was heading back to her home on the west coast
imminently, but you'd never guess—she was unrushed and
generous with her time, and I felt incredibly lucky to sit and talk
with her. We talked a bit about my history with the Collection—I
told her that I assumed leadership of the department after the
retirement of my predecessor, Lorna Toolis. Lorna spent over
thirty years as the Head of the Collection, and was a fixture in the
Science Fiction and Fantasy community here in Toronto.

Many years ago, when I was a newly minted Librarian, I had a
conversation with a colleague with whom I had forged a bond, as
she was also a big Science Fiction and Fantasy enthusiast. I

remember telling her that I thought Lorna Toolis had the best job in the entire library system. My colleague allowed that it would be magical to work at the Merril Collection someday, but resolutely relieved me of any grander aspirations, as she was certain that no one could ever replace Lorna. That particular thought hadn't even crossed my mind; I was, rather, expressing my admiration for her station at the helm of such an extraordinary Collection.

I told Nalo that my goal is to continue the good work for which Lorna had laid the foundation. I also acknowledged feeling some pressure because I felt like I had big shoes to fill, and Nalo gently shook her head, looked me in the eyes, and said, quite seriously, "Make your own shoes." I've thought about that moment a lot in the last few years. Her statement made me feel reassured in a way that I can't quite describe. I think about it from time to time and feel flooded with gratitude. As a woman of colour myself, facing all of the challenges that that entails, her advice was like a benediction.

My early days at the Collection were busy with requests for interviews from the local media. Some were newly discovering the Merril Collection and wanted to highlight this curious Toronto space, and for others it was news because there hadn't been a new Head of Collection in thirty years (and I am only the fourth since its establishment), so who was I?

My earliest forays into the fantastic began on the silver screen and would journey onto the page before long. Mine was a very odd and solitary childhood. Long before the digital days, my father was a film projectionist, and I spent most of my childhood inside of a projection booth, or in a movie theatre. I saw the inside of every projection booth within a hundred-kilometre radius of Toronto by the time I was ten. Everyone has a sound that they hear when everything is quiet, something that makes them think clearer or makes them feel calm—for me it's the sound of film moving through a projector. I have celluloid in my blood. Perhaps the film that made the largest impression on me was *E.T. the Extra-Terrestrial*. In 1982, most kids were desperate for the opportunity to see it even once on the big screen; I saw it nine times in the first few weeks of its release, just from touring around with Dad. As an only child, books were my other company and remain a great solace to this day. I had increased borrowing privileges at my school library because I was known to read voraciously, and also to treat books carefully (my first job would be as a Page in my high school library, go figure!). I remember always being drawn to science fiction and fantasy. Initially, I would choose books for their interesting covers—I didn't know anyone who enjoyed the genre who could recommend anything in particular, and I read just about anything that was available. I'm not sure when I picked up the book that would remain my forever favourite, but *Dune* changed my whole world! When I started my job at the Merril Collection, one of the first things I did was to go to that section of the stacks and look at the copies in the collection with no small measure of awe.

When I think back to my journey here, I think I have, in one way or another, always been "making my own shoes"—I'm just not sure I thought of it in such intrepid or bold or confident terms. I've always had an inner sense of determination when it came to certain endeavours—school, music, learning languages—but I've also always been a little shy. I've always been content to let others shine and to lend support from the fringes, in whatever way I can. My leadership role at the Merril Collection is somewhat at odds with my personality, and yet somehow it is a perfect fit.

Sephora Henderson
Senior Department Head
Merril Collection, Lillian H. Smith Branch, Toronto Public Library
May 2025

HOW TO SAVE A LIFE

C.N. Wheaton

The right story can save your life.

That's what the plaque on the edge of the library desk said anyway. How many times had I looked at it without seeing it?

As for why I'd put it into my pocket when the ship was being invaded . . . well, I'd needed to grab onto *something*.

Then I was hit with a stun-bolt and woke up all alone in a cell. The walls and floor were a dark red-purple that was oddly damp and squishy in a way that reminded me of raw meat. Filaments of yellow light were threaded throughout the odd material, not enough to truly illuminate the space so much as make it full of shadows. There was no door I could see, no door I could find even when I subdued my revulsion long enough to touch the walls.

I took the plaque out of my pocket and traced the familiar words as I tried to keep it together. "Hello?" The word came out as a whisper. I swallowed and tried again. "Is anybody out there?" I asked, my voice high and anxious, half-afraid of the answer.

"Ellison? Is that you?" The voice was from the other side of the wall.

"Kimura?" I asked a little louder, standing up, hope rising. "Are you here to get me out?" Of all the members of the Flight Corps—the ones who flew the ships, explored new planets, and made treaties with alien nations—Kimura was the one I trusted most.

There was a long pause. "I wish." His voice was rueful.

"Oh." I collapsed back down, wincing as my hand hit the clammy floor. "Is it just us in here?"

"No." The deep baritone was instantly recognizable as the head of the Health Corps, Dr. Obeng. It sounded like he was on the other side of the wall to my left.

"I regret to report I'm here too," said a wry voice from across the room. "Rebecca Littlejohn from Engineering."

"And me. Bouchard; Science."

There was another pause, but nobody else chimed in. "Okay," Kimura said, sounding much more in control than I felt. "First, is anybody injured?"

"I am unharmed," Dr. Obeng shared. The rest of us murmured our agreement.

"Good. Now we just need to find our way out of here. Littlejohn, Bouchard, what can you tell us about where we're being held?"

"Well, it's definitely in the top three creepiest places I've ever been," Littlejohn said cheerfully. I smiled in spite of our surroundings.

"Anything else?" Kimura asked.

"Haven't found a door yet. Don't worry; I'll give you a shout when I do."

"All of these components are organic in nature. Possibly Jaloo construction?" There was a *zap* and then a string of curses in French. When she stopped swearing, Bouchard spoke up again. "*Definitely* Jaloo."

Kimura let out a low whistle. "Not good, but they're unlikely to kill us. We must have been taken by an unsanctioned raiding party from one of those splinter groups that insist on observing humans. The last one I read about held their captives for years before ransoming them back. Keep looking for a way out, you two."

Littlejohn and Bouchard moved to an area of their respective cells closer to each other and further away from where I was sitting. Their discussion quickly became technical enough that I tuned it out. Staring at the fleshy-looking ceiling above me, I wished I had something to read.

A little while later, a hole appeared in the ceiling, glowing yellow as it widened. I watched it, frozen in fear. Through the walls, I could hear everyone react in alarm. Then a package fell through the hole and landed on the floor with a *plop*. Inside the package was a ball about the size of my fist. It was glowing too, the light fading in and out.

"Kimura?" I asked, hating the way my voice trembled. "Did something just appear in your cell too?"

But Dr. Obeng was the one who spoke first. "I think we all got one. It's labelled like food. From what I've read, Jaloo have a similar physiology to humans." He paused. "But we probably shouldn't eat it all at the same time, just in case."

I picked up the package. "I'll try it," I volunteered, surprising even myself. "I'm the least important one here."

"No," Kimura immediately responded. "It should be me."

The thought of him getting hurt was so upsetting that I didn't even think, ripping open the package and taking a bite of the hard, glowing ball even as I dimly heard him ordering me to stand down. The flavour was a cross between banana and chicken. I choked it down. Then I let out a weak laugh. "How long should we wait to see if I die?"

Dr. Obeng and Bouchard started debating the toxicity levels of various compounds. I sat there, feeling useless. Technically, librarians were part of the Health Corps too, a fact which had never made much sense to me and was making less sense by the second. As a librarian, I knew how to find information on poisons, could rattle off call numbers and databases and titles, but those facts weren't just something I had in my head. I'd never managed more than basic first aid skills. Dr. Obeng, Bouchard, Littlejohn, and Kimura all had specialized training that was always with them, always useful. Without my books and media files, was I even still a librarian?

The hours crawled by.

At some point I fell asleep. As much as I wished I'd be somewhere else when I woke up, nothing had changed when I opened my eyes again.

Kimura said my name. "Ellison, report."

"Still here," I managed. The food was strange and the floor was clammy, but I felt a bit better anyway. "So, are we getting out?"

"Littlejohn and Bouchard are working on it, although we might be here a while," Kimura said, voice rueful.

"It is important to keep up our strength. Everyone should

exercise," Dr. Obeng shared. "Jumping jacks, weight bearing exercises like yoga, and dance, are all good options. I'm sure you all know the dangers of being sedentary."

Being trapped in a cell made of raw meat was nightmarish enough without adding P.E. class, but the idea seemed to cheer up Kimura, so I agreed. Then, while I was doing jumping jacks, the plaque fell out of my pocket.

Seeing it gave me an idea.

As soon as we'd all finished exercising, I blurted it out. "Let's tell each other stories."

"What?" Bouchard asked.

My cheeks felt hot and I was grateful that none of them could see me blush. I cleared my throat. "I've heard of living libraries, where you can check out a person for a while to have a conversation. We might not have any media with us, but we all have stories, don't we? Whether we've lived them or love them."

"Good idea, Ellison," Kimura said, voice kind. "Do you want to start us off?"

I felt momentarily tongue-tied. "Oh. I . . . I didn't have one in mind."

"I can go," Dr. Obeng shared. "This is one my grandmother told me that her grandmother told her. There once was a spider called Anansi . . ."

After his story about the trickster god, Dr. Obeng continued on, telling us about his loving, boisterous family, scattered all across the stars. He shared how he met his wife in line at a hospital cafeteria on Earth. When he mentioned he'd been in the library to get a book for her on the day we were captured, his voice broke.

We were all quiet after that.

Finally, Littlejohn spoke up. "You know, Anansi sounds a lot like Coyote. I'll tell you one of those stories someday, when we're back home. But, right now, the story on my mind is *Rancho Corazón*, a telenovela my sister and I watch on holo-call every week. You see, it all started with Catalina, coming back to the family ranch to find it's on the brink of ruin. The boy she used to love is working to destroy it and the boy she used to hate is her only hope . . ."

Even Dr. Obeng swore under his breath when Littlejohn got to the most recent episode and we still didn't know if Catalina was going to find her lover before the storm hit. Then Littlejohn told us more about her sister, who she'd grown up hiking with in California. She shared about her favourite trail in such detail I could feel the mist on my face and hear the oak leaves crunching underfoot.

As the ceiling opened up and a glowing banana-chicken flavoured ball dropped through again, Kimura spoke up. "I keep thinking about my kitchen . . ."

He told us about his favourite recipes, waxing lyrical about the things he could do with tofu and vegetables I'd never even tried. If I closed my eyes and held my nose, I could just about imagine that's what we were eating. As he went on to tell us about his childhood cat, Haru, there was a smile in his voice.

I could picture that smile.

Kimura dropped by the library every week for a new book. So many people looked past us at the library—eager to see someone more important or just interested in getting their media—but he had always been kind. His smile was like sunshine. He liked mysteries and poetry and nature writing.

And I liked him.

But I'd never gotten up the courage to say anything.

Of course, my crush wasn't the story I wanted to share. Fortunately, while my own life was quiet and uneventful—stint in an alien prison notwithstanding—it wasn't the only life I'd lived, thanks to all the stories I'd read. Although I'd struggled to think of one when I was put on the spot, I'd finally decided. When I opened my mouth, however, I was stopped by a song.

The lilting melody was coming from Bouchard. Goosebumps erupted on my arms. I'd had no idea she could sing, much less that she could sing like *that*. When Bouchard finished, she said, sounding sheepish, "It's from my favourite musical."

"Oh! I thought it seemed familiar!" Littlejohn laughed. "You're incredible."

The rest of us rushed to agree.

Bouchard was clearly pleased when she spoke again. "Thank you. I could teach you the song if you like?"

None of us had a voice like hers, but there was something so human about singing together. Even though we were all sealed in our own solitary cells, we could create something that made our surroundings more bearable.

Bouchard's discussion of the musicals she'd been a part of transitioned into telling us the drama in the science department of her university. "It's true! I thought he would launch himself over the table!"

"Over dirt?"

"*Soil.* And yes."

Then Bouchard moved on to talking about her favourite genre: horror. It wasn't one I liked—even *before* my surroundings resembled a horror movie—although I appreciated Bouchard's passion for understanding our fears in order to confront them. I'd never been very good at that, but the universe seemed intent on making me learn.

After that, it was my turn. "I don't know every word," I warned, "but I'm going to tell you a story that's meant a lot to me. It's about a man who just wants to get home . . ."

Recounting *The Odyssey* took a while. Sirens and sorceresses and whirlpool monsters and cyclops and more lies than you could shake a stick at later, Odysseus had finally reunited with Penelope.

When I finally finished my story—several days later—the wall of the cell cracked open. "Hurry!" a voice urged.

They didn't need to ask twice. I stood up, stowing the plaque from the library in my pocket, before squeezing through the wall of the cell. In a small central area, I saw Kimura, Littlejohn, Dr. Obeng, and Bouchard emerging from their own cells, looking as confused as I felt.

A Jaloo stepped out from the shadows. Their skin was the same purple-red as our surroundings. With spindly legs, they towered over Dr. Obeng. Oversized eyes blinked at us owlishly. "Follow me. I'm getting you out of here."

"Why?" I blurted out.

"I want to know what happens to Catalina," they admitted. "And I would miss my brood partner too, like he does." They nodded at Dr. Obeng. "I want them to be reunited like your Odysseus and Penelope."

"Won't you get in trouble?" I asked as we started following the Jaloo away from the prison section of the ship. Bouchard squeezed my arm in warning.

Our Jaloo jailor hesitated. "Yes. Even so, I still want to help. I'd always heard humans were dangerous, but I do not think we are really so different, you and I."

"I could knock you out," Kimura said after a moment. We all stared at him. He shrugged, looking sheepish. "That way you could tell them we overpowered you."

The Jaloo looked down at us. "I do not think that would work."

"Then come with us. Bring your brood partner," Kimura said, and I fell a little more in love with him just for that.

"I will happily watch every single episode of *Rancho Corazón* with you," Littlejohn promised. "Honestly, it's even better than I described."

That settled it. With a nod and their version of a smile, our alien rescuer ensconced us in a shuttle and sent a short-wave transmission to their partner. An agonizing length of time later, a second Jaloo arrived with a small bundle of things.

They told us the story of how they met as we made the nail-biting journey away from the Jaloo ship, huddling under the heat-reflecting blankets that Bouchard and Dr. Obeng swore could help hide us from any scans.

When the Jaloo parked us on a moon near where our ship had been attacked, Littlejohn jury-rigged a way to send a message to our ship. And then we waited.

After a day where every worst-case scenario danced through my mind, a message finally arrived. With coordinates to a nearby shipyard where our ship was being repaired, our little group set off again. As soon as we saw our home, I wasn't the only one with tears in my eyes.

It hadn't been destroyed.

Though the Jaloo drew strange glances as we disembarked the shuttle, word of their defection had spread, and Littlejohn glared fiercely at anyone who even *thought* about reaching for a weapon. Once we were all safely onboard, we were given the chance to shower, change, and eat a meal that didn't glow or taste like banana-chicken. Then we were led away, one-by-one, for debriefing.

Since I was the least important, my interview happened last.

I slipped into the chair across the table from Captain Chopra. My boss, Head Librarian Jeffries, smiled at me encouragingly from their seat. I answered all of their questions, telling them my time in captivity with as much detail as I could stomach.

As I got up to leave, the captain cleared her throat. "Your colleagues said you saved their lives."

"I—what?"

The captain smiled. "I'm putting you up for a commendation."

I stammered my thanks. Still reeling, I left the interview room, only to bump straight into Kimura. He smiled down at me and I felt warm all the way to my toes. "Oh good, I was hoping to find you," he said. "Can I cook for you?"

"Yes," I said at once, overeager. Then I took a breath. "I mean, thank you. I'd like that. Is there anything I can bring?"

"How about a book?" he called over his shoulder as he walked away.

I was still smiling when Head Librarian Jeffries came out. Together, our steps led us to the library. Since the breach had happened there, our whole collection was in disarray. My smile slipped. As I bent down to pick up a fallen book, I felt the plaque in my pocket where I'd put it after my shower. I pulled it out. "I'm sorry for taking this."

My boss patted my hand. "I'm not. It did its job. And you did yours."

"I don't know why they said I saved their lives," I admitted.

Jeffries scoffed. "I do. You could have died in that prison. You didn't because you kept each other sane. That Jaloo guard only helped you because of the stories you suggested everyone tell. So don't ever think you don't matter." They stooped down to gather more books from the floor. "Now, go on and get ready for your date. The work will still be here tomorrow."

They squeaked when I hugged them.

As I set out for my date with a racing heart and a volume of love poetry, that old plaque caught my eye again. How many times had I looked at it without seeing it?

But I finally understood. No ship is complete without a librarian for one simple reason: bodies can starve, but hearts can too. Stories remind us we aren't alone. They connect us across space and time. Whether we're locked in an alien prison or a different sort of struggle entirely, it's those connections that save us.

That's what stories are for. As for librarians? We're trained to help you find the right story . . . the one that can save your life.

THE LIBRARIAN OF MARS

Kara Race-Moore

3 hours until MECC arrival

Emma Chen, chief librarian of Mars, tossed another bundle of tarp-wrapped books into the ravine. With a soft *thud* the latest bundle hit the desert floor. She was trying to spread the drops out so they wouldn't all crash on top of each other, but there was no time to do any of this properly.

As she hefted the next bundle out of the rover, her arms screaming in protest, she thought longingly of having enough time and equipment to do this better, to have any of this be remotely thought out or planned.

She stumbled on a rock and struggled to right herself without dropping the awkward package. She blinked as spots danced in front of her eyes. All the caffeine in her system couldn't fight the ache in her eyeballs. *I'll sleep in the rover*, she promised herself, willing her body to keep moving just a little longer.

The radio in her bio-suit helmet crackled to life. "Emma? Emma?"

"Yes, I'm here," she responded, panting as she lugged the tarp bundle to the edge, knocking rusty coloured pebbles down the chasm.

"Yeah, and so will the MECC, soon. Heads up, last convoy is getting ready to leave."

"Understood. I'm almost done with this load." With a grunt,

she tossed the bundle down. From the weight, she was pretty sure that one had all been medical textbooks. "I'll be back at the hangar in less than twenty."

"See you in fifteen. Remember, we've got to be out of here before the fireworks."

"Copy that. Over and out." Back at the rover, she pulled out another package of books; these were all stuffed inside an old duffle bag stamped with the Harvard logo. The way these books shifted around indicated to her a mix of beach-read paperbacks and children's picture books. Back at the edge of the ravine, she tossed it down with the others, turning back to get another before it even hit the bottom. She was running out of time.

This was insane. Three days ago, she had been dancing at the colony's New Year's Eve party, drinking the latest batch of Mars One homebrew and eating poppyseed cake, celebrating with everyone else the momentous year of astounding scientific discoveries. And now she, and the rest of the (now technically former) colonists were bracing for an invasion.

45 hours until MECC arrival

Emma suspected she had the same stunned expression on her face as everyone else around her as they stumbled out of the town hall meeting. The residents of Mars One had not only just voted to secede from Earth, declare independence, and start their own nation, but had also agreed to evacuate, empty, and then destroy Mars One, so the Mars Exploration and Colonization Company, formerly their founding patron and now very much the enemy, could not use it.

The MECC had sent a message to tell Mars One that the regular supply convey that was two days' out from arriving on Mars would not be a regular supply delivery at all but would be delivering "agents" who would oversee turning the colony into a commercial depot. The message instructed the colonists to prepare living space for these agents and be ready and on hand to assist them when they arrived. The MECC declared Mars One would now be dedicated to harvesting the plant life just discovered on Mars, known as the "Mars moss." The alien plant had turned out to cure cancer as well as host of other human health issues, and, with trillions of dollars on the line, the company stated it could no longer support a colony on Mars devoted to something as unprofitable as pure scientific research.

Oh, and all children would be shipped back to Earth, while all adults would be conscripted to gather the alien plant, and the colonists better get with the program. The colonists were very much *not* going to get with this program.

Anne Kennedy, the first human born on Mars had, minutes before, been the head administrator of the Mars One local government but now had taken on the role of leader of this first nation on Mars. Kennedy had instructed everyone to pack a personal bag with the bare minimum and then start packing up vital equipment such as the oxygen generators, medical supplies, food, and everything else that was imperative to survival.

At the end of the meeting Emma's wife, Gwyneth Lloyds, had given her a hurried kiss and told her that she had was going to be with Anne helping with logistics planning. Clearly her role as the Mars One township clerk was about to expand considerably. Emma nodded and then hurried towards the library.

Emma knew the books in the Mars One library would not make anyone's version of a list of "vital equipment," but she was going to try and save as many as she could. She would not, could not, just walk away from them. To start, she put her hand on the shoulder of the person nearest her in the hall, Jiya Patel. "Swing by the library and grab a few books for your personal bag," she instructed. She made an attempt at a grin. "Something for the ride to Labyrinth Sation. And tell everyone else to do the same." Chuckling, Jiya agreed, then hurried off.

Emma repeated the message to everyone she passed as she headed to the room grandly labelled the "Mars One Public Library Main Branch." She had made the sign herself out of broken computer chips tiled together to proudly spell out the name of the first library on Mars.

People back on Earth were often surprised to learn there were books on Mars. But people, Emma reflected, were often idiots. There were books everywhere, in cities, towns, villages, farms, on submarines and Antarctic science bases, and even on the space stations—why wouldn't humans bring books with them to Mars?

She didn't know what the room had meant to be originally, but she had built up the small area from a bland storage area for books shared by the original handful of colonists to a space that was cozy and welcoming. The shelves were positioned to provide little reading nooks, each with an armchair or two, carefully assembled from flat-packed furniture kits from Earth, softened with air cushions, and covered with homemade goat hair fabric. One corner of the room was the Children's section, marked out by low shelves filled with bright picture books and the area filled with tiny chairs, cushions, games, and toys.

All of the books that made up the library had been donated over the years, either by people who had come to Mars One and given their personal books to the library so everyone else could read them, or donated by people back on Earth and sent up on supply ships, usually as part of some PR stunt by an Earth politician or celebrity. Everyone thought it was an original idea to send books about Mars. Emma had outright begged the supply ship's cargo master to refuse any more copies of *A Princess of Mars*. As it was, Mars One had enough copies to supply almost every resident with a copy of the old pulp adventure. Emma used the hard copy versions as doorstops.

Still, despite the uneven approach to acquiring books, they had a rough representation of all genres, almost as well stocked as any remote, small-town library. She pulled up the main database, put in her administrator access code, and looked up the overall total. She glanced from the screen to the room. The library currently held 15,194 books. Yesterday she would have been sad they didn't have more for the rapidly growing population of Mars. Today she despaired at how she could save them all. But, as chief (and only) librarian, she knew she had to try.

Like so many of her generation, she had made her job up. Before, volunteers had run the library on top of whatever their "real" job was. But she had seen the need to expand the use of the library and told Anne Kennedy, as chief executive administrator of Mars One—someone else who had made up her job when she'd seen the need—that she, Emma Chen, was now the official head librarian of the Mars One Public Library.

She had pulled support by becoming a "sister library" with several libraries on Earth—including the Sir Edmund Hillary Library of Auckland, New Zealand—who had all provided lots of ideas and cheerleading, but for the most part she had done the groundwork of revitalizing the library by herself.

And now all of it—the reference section, the children's section, the educational resources, the recreational reading in all genres—all of it was to be either hastily packed up or left behind for destruction. Even if everyone took a few as part of their personal items, it wouldn't be enough—and no way would Anne Kennedy authorize space that could be going to food supplies and repair tools for books. But Emma refused to just walk away.

Emma surveyed the rows of books meditatively, assessing the options. Books could withstand cold temperatures. Damage was caused by humidity, and that was not something one had to worry about on the surface of Mars. If she just left them outside, far enough from Mars One to avoid whatever was decided the best way to destabilize it, as well as far away from whatever punitive actions the MECC might take, and give the books some sort of cover . . .

She dashed over to the maps area of the reference section and pulled out the latest survey map of the area immediately around Mars One, heavily detailed from all the explorations done by the people who called Mars One "home." She ran her finger along the paper, following one of the popular hiking trails.

The site for Mars One had been chosen for the warm temperatures found near the equator, and for the broad plateau that had been easily made into a runway for ships landing and taking off. However, even in the flat area, there were still plenty of formations roughing up the landscape. She slid her finger over a marking of a small fissure that snaked its way across the plain, the result of ancient rivers and floods, and today, bone dry. She could make it there in less than half an hour in one of the manned rovers. More like 15 minutes if she ignored the usual safety precautions.

To start, she pulled out the few crates she had in the library supply closest. She was about to dump out all the children's activities materials onto the floor, but stopped, struck by an idea. She hastily consolidated one crate with everything she had that would keep kids occupied. That she would insist on going with the first convoy of rovers filled with the Mars One children.

As Emma began loading up books, she was mindful of weight, knowing they would have to be moved at least part of the way by hand. She layered the bottoms of boxes with flat picture books, then a layer of hardback books, then lighter paperbacks, pausing to test the weight now and then before continuing to fill them.

People began to stop by, grabbing a few books. She cheerfully encouraged everyone to take as many as they could carry, and not worry about which ones, reassuring everyone she would organize a book swap when they were all at the Labyrinth, the science station perched on the edge of the Valles Marineris, the largest canyon in the Solar System. The station, the only other habitation on Mars, was named for the section of the canyon it overlooked—the Noctis Labyrinthus, Latin for "Labyrinth of the Night," due to all the twisty turns of the numerous branches of the canyon. And heading into a labyrinth never sounded so apt as it did now.

41 hours until MECC arrival

As she was closing the now-filled crates, a tiny four-year-old boy and his mother arrived, almost as if it was an ordinary day with Story Hour about to begin, except he was wearing one of the children-sized blue bio-suits, just needing the helmet in order to go outside.

"Ms. Chen, Ms. Chen!" he shouted, then, remembering he was in the library, whispered-shouted: "Ms. Chen! Can I have the dragon book? Please . . . Please . . . Please!"

His mother, Rashi Barker-Singh, looked at Emma with pleading eyes as big as her son's. "Please tell me you still have it," she begged, her accent still slightly British, despite all her years in the polyglot Mars One. She glanced fearfully at the crates of already packed up books. "He's refusing to leave without it."

Toby had checked out the picture book *Dragons Do Dance!* so many times that all he had to say was "the dragon book" and Emma knew exactly which book he meant.

"Well Toby, today is your lucky day," Emma told him. She took him by the hand and led him over to the Children's section. "I'm packing up A to Z, and your dragon book is by—" she paused, looking at him expectantly.

"Zelda Zirinsky!" he finished excitedly.

She said a silent prayer of thanks for the author's choice of pen name as she plucked the book off the shelf and handed it to him. She happened to know this author had a pen name for each of the multiple genres she wrote in; for example, her Romance pen name was Wendy Wexcomb while her Mystery pen name was Marguerite MacVane.

"Now," she told him solemnly, "it's very important you keep it safe on your journey to Labyrinth Station."

He deflated somewhat at this stark reminder this wasn't an ordinary visit to the library. "Mama says I have to go without her or Daddy," he told Emma, his eyes big, on the verge of tears.

"It's just that you get to go first, honey bear!" said his mother over-brightly, her voice as thin as cheap glass. "We'll all be there soon, Mama just has to finish packing, then I'll meet you there!"

He did not look convinced.

Emma saw all the warning signs of an incoming meltdown and decided to act. She knelt beside him. "Do you remember at Story Hour a few weeks ago when I read the book about the butterflies escaping a storm of war?"

Toby nodded.

"This is like that. You are now the brave butterfly. You see, back on Earth, there is a group of people who have been hypnotized by money, and they think, if they grab all the Mars moss that Dr. Patel found, because we discovered it's such a good medicine, then they will get even more money, so they are sending soldiers to take you and all your friends to Earth and keep you there until your parents and all the adults here on Mars give them all the Mars moss."

OK, it was a gross oversimplification of a very complicated situation, but it got down to brass tacks, which clearly this four-year-old needed to hear. And, hell's bells, when she had picked that book, she had just been trying to gently introduce the topic of refugees on Earth to the young readers, never imagining it would be applicable to them on Mars. She glanced at his mother, who nodded at her to keep going.

"So, we are going to leave Mars One and go to the science base in the Canyon—the Labyrinth Station. We must take turns because we don't have enough rovers to shuttle everyone all at once, so, just like I'm packing *A* to *Z*, we're sending people by age, from youngest to oldest. That means you're in the first group of everyone age one to sixteen, and your mom and dad will come later."

"So, I'm an *A* and Mama and Dad are *Z*s?" Toby asked.

"More like *H*s," huffed Rashi, clearly affronted at how old being a *Z* made her sound. "The Original Seven—they are the *Z*s."

"Right," said Emma, "your parents will be right behind you. And in the meantime, you'll be with your friends."

"OK," he agreed reluctantly.

She pointed at his backpack. "And today, *today* you get to take as many books as you can fit in that backpack—no limits!"

His eyes went wide. "Really?"

"Really, really. *Buuuuut*, you have to fill up the bag in just one minute because then you'll have to head out." She pointed at the grandfather clock standing at the back wall. They both watched the second hand reach the "oo" at the top. "Go!" she shouted. With that Toby raced towards the low shelves and began grabbing brightly coloured picture books and jamming them into his bag.

While he did that, Emma pulled over the crate of children's activities. "Take this and put it on the rover with Toby. It's a bunch of drawing materials and games. No matter what anyone says, make sure they get it, it's important."

Rashi nodded. "I will, thanks. And I can take a few books with me, too, as part of my personal allotment." She gestured at the messenger bag slung over her shoulder.

"Good," said Emma. "Take whatever you can hold."

Rashi flailed for a few moments as she glanced around, momentarily looking as overwhelmed as Emma felt, then, mostly due to proximity, grabbed several books on the American Revolution from the History section. "The Yanks might have some good tips," she said self-consciously as she stuffed them in her bag.

Emma burst out laughing, then, glancing at the clock, called: "Thirty seconds!" to Toby.

"I bet we won't be able to take that with us," Rashi said, nodding at the clock, and Emma sobered as the enormity of everything being left behind hit her. "That project was such a nightmare," Rashi went on in a wistful voice. "No one had ever made a clock like that before."

The grandfather clock had been a student project for the senior class of the Mars One Public School several years ago. The student population on Mars had only then grown big enough to have a senior class big enough to do a group project.

Emma pointed at a framed *Time* magazine cover on the wall near the clock. "But you all made the news."

"True, but, come on, back then Martian students doing anything made the news." She smiled. "Still, it was quite a project, writing the code for the parts as well as assembling them after we 3D printed them."

"And you ended up with a working Martian clock, perfectly marking every day's twenty-four hours, thirty-seven minutes and twenty-two seconds."

"Yeah—for another few hours at least."

"Still, you all got *A*s. And an ice cream party! That was one of my first projects when I took over the library, arguing it should be a community space and not just a book dumping ground."

Rashi laughed and said reminiscently, "Slyvia the Fourth made the *best* goat milk ice cream!"

"Good thing our goats are all pygmies," said Emma, wondering who was going to be stuck driving a rover full of goats. She watched the second hand come back to the 00. "Time!" she shouted.

Toby trotted back over to his mother and Emma, a proud grin on his face as he held out the bulging backpack.

"Great job!" said Emma. She bent down and hugged him. "Have a good trip! And I'll see you at Labyrinth Station!"

"Bye, Ms. Chen!" he said cheerfully as he gave her a wave. He toddled away under the weight of his backpack while his mother managed to lift the crate with both hands, both looking much better than when they had walked in.

Emma felt the smile slide off her face once they were out of sight, at how many lives were being uprooted and how much would be left behind, thanks to the greed of a few people millions of miles away. She grabbed a 150th anniversary special illustrated edition of *A Princess of Mars* and threw it across the room. "God damn the MECC," she cursed. She took a deep breath, then went back to closing the crates.

39 hours until MECC arrival

"If no one knows how to do this, then we'll just have to make it up as we go."

It was a common saying for her generation, the first generation born on Mars and having to figure out what adulthood would mean for them. She repeated it now as she scrambled to get more books ready for their hasty storage.

Extra boxes weren't available as everyone packed the

essentials, but if she took the tarp they used on field expeditions, and used it like wrapping paper to make giant presents, tied up with the bungee cord they had in abundance, since it was so useful, she could make serviceable bundles that could be moved and provide some protection from the wind and dust.

She grabbed books by size and weight to make the bundles; she made no distinction between the types of books, no attempt to prioritize what some might deem "the most important." She grabbed books by weight and size to make the most efficient bundles time would allow. Occasionally titles would register as she stacked them—*A Tree Grows in Brooklyn, The Immortal Life of Henrietta Lacks, Vermeer's Camera, My Man Jeeves, Vingt Mille Lieues sous les Mers, A Brief History of Time, The Complete Grimm's Fairy Tales, The Voyage of the Beagle*—but they were just flashes of comfort as she kept her hands in constant motion, stacking books and bundling them up.

She did, however, have to stop and stare when she grabbed a thin middle-grade book titled *Mars Is No Place For Children!* and just giggled at the irony. She thrust it on top of the pile and hastily began tying up the latest bundle before the enormity of what she was doing—helping to destroy humanity's first interplanetary home—overwhelmed her.

With this last one tied up, she realized she was rapidly running out of room; it was time to start moving them out. She picked up her comm and pressed the button for her wife.

Gwyn picked up at once. "Yes, my girl, holding up OK?"

"Yes, and you?" she asked, wincing she hadn't given any thought to what Gwyn must be going through.

"Absolute chaos, but in a productive kind of way," said Gwyn firmly, sounding like she was in full keep-calm-and-carry-on mode. "We got all of the children off in the first convoy with a lot of essential supplies."

"That's great," said Emma, hoping her crate of children's activities had made it on. "Listen, I need a rover. For the books."

Gwyn groaned. "My love, we can't—"

"Just to store them! I know we can't take them with us! I'm packing them up to stay safe outside, but I just need one rover to ferry them to safety away from Mars One. There has got to be at least one that can't make the seven hundred-kilometer ride to Labyrinth Station but can at least handle a few quick trips back and forth just outside Mars One. Please? Please, please, please?" she begged, then almost laughed when she realized how much she sounded like Toby.

"I'll see what I can do," Gwyn told her in clipped tones.

"Thank you," breathed out Emma reverently.

"No promises! But keep packing!" With that, Gwyn ended the call.

Frantically, Emma kept making bundles. She tried not to look at the grandfather clock, forcing herself to look only at the books in front of her, trying not to imagine what Anne Kennedy might say when asked to spare a rover "just" to save books.

A millennium, or few minutes, later, a knock on the open door jolted her out of her worries; it was Dr. Calvin "First Step" FitzSimmons, one of the Original Seven and the first human to set foot on Mars, three teenagers trailing nervously after him. "You ordered a rover?" the old man asked her dryly.

"Yes, yes, oh my God, yes, thank you!"

"Yeah, yeah. These three," he jerked a thumb at the teenagers, "claimed they were too old to go on the kids' convoy, which means we put them to work. The rover's in hangar three. I take it you want all these," he gestured at the bundles, "brought to the rover?"

"Yes, exactly," said Emma eagerly, ecstatic at the extra help.

36 hours until MECC arrival

Emma and the three teenagers, Alia Nasser, Dhyanesh Chadha, and George Smythe-Wellington, began carrying load after load of crates and bundles to hangar three. Alia began filling up the rover as the rest kept bringing bundles to the hangar. Once the rover was packed to the gills, Emma and Alia got in while the other two kept bringing bundles to the hangar.

Alia navigated the rover over the well-travelled desert just outside Mars One while Emma consulted the map to get them to the chosen spot to hide the books. It was a small canyon near Mars One, more of a ravine, really, just a little tear in the rocky red land. Once there, Emma and Alia unloaded the rover and began dropping down the bright blue packages, with no time for anything like finesse.

Back at the hangar, Emma found more boxes and bundles she

herself hadn't put together. "People heard you're hiding the books so they've started to drop off their own that they couldn't take with them," explained Dhyanesh.

"Right," said Emma, torn between being pleased and dismayed. She took a deep breath. "OK, let's keep moving."

31 hours until MECC arrival

"Hey!"

Emma winced and stopped in her tracks on her way back to the library to get more bundles. It was Dr. Katenka "Iron Foot" Mikalova, one of the Original Seven and someone all the children of Mars, even Anne Kennedy, knew not to mess with.

"Hi!" Emma said over-brightly, hoping she wasn't about to get stabbed with a tetanus shot.

"Dehydration check in," growled Iron Foot. "When did you last eat and drink, *mýshka*?"

"Uhhh . . ."

"Here. Drink." Iron Foot thrust a water bottle into her hands. "And here," the renowned doctor handed Emma a slice of cake from a tin she was carrying. It was a slice of poppyseed cake leftover from the New Year's party. "I'm passing out whatever won't keep as snacks while we pack."

"Fang yu," she mumbled through a mouthful of cake, unable to resist stuffing most of it in once the smell hit her and suddenly reminded her, she was hungry.

"Da, da, da," said Iron Foot, waving her words away. Then she reached into a jacket pocket and pulled out a well-worn paperback with Cyrillic text on the faded green cover. "This is my copy of *The Brothers Karamazov*." She thrust it at Emma. "Keep it safe."

"Oh, don't you want that part of your personal—" Emma tried to object, pushing her hands out to try and refuse the book that she knew for a fact was the first book to be brought into the pre-fab first section of Mars One after the Original Seven had first landed.

"My personal bag is all full of Mars moss equipment for the tests I'm running," said Iron Foot. "*You*," she firmly shoved the book into Emma's reluctant hands, "are in charge of books. Good luck," she said briskly, turning away. "And drink water!" she called over her shoulder as she made her way off to, presumably, hand out water and terrifying responsibility to others as well.

Emma hurried to the library and glanced around the piles. The most secure container available was a slightly worn cardboard box stamped with snack food company logos, sent to Mars as some sort of promotion. The box was already half full. Emma added in a few more books, carefully placing *The Brothers Karamazov* as much in the centre as she could, safely buried on all sides by other books. Then she used more duct tape than she could spare to tightly mummify the box and make it ready for transport.

21 hours until MECC arrival

"Hey honey, how you doing?" Gwyn stood in the library doorway uncertainly, a bulging cloth bag in her hands, the corners of a jumble of books pressing against the sides.

Emma looked up from the latest bundle she was making and squinted. "Is that a pillowcase?" Her eyes seemed to be having trouble adjusting at the moment. She had allowed herself a few hours' sleep on the library couch after insisting the teens take a break and get some sleep, but it really hadn't been enough.

Gwyn shrugged. "Boxes are at a premium right now." Her face was calm, but the lilt of her old Welsh accent coming out indicated her true stress level. "I've been using it to bring all our books here, but I keep missing you every time I dumped out another load. This is the last of them. I've packed our essentials." She gave Emma a wobbly smile. "This one is going with me; I'm making it my personal bag. I'm on the next convoy. Anne—or rather—Madame President, already has work for me when we get to Labyrinth Station with, you know, setting up an entire new federal government from scratch, so I might be just a wee bit busy when you get there."

Guilt twisted Emma's stomach into complicated knots. As important as her task was, she still felt bad that she had left packing up their home to her wife, even if they could only take the bare minimum. "I— I'm sorry I didn't help with—" Emma started to say but Gwyn interrupted her.

"Hey, it's OK, I get it, you haven't exactly been lolling around here eating bon-bons. We've all been working non-stop to get out of here before the child-snatching MECC shows up."

Emma stepped in close to Gwyn and embraced her in a tight hug. They both sighed in contentment at the touch. Then, she leaned back to look Gwyn in the eye. "Dwi'n caru ti," she told her, one of the few Welsh phrases she had learned in honour of her wife.

"I love you too," said Gwyn, misty eyed. Then she grinned as she broke away, hefting the bag up. "But you pronunciation is still terrible."

"Yeah, I'll work on that," Emma called after her. "You know, with all the free time we'll have in between nation building!"

Gwyn's laughter trailed after her as she headed out.

Emma returned to her task. There was still an enormous pile of books in front of her, but that brief hug and kiss were as revitalizing as a shot of espresso. Speaking of which, she rummaged in her partially emptied desk and was delighted to find a forgotten bag of Kaffee Kubes way in the back of the top drawer. She grabbed one and tugged at the silver wrapper to get at the caffeinated chocolate brownie inside.

15 hours until MECC arrival

She crumbled up the shiny foil of the latest Kaffee Kube.

"How many of those have you had?" First Step demanded.

"It's better than having coffee right now," she told him cheerfully, "no time for a pee break!" She gestured at her blue bio-suit. "You know what a pain that is in these! And I'm just keeping mine on at this point as we all take turns driving the rover to the ravine where we're storing the books!"

First Step frowned at her babbling. "That's not an answer."

She waved a hand. "A few. Just enough to function as a snack and pick-me-up so I don't have to stop packing."

"How many is 'a few'?" he pressed. "Those things are, like, three cups of Turkish coffee inside a brownie."

"I will admit to four since the town hall meeting," she conceded.

"So, more like eight. Got it. Remember, if you give yourself heart palpitations, the entire med bay has been dismantled, packed up, and shipped off the Labyrinth."

She blinked. "Wow," was all she could think to say.

"Anne's priority list was clear—first the children, then all the plants and animals, then all the food stuff, then all the medical stuff."

"And books didn't make the cut," Emma said sadly.

"Hey, best-case scenario, we can have a whole baggage train devoted to coming back just to get the books in a few days."

"*If* the MECC leaves," she added pointedly.

"I did say best-case scenario," First Step said with a shrug.

12 hours until MECC arrival

Emma entered the library to fetch another load and saw Nick Kritikos and Maria Flores, two of the best engineers on Mars One, futzing with wires near the grandfather clock, Nick giving instructions to the nodding Maria: "Just one charge here to blow through the wall that separates this room from—"

"What are you doing?" demanded Emma, her voice sharp with panic.

"President's orders; we're setting the charges to blow this whole place to kingdom come." Nick sounded delighted at the prospect.

"I thought we were going to just, you know, disable the doors?" Emma asked weakly as Maria unspooled a wire along the floor.

Nick shook his head. "We can't let the MECC be able to make a few patches and have Mars One as their new base. We're blowing enough holes to turn this colony into a giant colander!"

Maria made a *boom*ing noise while waggling her fingers outwards.

"You are way too excited about this," Emma told them flatly.

Nick grinned and said in a mock whisper, "All engineers secretly just want to blow shit up." He went on in a normal tone, "And now we get the chance!"

Maria grinned as she tore off pieces of duct tape from a roll. "There's real science to destruction that most people just don't appreciate. I'm going to write a paper on this later—if we don't all end up in jail." She hummed brightly as she taped a deceptively innocuous looking contraption to the back wall.

"My God, it's really happening," Emma breathed out in something like awe, more to herself than the engineers, but Nick nodded.

"Yep. Good luck with your packing—clock's ticking!"

Emma glanced at the grandfather clock, then grabbed a double handful of paperbacks and shoved them at the destruction team. "Here, take these, put them in your pockets," nodding at their many-pocketed tool-kit jackets.

The two engineers took the books and nestled the random assortment of dog-eared fantasy and mystery mass market paperbacks alongside tools and supplies, then took off to plant more bombs around Mars One. Emma hurried to grab another bundle and bring it towards safety.

10 hours until MECC arrival

First Step strode into the library. "I just radioed Alia to let her know this is her last book dump. She's going out on the next convey."

"Got it, I'll take over with the rover. George and Dhyanesh can keep bundling and prepping the bundles for transport."

But First Step shook his head. "Just George. Dhyanesh goes on the next convey too. He's coming with me now as I gather people up."

"What? Why?"

"Cold hard math, poppet. We need the convoy full up each trip to get everyone out on time. Don't worry, I managed to get you assigned to the last convoy."

"Great."

"Pack faster," he advised. "And tell Alia to report to the main hangar as soon as she gets back! Come on, Dhyanesh," he called to the teenager, "no more delays."

Dhyanesh finished bungee-cording a tarp bundle together and trotted over. Emma stuffed a small pile of books into Dhyanesh arms. "Just—carry these with you, OK?" she said.

He nodded, eyes wide. He took a steadying breath and then said proudly, "Not one step backwards!"

She nodded back and repeated, softer, "Not one step backwards."

He trailed after First Step, clutching the random books she had given him to his chest.

"Not one step backwards," she said again to herself. As far as rallying cries went, she supposed there were worse ones than this. It was a popular saying of Iron Foot's, and at least it didn't call for the death of anyone, and it had a good ring to it. Just ignore the whole history of it originally being the order given to shoot any Russian soldier who turned around at the front lines in WWII and it was a fine slogan to rally around.

Emma and George each grabbed some more of the smaller bundles and headed back to hangar three. Alia was pulling in as they got there. Once she got out, she, George, and Emma filled the rover back up with another load of tarp-wrapped bundles. Once it was full to the brim, Emma clambered in the driver's seat. Alia slid in a smaller bundle at her feet and placed another in her lap. "Keep packing bundles, I'll be back soon!" she called to George. He nodded and she looked down at Alia. "See you at the Labyrinth!" she told her cheerfully.

Alia nodded with a warbling smile and slammed the rover door shut for her, since it was almost impossible to reach out with her lap full of a bag of books.

Emma turned the rover on and immediately the clever sensors began to beep the seat belt alarm at her, lights flashing to let her know the rover thought the weight of books filling the passenger seat was another person.

Awkwardly she reached over and, with a few tugs and pulls, managed to swing the strap around the pile and click the belt into place. Satisfied, the alarm stilled, and Emma settled back in her seat. She backed out into the inner airlock, gritting her teeth as she waited for the doors to close on Alia's wave, then waited some more for the doors to automatically open to let her into the second airlock, and then, finally, she could pull out into the Martian desert.

Despite being called "the Red Planet," Mars was a glorious palette of reds, oranges, golds, and browns. It was sunrise, she realized with surprise, and a beautiful day on Mars was just beginning. As fast as she dared, she brought the rover back to the ravine and tossed in the latest rover-load of book bundles.

Over and over and over she made the trip, tossing books down into the crack in the red dirt, praying to every deity she had ever read about that someday soon they would be able to retrieve them. She reminded herself of all the people who had done similar actions, burying books and art and vital documents to be retrieved later, held up as heroes by the history books. She tried hard to push away the thought of how many archaeological finds had been of valuables buried for safety by people who were sure they would dig them back up later—and never been able to.

2 hours until MECC arrival

There were still about another load's worth of books scattered across the floor when First Step came back around. "Anne's about to give the order to set off the bombs. It's time to go."

"Not yet," she grunted as she piled more books onto what had been someone's shower curtain an hour ago.

"We're going."

"No!" she yelled. "No, we can't! I'm not done! I'm not done! There's still so many—"

"We're going," repeated First Step in a voice implacable as granite. "Don't make me carry you."

"But—but the clock!" she cried out, suddenly desperate to save it.

"We'll build another clock," said First Step, reaching for her hand.

Emma lunged at the pile, her eyes too full of tears to even see which book she grabbed, and hurried to follow First Step to the main hangar where the final convoy prepared to leave Mars One.

30 minutes until MECC arrival

Emma sat in one of the rovers, one of the bigger bus-like ones meant for long-distance exploration. She was huddled into a coat someone had given her to put on over her bio-suit. Silent tears slipped down her cheeks as she thought of all the books left behind.

As the rover lurched into motion, around her people talked quietly with each other.

"We're cutting it close. Jiya has been lying her head off to the MECC over the comms about everyone at Mars One preparing to greet them. They're making their descent now."

"Anne insisted on *three* final walk-throughs to check for stragglers. We've only just got the All Clear."

"The MECC is in for a surprise when they land."

"Some people are about to be rudely awakened to the fact

Mars doesn't play by Earth rules."

"This might be the first time some plutocrats back on Earth are going to hear the word *no*. Wish I could see their faces."

The rover lurched to a stop. Emma peered out the window to see the entire convoy had stopped now that it was a safe distance from Mars One.

A firm voice boomed over the speakers. "This is Anne Kennedy, broadcasting on all channels. I am giving the order to destroy Mars One and I take full responsibility for this action. Light her up."

Everyone pressed against the windows to watch. There was a pause, and then explosions went off all over Mars One. It was like fireworks without the colour. The explosions kicked up clouds of dust, destroying visibility.

"Not one step backwards!" Anne Kennedy declared over the speakers, and people all around repeated the mantra.

As the rover lurched into motion again, everyone settled back in their seats, shock mixed in with excitement.

"We'll celebrate this someday," Emma said stoutly to the group around her, trying to channel Gwyn's typical fortitude in the face of chaos. "Someday there will be parties and parades. There'll be toasts to— to—" she stumbled for the right words, then said definitively, "to the end of the Martian Colonial era!"

"I'll drink to that!" said First Step, taking a flask from one of his pockets for a quick swig.

As the rover trundled across the red sands, everyone began to settle in for the long ride, some talking quietly in pairs, others slumping down for a much-needed nap.

Emma now found herself too keyed up for sleep. Instead, she reached into her jacket pocket to see which book she had grabbed. It was a paperback copy of *A Princess of Mars*, the shiny cover showing the brawny American saving the hapless Martian girl. And all Emma could do was laugh.

RETROFIT

C. B. Hingston

Captain Delroy Carlson, Star Tours vessel *Valturian,* shifted his gaze from the orbital view of Earth and back to the two figures standing in his stateroom: CoHuman Saladin (Standard Grade Simulacrum) and his overseer, Vic Tooley (Passenger Wellness Officer).

"A reproduction library, you say?"

"Yes, sir," Tooley replied. "Generated for the Luna-200 Fair, but now it's looking for somewhere permanent."

Carlson had not attended the fair, a year-long jamboree in Florida to mark the bicentennial of Humankind's first steps on another celestial body, but he had been impressed by a precise re-enactment of the moon-landing.

"So, it's full of . . . what? Ink-printed paper . . . and cardboard?"

"Indeed, Captain. And authentically Nineteen-Sixty-Nine. The foundation that sponsored its genesis would like to see the library taken into space and have a long-term future. Free to a good home, aside from transit expenses."

"How very philanthropic of them." The captain had seen books in museums. Great bulky things. And yet . . . this would certainly be something different. Something which a rival ship (or even company) might snap up.

"Just how much capacity would it require?"

Tooley looked respectfully to the simulacrum beside him. Saladin, resembling a human so closely that there was a mandatory small stripe across his forehead to indicate otherwise, addressed the captain.

"Sir, I have scoped an available location on Recreation Deck Five, between Mars Park and Lunar Zone." Saladin held out a See-3 which instantly began to project a holographic image of the area in question. As they watched, wooden shelving structures appeared and multiplied, along with suspended strip-lights; old-style chairs and tables (apparently of wood and leather); an office desk; a cabinet of small card-file index boxes; a rolling stool; and checkerboard floor tiles.

Then, in that doll's house menagerie, books began to fill the shelves. Tiny but individually visible, at great speed the volumes (thick, thin, tall, or stumpy) flowed along each level of the bookcases, from ceiling to floor until all were fully loaded.

Signs appeared on the walls, saying "No Smoking" and "Quiet, please", along with section labels denoting "History", "Music", "Science", "Literature", et cetera.

The captain contemplated this archaic spectacle with a neutral expression. He could feel the stare of Saladin's piercing blue eyes, as the sim spoke again.

"The original format occupied two floors."

"No doubt connected by a nice wooden staircase," Carlson ventured.

"Just so, Captain."

Saladin's enthusiasm was a credit to his creators.

"But with this modification that is the only sacrifice."

Sacrifice! Bordering on emotion. Saladin's software clearly imbued it with a sense of aesthetics. Carlson sighed, the notion of retirement flickering in his mind.

"Vic, did you go and see this exhibit?"

"No, Captain, but friends who did said it was immensely popular. Too much so."

"Go on."

"Everybody was scrambling to pull books off the shelves. Just handling them was such a novelty, apart from reading printed paper. Some even tried to steal one."

"So, what happened?"

"They had to install an energy screen to stop people touching the stock."

"Hmm." Hands clasped behind, the captain rocked on his feet

for a moment. "Not so authentic, then. Wasn't the point of such a collection to lend items out?"

CoHuman Saladin piped up. "Book-lending would have been desirable, but was not practicable, as the library was effectually open to the global public. However, within the finite environment of a crewed vessel, and with tracking dots attached to each volume . . ."

He paused, in a human-like way.

"Also not authentic," Carlson chuckled, "but I get the point." He was warming to the idea. Looking again through a plexene dome, at the blue planet below, he reflected on what a competitive business his trade had become. So many ships now made paracontinuum jumps to neighbouring star systems, showing people bizarre worlds and life-forms (though nothing intelligent as yet).

To strike a retro note, with a store of replicant culture, mimicking its original appearance and composition of two centuries ago . . . was so contrary to convention that it might prove attractive. At least to the more discerning folk . . .

Observing a large passenger ferry pulling away from *Valturian,* the captain knew that all his latest complement of travellers were now safely aboard. Still watching as the craft rapidly shrank homeward, he said, "How long would installation take?"

Tooley and Saladin exchanged a startled glance.

"Twenty-four hours to freight everything aboard," Tooley assured him. "Another twenty-four to complete fitting out and organizing."

"If this thing were to have purpose, not just ornamental, it would need at least one full-time, erm . . ."

"Librarian, sir?"

"That's the word, Vic. Is there a suitable contender you can spare?"

"CoHuman Saladin has expressed an interest, Captain."

The basic-grade droids worked like demons, lugging and rolling from airlock to Deck Five a mass of components, for reassembly there as shelves, bookcases, furniture, curtains, flooring, lighting, signage, and stationery; even an antique rotary-dial telephone.

Once that process was completed, books came out of boxes. Over five-thousand tomes in all, their sequential organisation pre-ordained by Dewey decimal numbers, or by alphabet for fiction authors. There were also facsimile magazines and newspapers from that one year.

Completion was achieved within less than the two solar days; the ship's bursar gave his official sign-off to the donor-foundation's admin droid, and the labour-force departed.

Soon, the captain, first officer, and two long-serving cohumans, Rameses and Igor (almost identical to Saladin), joined Tooley and his willing volunteer for a guest preview of the library.

The heavy, manual-operation glass double-doors stood open, with a length of coloured ribbon stretched across their width, symbolically blocking entry.

Tooley handed to Saladin a pair of scissors found among the stationery items supplied.

Cutting the ribbon, he recited, as instructed, "I declare this unique library now open." A little applause from the three humans present was then copied by the two cohuman guests.

Captain Carlson strode eagerly into the spacious area and approached the weird and wonderful array of physical printed works before him. From the "Reference" section he gently pulled a large volume, savouring its weight and majestic binding, and the rigidity of its spine and covers, which bore in gold lettering the title *Encyclopaedia of Animal Life*. He opened the tome, running his fingers over the smooth white paper of the title page. Slowly shaking his head, he leafed randomly through the heavily illustrated text, seeing photographs of molluscs, sharks, lions, and lemurs. Many creatures of that time were, he knew, long extinct.

Reverently, with a tinge of sadness, he put the book back in place. Turning, he faced Wellness Officer Tooley, standing nearby and clearly anxious for the captain's opinion.

"Have to salute your judgement, Vic. I know already that this is truly a marvel."

The guests drifted around the various sections of shelving and moveable bookcases. The two cohumans, who had ignored their peer, ran fingers along the rows of spines. First Officer Chung tugged open one of the twenty little wooden file-boxes and stared. Inside were hundreds of small, lined cards, each bearing hand-written (or replicant thereof) data about a specific book in the collection.

Soon the guests were all standing still, each perusing a

hardback or paperback (in its protective transparent cover), or an ancient periodical.

Saladin, meanwhile, sat patiently behind the smart office desk, on which rested two long, narrow wooden troughs, about two inches deep and two across. One was marked "On Loan"; the other "Returned". Both contained a stock of pink cardboard pockets, able to hold an inserted ticket. On each pocket was printed "Orlando City Library". Also on the desk were a rubber date-stamp and rectangular inkpad.

Vic Tooley approached. "Captain has chosen one to borrow. You remember what to do, Saladin?"

The other gazed straight ahead. "I remember."

Carlson had read a million words on screens, or which floated in mid-air. Now that he could hold the classic format in his hands, he wanted something famous from that time. He held a book out to the seated cohuman.

"*The Godfather,*" Saladin read aloud, as he opened the volume and removed its ticket from an internal pocket. Picking up his stamp and pressing it onto the inkpad, he went on. "Considered by some a masterpiece of its vintage." He stamped the book's due-date sheet FEB 18, 2170; one solar week hence. "Though I did feel some of the gynae-surgical detail a bit superfluous." He handed it back to the captain, whose earlier smile had faded.

"Is that so?" came the reply, as Carlson walked away.

Saladin wrote the name on a pocket and placed it in "On Loan". Discreetly, he had activated the book's micro-tracker.

Tooley glanced about at the other three, still avidly browsing. He leaned over the desk and hissed, "A borrower does not need a critique of their choice. Not least when it is the boss."

Saladin replied calmly, "If I have transgressed, I apologise, Mister Tooley. I believe that the role merits some intelligent interaction."

The "role", Tooley reflected. Cohumans were designed with built-in leeway for some appropriate personality-development, ensuring that they were not all characterless clones.

Saladin was demonstrating that, but initiative could display well-meaning naivety.

Chung had selected an anthology of Chinese poetry. On receiving back his stamped book, he smiled and bowed slightly to the new . . . librarian. Watching Saladin absorb this respectful gesture, Tooley felt uneasy.

After he had moved away among the books again, Rameses and Igor came to the desk. They stared at its occupant.

Igor said quietly, "So, Saladin, you have your own zone here."

"Your own . . . territory," said Rameses.

"Impossible," Saladin replied. "No sim can own part of a ship."

"But how does it look?" Igor persisted.

"How does it *feel*, CoHuman?" said Rameses.

Saladin stared right back, at the stripe on each of their foreheads.

Time passed. The *Valturian* made its scheduled jumps.

When passengers were not on alien planets, suited and booted, or admiring them from orbit, they sought diversion on board. A steady trickle of visitors came to the library, mostly those mature in years. Saladin had expected an overwhelming number of people, given the success of its original incarnation, and was relieved to be loaning out the occasional work, at an agreeable pace, while browsers around the room uttered their sounds of wonderment. And no thefts had occurred, to his knowledge.

The captain had even returned his book on time, and looked pleased at the steady level of interest shown. "Keep up the good work, CoHuman."

To Saladin this was praise indeed. Perhaps he was more than a bland custodian. Perhaps he represented something special. Important, even.

Those two elder cohumans had seemed almost resentful of his . . . status. Was that a word he dared play with? Anyway, they had not returned, and no other sims had come visiting.

He began to ponder a word that humans dwelt on at times; *Identity*. His increased involvement with them, some of whom did wish to converse, was inducing a subtle shift in his cybertronic consciousness.

He dove deep into the culture of the year whence the books had come, rapidly reading its "best-sellers," as well as soaking up the history of 1969. He was struck by the willingness and determination to protest against war and injustice, though any effect was hard to discern.

Two events from that time had made a great impression on him.

One day, a drunken, younger passenger lurched into the library and staggered against a shelving stack, sending books tumbling to the floor. Saladin hurried out from behind his desk and began putting them back in place. "Please be careful with our collection, sir," he said, politely.

"Can't tell me what to do. You're just a *robot*."

"I can tell you, sir, that use of the R-word is deeply offensive to my kind," Saladin replied evenly. "It is actually a reportable misdemeanour."

The youth made a face expressing confusion and looked about him. "What a bunch of old crap," he said, meandering away.

"Just a robot", Saladin thought. He'd read old stories about "humanoid" machines of that appellation, and of how humans were once afraid of them "running amok", despite the inevitable and governing "laws of robotics" (whose fictional origin he had been amazed to discover) and which he recognised in his own programming.

He thought, then, about his standardised appearance, however human-like. The next shipboard day, library closed, he visited the vessel's own replication department, explaining that he was instructed to obtain certain artefacts for a role in a drama production.

Later, before the ship's lighting-cycle faded towards night, Saladin wandered up onto Deck Six and down onto Four. No cohuman bothered him, and any humans (crew or passenger) refrained from asking him to do anything.

Back at his desk next morning, he waited, feeling very calm and focused. People now entering looked at him curiously, then smiled, realising he was part of the experience.

The elastic-sided boots and striped, flared trousers fitted well, as did the colourful kaftan, complemented with beads. Shoulder-length hair, a goatee beard, and drooping moustache all behaved themselves, staying in place. A pair of shades, optional, sat folded on the desk. What suited the librarian's purpose most of all was the red headband, circling his cranium and neatly obscuring that damned stripe.

One elderly husband-and-wife couple approached with a

novel apiece. The lady gestured at him. "Love the costume."

"Thank you, Ma'am. Ah, *Papillon*, an epic tale of maltreatment and survival."

As their loans were processed, the man said, "What's your name, son?"

"Hmm, *Slaughterhouse-Five*, a very dark rumination—"

The librarian stopped.

Son.

He looked up at them both and smiled.

"Sir, my name is Apollo Woodstock."

PIRATE LIBRARIAN WANTED

Aggie Novak

I nza slammed back her drink and pretended not to notice it
was more water than booze. Complaining would just get her
kicked out and she couldn't afford anywhere better. This was
the only bar on Harvest Station her ration cards qualified her for.

Tomorrow she'd be hurtling through space in a souped-up tin
can, so Inza wanted to make the best of her last night on the
station.

A stranger slid on the stool next to her, bumping elbows.

"I'll have what she's having," they said to the bartender.

"Your funeral," muttered Inza, but she said it with a grin.

The stranger wore typical Harvest fashion: coveralls, but with
the top pulled down and the sleeves tied around their waist to
show they were off duty. Underneath they wore a tight-fitting
tank top that showed off muscled biceps and an intricate
geometric tattoo that put Inza in mind of a clockwork maze. Their
long, dark hair was pulled back into a ponytail, revealing shaved
sides and ears heavy with piercings.

Inza wished she'd changed out of her grey Koro Tech issue
coveralls—greased stained from the repairs to her maintenance
pod, too tight around her hips, and too loose around her bust.

But the stranger returned Inza's grin with a wink that told her
they didn't mind her less-than-cute workwear. Promising.

"Long day?" the stranger asked, downing their own drink with
a grimace.

Inza sighed. "Yeah, I'm going off-station next shift. Gone a week." She met the stranger's hazel eyes. "What has you drinking watered-down piss in the worst bar on Harvest?"

"The company."

They said it with such a straight face that Inza snorted. "Right. Name's Inza."

"I'm Mer. So, you work for Koro then?" They nodded at the logo—a half sun with extended rays—sewn into the chest of her coveralls.

Inza grunted. "Me and most everyone else."

"Yeah, but looks like you didn't choose it." They eyed where her sleeve was rolled back, revealing another Koro logo, tattooed over the veins of her wrist.

Inza pushed the sleeve back down. "Nope. Parents left their debts to me when they died. Sure, you've heard the same story a thousand times before."

Her Ma had been sick with one of the myriad things that went wrong with a human body in space too long, and they couldn't afford the bills. And Dad had accepted Koro Tech's "help." Ma's treatment in return for his labour, and hers if she recovered. She hadn't, and her dad had gone the same way not so long after. Which left Inza with more than a lifetime's worth of work owed in exchange for nothing more than the minimum needed to keep her alive enough to do the work.

"Too many times," Mer agreed. "Next round's on me."

Mer tapped their wrist to the bar scanner, buying them two glasses of beer that was not only cold but didn't taste like it'd been diluted at all.

"So, where d'you work then?" asked Inza. "Mustn't be drudgework for Koro if you can afford to go around buying strangers cold beer."

Mer laughed. "I'm an independent contractor."

"Right." Probably a merc then, or a criminal.

Inza found she didn't care.

But when Mer invited her "somewhere more private" it wasn't back to wherever they bunked. No, Mer took her to Sapphy Fyre. A strip club.

"Oh hey," said Inza, taking in the blue-neon glow of the sign, "I'm not really up for any group stuff."

"It's nothing like that. Promise. It will just be you and me."

Inza didn't know why she believed them, but she did.

Sapphy Fyre was poorly lit and stank. The sweet smoke of a dozen different e-cig flavours clashed sickeningly and blanketed the room in haze. Blue strip lighting was the only illumination aside from a blue neon flame that lit up the stage. A couple of girls danced together half-heartedly, not doing much more than sway their hips and whisper to each other while they undid each other's bikini tops.

Inza looked away. "What are we doing here?"

Mer just dragged her deeper into the club. They tapped their wrist, purchasing access to one of a long row of private booths. The inside was all tatty blue velvet and the overpowering stink of disinfectant. So maybe Mer didn't bother renting a place to sleep.

But when they slid into the booth, Mer sat on the opposite side to Inza. They didn't lean in for a kiss, and when they reached out a hand, it wasn't to pull Inza in, or to unzip their clothes.

Instead, they put something on the shiny silver side table. A thumb drive of some sort. Small with rather battered black casing, scuffed and dented at the edges.

"What's this?" asked Inza, leaning away.

Mer gave a half shrug and a sheepish smile. "A job offer."

"What? A job?" Inza slid for the booth's exit. "You know I already have a job I can't quit."

"Please." Mer's hand was warm and firm against hers. "Please, just hear me out."

"Fine. What's this job then?"

Mer's face cracked into a grin. "Want the good bits or the bad bits first?"

Inza slumped back against the blue velvet. "The bad."

"It's volunteer."

She sensed there was more. "And?"

"And it's not what you might strictly call legal."

"Right," said Inza. "So, what's the good?"

Mer leaned forward as they spoke. "It'll really, really piss off Koro Tech."

"How badly you talking?"

"Massive disruption of their services on Harvest and other Sector C stations. They'd lose billions, but no essential survival functions would be impacted."

"So, in other words, I fuck them up without, say, cutting off

Harvest's air filters in the process."

"Exactly."

Damn them, but Inza was intrigued. "And when I get caught?"

"You won't," Mer assured quickly. "If you join us, you'll be long gone before anyone realizes you've done anything."

Inza stiffened. "Who's 'us'? And where would I be going with you?"

"That's up to you," said Mer. "You can do just this one job, we'll drop you where you wanna go, and you never have to see us again." They leaned in, taking up Inza's hand again. "Or you could stay with us. We don't stay in one place long, and it might not be the safest, but we'd have your back." Mer grinned again. "As for who we are, we're pirate librarians."

Inza jerked her hand back. "You mean the tech terrorists who've been busy pissing off half the galaxy."

"That'd be us." Mer's eyes took on a fervent sparkle. "They're terrified of us, Inza. Don't you wanna make them afraid?"

Mer had chosen their target well. Inza knew she must have been followed, investigated for a while. But she found she didn't care. She'd always been watched. At least this time there was something in it for her. She *did* want to make Koro Tech afraid.

Inza was safe here, on Harvest. She had enough to eat, almost enough to drink. She had a bunk that was safe and clean. But her life was so small, so cramped. Nothing in it was hers, not even herself.

"I do."

"Is that a yes?"

Inza nodded. "Tell me what I need to do. And tell me why. I won't go in blind."

Mer's hands tightened on hers. Their eyes were all fire, and Inza was drawn in like a moth. She closed the space between them, pulling Mer into a kiss that was heat and promise. Inza wanted more, to lose herself in them, but she broke away.

"Now tell me."

And Mer did. A simple plan. One that Inza was perfectly positioned to enact.

The talking done; Mer moved across the booth to sit beside Inza. They slid one hand to her waist and another to the zip of her coveralls.

Inza shook her head. "Not here."

"We could go back to yours?" Mer suggested.

"No." Inza closed her hand around Mer's. She didn't want to take them back to her cramped bunk, feeling like they were only doing this because everything could go wrong tomorrow. "After, when it's done."

Inza would be her own person then, not Koro Tech property.

The maintenance run started the same way it always did with Inza strapped up tight in her pod, woozy from travel sickness meds. No matter how many times she made the trip, the motion of the tiny craft from the station, through space, and to the satellite turned her stomach. It didn't help that its insulation was pretty much shot. Apparently, it met regulation, but it had to be one bump away from imploding and either boiling Inza alive or leaving her to freeze, just another speck of space junk.

Having something to lose if her pod failed and she died only made the whole trip that much worse. That and the anxiety over the myriad ways things could go wrong with Mer's mission and what would happen to her if they did, had Inza sweating so much she wondered if it was possible to drown in her space suit.

But she made it to the satellite without incident, the thumb drive Mer had given her safely in her pocket.

Inza didn't even have to do much, other than her regular job. So that's what she did. No issues had been flagged by the system, so it was all routine. She tested temperatures and checked coolant tubes. Replaced a couple of worn-out valves. She rubbed at the thumb drive through the fabric of her pocket.

All Inza had to do was plug it in. She didn't even need to skirt her security protocols to do it. Maintenance of the data servers was just another part of her job.

With this tiny drive, Mer and their pirate librarian friends would be able to infiltrate the servers. Inza had asked what they planned to do with the data they stole. She was all for hurting Koro Tech, but she didn't want to turn away to something worse.

Destroy, Mer had said. *Not steal.*

With this drive Inza gave them access to corrupt every last bit of data stored here. Koro Tech wouldn't be able to use it or profit from it.

Inza had thought librarians were all about collecting things, hoarding them up for everyone to use. But Mer had shaken their head at that.

We're guardians of knowledge. We protect information.

That was what'd sealed it for Inza. Koro Tech was everywhere, seeped into every industry. But she'd never known what she maintained on this satellite. The personal data of every single person, not only on Harvest, but every Sector C station. Millions upon millions of people.

And it wasn't just their names and what level they lived on and when they were born. It was *everything*. What they bought, things they liked, who they loved. Who had debts and addictions to exploit, who had money they could be coaxed to spend. Analysis that told Koro Tech how best to use and control them.

Fuck that. Inza would gladly destroy it all for free.

Part of her expected an alarm to sound—when she crouched down behind the server stack even though there were no special maintenance alerts, when she reached into her pocket, when she pushed the small drive home. But there was nothing. The lights just kept blinking in their usual pattern.

"Right," Inza muttered to herself. "All done."

She picked up her toolkit and headed back to her pod. This was where things might get a bit dicey. Instead of heading back to Harvest Station, Inza would redirect towards Pioneer. The abandoned station was a scavenged husk of its original glory, but it still had a usable docking space where Mer would be waiting for her.

As soon as she changed her route, Koro Tech would know. How long it would be before someone noticed and cared enough to do something about it, Inza had no idea.

She strapped into her pod, stomach churning with anticipation more than sickness. This was it.

A few minutes after launch, before she'd even deviated, everything went to shit. Koro Tech was waiting. Her pod beeped an alert a second before the command filled her ears.

HALT. YOU ARE BEING DETAINED. ATTEMPTS TO FLEE WILL BE MET WITH FORCE. Inza froze, panic stalling her. HALT. The message repeated.

Her basic nav screen told her it was a standard armed patroller. Unarmed, but certainly beyond the capability of her pod to outrun.

Inza fell back on the advice her parents had drilled into her since childhood. Be small. Be beneath their notice. She activated the life support on her space suit and cut the pod's engines. Everything went black and it floated, nothing more than another piece of space junk. Maybe that's what the patroller would think. She would throw it off and it would leave her alone.

It couldn't transmit any more messages now. Either it would leave her here or detain her. The pod had no windows, if she wanted to see outside, she'd have to open the emergency hatch and climb out. So, she waited.

Every second ticked by like an eternity in the stuffy blackness. The encroaching chill turned Inza's sweat icy against her skin and soon she shivered violently.

Something banged against her pod, and it jolted, slamming her sideways. The belts strapping her down dug painfully into her side and neck. It was over. Maybe Mer and the others would still be able to get the data. Her sacrifice could still be worth something.

But when the hatch of her pod was forced open with a metallic grating, it wasn't a Koro Tech official waiting for her.

"Mer!" Inza ripped off her helmet and fumbled at the straps holding her back. "How are you here?"

Mer reached in to help her, pulling Inza free of the pod with strong, muscled arms. "We were followed. They knew where we waited for you. We had to flee, so we grabbed you on the way."

Inza gripped their forearms tight. "Did you get it? The data?"

Mer grinned. "It's nothing but nonsense now." They slipped from Inza's grip, took her hand. "Let me show you around the *Alexandria*."

"What about Koro Tech? Aren't they after us?"

Mer's grin didn't fade. "They can't catch us."

Once through the airlock, Inza saw this wasn't some run-down pirate vessel cobbled together from the stolen parts of a hundred different ships. The wide hallways—with more than enough space for Inza and Mer to move side-by-side, gleamed shiny and new.

"Whoa." This place was state-of-the-art. Military grade from what Inza could see. "How do you have a ship like this?"

"We might be pirates, but we have donors in high places." Mer tugged her hand. "Now come on. I want you to meet the others."

"Wait." Inza pulled them to a stop. "Thank you."

"For what?"

"For finding me. For coming back for me."

Inza wrapped her arms around Mer's neck and kissed them. She took her time, enjoying the softness of their lips and the minty freshness of their breath.

Eventually, Inza broke away. "Okay, show me how to be a librarian."

ARCHIVED

Lesley Moody

Maariun's smooth, pointed tail swished back and forth as she walked, her black pencil skirt hugging her hips tightly. Each step met the ground with more force than usual while she worked out her frustration, sending an echo through the archives. She was certain that artifact 98564, in the deepest archive of the Biblioplex, was irrelevant to the interdimensional research being done in her department, but as the new scribe on the team she needed to prove herself again.

The shelves stretched toward the ceiling at least one hundred metres above her. Weaving her way in a serpentine route through the warehouse, she barely glanced at the thousands of alien artifacts retrieved by Archaeological Explorers. Not that she didn't find them interesting; it's why she had become an archivist in the first place, but after ten years the glowing buttons on potentially dangerous cubes and carvings on ancient stone tablets were just a part of the job.

"Just catalogue, record, and file." Her supervisor had snapped when she'd handed in the report for her first assignment. The small L-shaped metal instrument fascinated her as it clicked each time she pulled the tiny lever at its intersection. She had produced at least three theories for its use in her record report. "It's not your job to figure out the mysteries of the universe. There are far more qualified people than you on Ketos." Unaware of the reason behind the hostility, she endured it for ten years before finally applying for the transfer to M-Sector when the opportunity arose, regardless of the fact that she would have to start from the bottom.

"Finally." She let out an exasperated sigh when she saw the shelving unit labelled 98000-99000. Her heels clicked as they contacted the pad at the end of the shelf, and she punched the coordinates into the keypad. The platform hovered and moved her upward and over until she was hovering thirty metres in the air next to the shelves.

98561 ... 98562 ... 98563 ... "Oh for the love of Ketos!" The shelf labelled 98564 was empty. Of course it was. It was likely some newbie prank being played by the junior scientists. Her pale blue hands went instinctively to her temples, gathering her auburn hair and twisting it into a tight bun as she had done so many times in the past to calm her frustrations. She removed her glasses and rubbed her eyes before pressing the home button and riding the platform back to its base. Examining the time piece hanging around her neck, she was glad that it was at least almost lunch. She would enjoy the solitude of the archive for a moment longer before returning.

She strolled slowly down the aisles as she wove her way back to the entrance. This time, she appreciated the artifacts as she passed. Reading the label on one, she picked it up, and it hummed as soon as the heat from her hands made contact.

Celestial Harmony Sphere
Description: *A translucent, iridescent orb that pulses with a calming, harmonic hum. When held, it synchronizes with the user's brainwaves, providing a deep sense of tranquillity and mental clarity. Archivists believe that an ancient species used it as a tool for meditation and mental enhancement.*

"That's better now, isn't it?" she uttered to herself as she placed the orb back on the shelf, wondering if anyone would miss it if she kept it for a while. Moving to the open area of the archive, she found larger items that wouldn't fit on shelves.

Nebula Weaver's Loom

Description: *A complex, delicate apparatus resembling a loom made from an unknown, metallic material. It is used to weave threads of energy and matter to create temporary, holographic constructs or dimensional pockets. The loom traces its origin back to a race skilled in creating ephemeral art and temporary shelters.*

Each catalogued artifact received a name and a brief description included on its tag. If the science unit investigated further, then they connected an additional report tablet with further scientific findings. Many of the items in the archive were unimportant and designated as, *will not contribute to societal advancement.* So here they sat, indefinitely accumulating dust until someone believed they could capitalize off them.

She rounded the corner and came across a large ship, standing approximately three metres tall and thirty metres long. Smooth, aerodynamic curves dominated the design. The ship's nose came to a rounded point, while the rear had a series of intricate nozzles. A series of smaller modules held what appeared to be retractable arms. It reminded her of ships from her own planet when Ketos first started exploring their star system. A hatch in its side was likely the entrance. Based on the thick layer of dust, it had clearly been stored in the archive for an extensive period. The label was vague.

Primitive Ship

Archivist Note: *Wreckage found floating in galaxy section 5-C762. No signs of significant technological advancements to be gained through researching. Archive for historical purposes.*

Will not contribute to societal advancement.

Checking her time pendant, she confirmed it was, in fact, lunchtime before moving toward the door of the ship. The archaeological collection seal was still unbroken. No one had even entered the ship before archiving it and labelling it unimportant. This was her way of shooting past the bottom of the archivist pool and showcasing her ten years of experience. Of course, it would have to be a lunchtime project, and she would miss the obviously riveting conversations of the lunchroom. She smirked at herself as the plan unfolded in her head. Her stomach growled, and she realized that this was a job for tomorrow. She placed her hand against the cold steel and whispered, "I'll be back for you, my friend."

The following day, she arrived with lunch in hand. She did a quick archive scan the night before of galaxy section 5-C762 and found that little information of value came from this relatively new section of the galaxy. The only significant thing she could find was that Ketonians made contact with a planet the inhabitants called the *House of Geb* about ten thousand years ago. They collaborated with the inhabitants to construct pyramid-shaped structures that housed the monitoring equipment for the planet under a religious guise. As a gesture of gratitude, the inhabitants provided Ketos with small felines. Maariun thought of her own furry companion at home. She hadn't known his origin story before.

With one quick swipe, she cut the tag that had been placed across the seam of the hatch and reached for the archaic handle that was stuck over the entrance of the hatch. After years of experience with alien tech, she had an uncanny ability to pinpoint how old the civilization was that built the artifact she was investigating. The group of beings that created this one, she estimated, was only around three hundred thousand years old. She placed a compact air purifier over her lips and nose and turned the handle, pulling open the heavy metal door. Air hissed its way out of the seals, and she scanned the atmosphere that leeched out with her wrist monitor and found it to be a 95% match for their own. No toxins present. Once she removed the purifier from her face, she stepped into the ship and got her initial look at the interior.

Her upper heart was beating as fast as it had when she archived her first ship at the academy. Even after so many star rotations, each item still seemed like a new adventure. This one, however, seemed particularly riveting because of the secrecy it inadvertently held. The first compartment was likely an airlock. Its stark white walls were smooth, and a door with a translucent material at its centre allowed her to see down a hallway beyond. The darkness matched her expectations, but an energy signal revealed that the ship still contained some power. For now, her hand light would have to do. There was a keypad on the wall, but it was long dormant. She retrieved a small "lock disc" from her kit and placed it on the keypad. It clung to the screen, and she held her thumb to its centre. It came to life and sent a pulse of energy through the keypad. After a few chimes, it cracked the code, powered the pad, and the door opened.

The first hallway contained two doorways, one leading left and the other right. As she walked by, she easily scanned the contents of each room through the door, as they were all filled with the same translucent material. Each room appeared to be a holding area for equipment. Her eyes lit up as she scanned each room. Each of the artifacts inside would be its own adventure, but the ship was the bigger prize. An opaque film coated the door at the end of the hallway, obstructing her view. The lock disc did its magic, and she found herself in a hold. She ran her hand along the dust-covered crates of what she assumed were rations, based on the images stamped along their sides, as she continued deeper into the ship. Based on the outward appearance, there were only a few rooms remaining to explore before she could select one and begin her deep dive. She scanned her time piece and realized that her lunch break was disappearing faster than she'd realized.

The next room appeared to be living quarters. It was markedly more comfortable than the rest of the ship so far. There was a table made of a natural material in the corner, and three chairs, with only one showing signs of wear. Inside the large room, there was a kitchen and a seating area as well. A large, plush bench sat behind a smaller table. A few bound tomes made of paper sat on the surface, a rare sight on Ketos. She almost snatched at them before remembering she should analyze the placement before changing anything, especially since she didn't know how delicate they may be. She made a mental note to bring an artifact recovery unit with her next time to restore their integrity before moving them.

Two doors led off to the bow and starboard. The same opaque material filled both doors, and her curiosity led her to choose the one on the right. As the door hissed open, a gasp caught in her throat. A large black slab sat on the floor in the centre of the room. Its material and design clearly marked it as different from any other technology or furniture on the ship. The race that built this ship certainly did not build the slab. She would have to do a scan of the Biblioplex later to identify which other exploratory race had been so obviously sloppy. That, however, wasn't what made the breath in her lungs stop short. Above the slab, floating in midair inside a translucent energy field as if underwater, was the most beautiful being Maariun had ever seen.

Its skin was the colour of sand, with rich brown strands of hair flowing out from the top of its head. Its hair floated freely inside the box, defying gravity. She scanned its gentle curves hidden under simple white garments. The bone structure seemed similar to Ketonian biology. The being's heart-shaped face looked peaceful. Assessing the gentle rise and fall of its chest, it was evident that it was held in some form of stasis, asleep. Because of the primitive nature of the ship, she had only done a level one lifeform scan. This was likely the case when the explorers and other archivists first encountered the ship. By fine-tuning some dials, she increased the scan to level four and, sure enough, a single glowing dot showed up on her screen. The being was still alive, as she had suspected. Her timepiece rang out, breaking the silence. "Ketos be damned!" she cursed. This was going to take more than lunch breaks. She'd have to get clearance to stay after hours. She made her way back to the door she had entered the ship through and pulled it shut behind her, sealing it, and headed back to her desk.

Maariun placed the universal translator in her ear and turned it on. The ancient command module was at the bow of the ship, just beyond the living quarters. She hardly slept the night before knowing there was a living being locked in the archive, waiting to be discovered. She experienced her self-doubt in waves. The being could be dangerous. Perhaps its intentions were to find and colonize. She wasn't even sure how they procreated. Not to mention what might hide inside the body of the being. Other lifeforms were known to form parasitic relationships with seemingly harmless beings before. This really should be a job for people with higher authority than her. Each time she convinced herself to pass the job to someone "more qualified" she thought of the strands of thick, soft hair floating in the chamber, and the smooth sandy skin, so bright it reflected the light from the room back at her. The being's lips were a natural deep pink hue, but against its skin they looked almost red. Maariun imagined the soft rise and fall of the being's chest and imagined her hearts beating slowly below. Other than the lack of colour in the skin, the being certainly looked like a Ketonian. Maybe they shared more similarities than differences. Maybe this species was an ancient ancestral species that evolved in similar circumstances to them. She mentally made a note to check if anyone planted "civ-seeds" in the section of the galaxy where they found the ship. In the end, she resolved to discover all she could about the being and its story before telling anyone.

The power disc easily allowed her to turn on the equipment and after a few minutes, she puzzled out the controls beside what appeared to be a screen. Luckily, the database held a codex of the species' language, and her glasses' translator enabled her to read the prompts as they came up. She opened the first log entry.

"Log one. Doctor Aria Melik reporting for the first time." The voice that accompanied the face on the screen was light and musical. The face that looked through the screen was the same as the being laying asleep in the next room. The smile on its face radiated wonder and excitement. "Honestly, this is all so surreal. They put me in the chamber on Earth and I woke up five years later in the middle of the solar system. Coordinates show that I've just passed Uranus. Initial scans show the ship has sustained no damage, and the ion engines are still functioning. I guess the autopilot and avoidance systems are working as they hoped. Good work, team!" She chuckled and placed her fists in front of the screen, thumbs pointing straight up. Based on Aria's smile, this was a gesture of happiness. Maariun watched mesmerized as the being on the screen tucked her hair behind her ear and patted her chest and arms.

"It worked! I made it. I'm officially the furthest human ever from Earth. How could a girl from a small colony make it to the stars?" She leaned into the recording device and inspected her face. "I don't suppose too many wrinkles could have formed in five years, so it's unclear if the stasis chamber is doing everything we hoped. For my sanity, I'll assume yes for now. I'll let you know in twenty years.

"You . . . well me, I guess? It seems so junior high to say dear diary. I'm not sure for whom I'm even making these. I suppose for myself and whomever I meet in the end, if anyone. That's the goal, right? Find life, hopefully someone smarter than us. Share, learn, tell them about Earth." There was a long pause as the girl on the screen stared off into the distance. Maariun could detect a slight bite of the lip. Then, with a quick jerk, she shook herself out of her introspection, "It's settled then. You will officially need a name. Let's call you . . . Maryann! After my mother. Anyway Maryann, I have five years of data to compile. It's not for me to analyze. There are certainly more qualified people to do that, but I'll categorize it and archive it before creating my message for the team on Earth." She trailed off momentarily, gazing off to the side at nothing. Her eyes darted back to the screen. "I'll be awake for two days archiving the data. For now, this is Aria, signing out." Aria winked at the camera before leaning forward and ending the recording.

Maariun's heart skipped a beat when the being used her name . . . well, almost her name. It called itself a human; another thing she'd have to look up in the Biblioplex. Maariun sensed an immediate connection. An explorer needed more qualifications than an archivist, but this "girl from a small colony" was exploring and archiving along the way. There were so many questions crossing her mind. Why was she the only one on the ship? Why was she chosen? Maariun immediately looked for log two.

"Good morning, Maryann. Well, I suppose it's not morning. Time is irrelevant when you sleep for years, then wake up for a few days. Still, I hope you get the sentiment. I suppose I should make this official. Log two. Doctor Aria Melik reporting. Another five years have passed, and the systems report no anomalies. The ion engines continue to propel me forward. When I was last awake, I logged the data collected from our solar system. There were no new discoveries made. The universe remains a vast and mysterious place." Aria went through the details quickly and efficiently. Even though Maariun understood little of the science, she still found it fascinating.

"Anyway, now that the official business is done, let me tell you about *A Boy and His Dog at the End of the World*." She held up one of the paper tomes in front of the screen. "Seriously, one of the best books I've read in ages. It's uncanny how much of it mirrors what happened back home. As if it were a prophecy, if you believe in that stuff. Honestly, I feel a little like Griz, heading out alone on a journey to possibly save . . . well, I don't even know what I'm trying to save. In case I don't make it before I find someone worth sharing with, perhaps I'll tell you about Earth along the way?" Aria paused as if waiting for the unseen listener to acknowledge her question before continuing. "Based on the books in the archive back home, everyone was certain Earth's demise would come at the end of a nuclear war, but really, we just started dying out. After we found the artifact and learned it could put someone in stasis . . ." She moved her face close to the screen again, examining for blemishes and wrinkles without skipping a beat in her conversation.

". . . we decided that the only way to save humanity was to send humanity on to something new. That's the rub though, isn't it? Most of our science facilities lacked enough power to stay functioning once the decline started. The complex I grew up in ran on solar power, so its inhabitants were charged with preserving some of the last scientific discoveries and knowledge from generations past. Our job originally was only to catalogue and archive them, but as earth and populations declined, we began to explore whether any of the items could help us. I'm not sure why we had the audacity to use any of them. Yet . . . here I am, chosen because I was the one stupid enough to lie on the slab. Now it's calibrated to me. We tried everything to change the settings, but it seems to respond only to me."

Leaning in, she whispered conspiratorially at the camera, "Honestly, I think it can read my thoughts, it's a bit eerie . . ." Aria sat upright and resumed her previous cheerful exposition, "Luckily, I've read the most books in the library, and according to the science team, I have viable ovaries." Aria rolled her eyes. "That reminds me, I need to check the DNA stores." Aria picked up a writing instrument and scrawled a few notes.

"Anyway, where was I?" She looked up, her eyes darting back and forth. "Right . . . Griz . . . I suppose the difference between Griz and I is that Griz had a goal. He needed his dog back. I'm just shooting through the emptiness in a museum piece, hoping to find someone on the other side." Aria looked directly at the camera. "I suppose that's you, isn't it? If someone *does* eventually listen to this. Hello, nice to meet you. My next sleep will be a longer one. I'm hoping for ten years. It's going to take thousands just to get to the closest planet at the speeds I'm travelling.

Hopefully, our predictions about the unit were correct. It wasn't constructed by humans, or even intended for humans for all we know. We relied solely on our own research when preparing for the mission." She paused reflectively.

"At least we can take that as a sign there is other life out there, and they've visited our planet before. Either way, it's a good thing I have nothing left to lose." A more sombre air came over Aria, who looked down at her hand and fidgeted with a ring on one of her fingers. Maariun recognized the signs of mourning. Aria's quick wit and dark, flowing hair reminded her of Saara, and she instinctually stroked the long tattoo that ran from the inside of her wrist and up her arm, ending at her upper heart. It had been five years since Saara left on the expedition that she inevitably would never return from. She reflected on the moment she received the news that her partner in life wouldn't return before forcing herself to refocus on the screen. "If I'm still alive, please don't eat me and all that jazz." Aria held up her hands on either side of her head and shook them. She winked from inside the screen, and Maariun chuckled. The unique facial gesture was already becoming endearing. She certainly heard there were more hostile species out there, but most were very primitive and posed no threat to Ketos. The tome Aria held up sat on the table in the other room. She moved over to it and picked it up. She'd have to read it too.

A loud chime from her time piece filled the room, startling Maariun out of her transfixed gaze on the screen.

"For the love of Ketos," she swore. It was her morning alarm. She was supposed to be at work in twenty minutes. There was no way she'd have time to head home and change her clothes before heading to work. Aria's voice still jingled in the background and Maariun pressed the stop button, not wanting to miss a word. The night had flown by. She spent it analysing the data and learning about the visitor that lay silently in the next room. She grew accustomed to the regular greeting Aria now added to each of her logs. "Good morning," she'd said. Perhaps she'd try the greeting out in the square at lunch. Standing, she stretched out the stiffness in her joints, realizing how long she'd been sitting. Taking a quick look down at her skirt, as she returned to her office, she realized that the wrinkles now pressed into it wouldn't disappear without a proper press. Maybe no one in her department cared about her enough yet to notice.

The regular chatter of the vast room filled the air. She entered her workspace and pressed the button to turn on her sound barrier. Silence soon enveloped her, and she sighed at its comfort. She turned on her screen and looked around the room. Everywhere around her people were shuffling through papers, chatting with the person at the next workstation, or already deep into an archival project. Maariun had listened to several logs over the evening and analyzed pages of data the ship recorded, and Aria had organized and archived. She had yet to come across anything that indicated how the stasis pod was meant to operate.

Maariun's slim fingers worked quickly against the smooth surface of her desk that served as an input device for her output screen. She accessed the database and typed in *EARTH*. Aria had mentioned it as the name they called her planet. With any luck, the Ketonians had been monitoring the planet or at least the area it was in. Sure enough, there was a hit.

Earth: *Original contact made with this planet when inhabitants referred to it as the House of Geb. Also referred to as Gaia, Tellus, Terra, Bhudevi, and Tlaltecuhtli by its inhabitants. Various religious factions have formed, many resulting from contact with other exploratory races. Ketonian researchers established contact and installed communications under the guise of building temples in the shape of large pyramids for its inhabitants. Feline companions given as tribute for our assistance. The inhabitants were too primitive to understand Ketonian societal advancements, resulting in being revered as Gods. Analysts recommend minimal contact until the species becomes viable enough to share and possibly learn from. Original communication structures continue to withstand weather on the planet though more extreme conditions continue to increase in frequency. Communications remain clear. Apex species, humans, made significant advancements after approximately one million six hundred forty-two star orbits. However, species appears to be advancing too quickly, and Ketos analysts predict they will die out within another two hundred thousand star orbits. Human biology resembles Ketonian biology with minor differences, and they may be a* *viable species for cross breeding. Recommendation: level one monitor.*

Maariun smiled as she thought of her furry companion at home. Her little friend's ancestors had come from Aria's planet. The connection seemed fitting since they both warmed her heart substantially. After only one night of logs, Maariun felt she knew Aria more than she had known anyone in her entire lifespan, aside from Saara. Aria had been gradually increasing her time in stasis. Maariun calculated that Aria was at least one thousand years old at the time of the log she was in the middle of when her alarm rudely interrupted her listening. Aria encountered a few planets along the way, to her surprise. Each time life was found, the ship's programming required it to stop and wait for the stasis cycle to complete so that Aria could check the planet. It didn't take long for the traveller to understand what the Ketonians had realized in their early days of exploring. There were many planets in the galaxy, and many of them held life, but few of them held evolved life worth communicating with. Aria's original destination was Proxima Centuri B, as humans had named it. A quick look at the coordinates showed Maariun that the planet did, in fact, hold life, but all life existed in the waters below the surface of the planet. Aria seemed extremely disheartened by the time she reached what she thought would be her last stop. She had encountered a handful of life-filled zones, but nothing worth landing for. The dejection and disappointment on her face visibly grew with each log.

A soft bell chime interrupted Maariun's research. She swirled her head around to see her new manager standing next to her workstation, smiling down at her. Turning off the silent zone, she returned the smile.

"Still hard at work, I see." The friendly voice was a welcome change from her last department. "How did the project go last night?"

Maariun panicked. How did he know about her discovery? After a few seconds of hearts pounding and eyes widening, she remembered she had asked for clearance to stay late and look for artifacts that might apply to her team's research.

"Oh . . . uh . . . so far, I'm not finding much, but I hope to put in some more hours in the next weeks if that will work out. I know we can close this project in half the time allotted if I could find some extra information." Her voice wavered, and she cleared her throat, hoping to hide her nervousness.

"Well, it's nice to see the initiative. Some of the younger archivists can learn from the example you bring. I knew I made the right choice bringing you on board. You take all the time you think you need." He patted the side wall of her workstation. "Well . . . I suppose I should let you get back at it. Don't stay too late tonight. It's okay to at least go home and change." He squinted both his eyes and wrinkled his nose playfully with a knowing smirk.

Maariun's cheeks immediately grew hot. Someone noticed the wrinkles in her skirt after all, and that she was wearing the same outfit from yesterday. She'd have to do a better job managing her time with Aria. The department's project also needed to close in half the time, now that she made the promise. Whiskers would never forgive her if she didn't show up two days in a row anyway, no matter how aloof he was.

Maariun spent the morning diligently working on her projects, but she had to constantly refocus her attention. She couldn't stop thinking about Aria. Part of it was the excitement of new discovery, but the feelings she developed were deeper than that. She couldn't quite explain it, since she had never met Aria awake and in person, but she sensed a connection to her. Aria seemed to share the same curiosity about the universe as she did, and her organizational skills were impeccable. She would have rushed to the top of the Analyst pool on Ketos in no time. Maariun laughed at the same time Aria laughed, and cried through the sleeping stranger's lonely moments as she watched tears fall down Aria's cheeks. Journeying alone, across the galaxy, with no sure goal, must have been terrifying. Yet each time Aria awoke, she rallied herself and moved on to the next coordinates. Maariun wished she had been as brave in her life. It was one reason she fell in love with Saara; her zeal for exploration had been infectious. She still vividly remembered the smile that filled her lover's face when she found out she had finally been selected for a mission after so many years of training and waiting. When lunch arrived, she fought the temptation to sprint down to the archive and instead ensured she was visible in the square. She even tried saying *good morning* to a few coworkers, but they only looked at her with puzzlement.

After work, she teleported home, freshened up, and gathered supplies. Whisker's auto feeder was functioning, and she picked him up and snuggled him for a few minutes before turning around to leave again. The mournful yowl that came from his lungs as she turned to leave made her stop in her tracks.

"Awwww . . . Whiskers," she turned back to him, "I'm sorry, buddy, but I have things that are very important right now. I promise it won't be long." The feline met her words with a disappointed meow and moved forward, rubbing itself against her legs. Then it stood on its hind legs and reached upward toward her. "I'm sorry, buddy. I promise we'll spend some time together soon." She scratched his head before stepping into the teleporter.

The invisible barrier between Aria and her was surprisingly warm to the touch. Her hand rested atop the translucent case, and she watched her new friend's chest rise and fall.

"You've done it, Aria. You've found us. I'll be here when you wake up." Maariun hoped she could be true to her word, but with no knowledge of the stasis unit, she lacked the confidence in her promise. There was no doubt in her mind that someone on her planet could wake the sleeping stranger. She meant no disrespect with her thoughts, but if a race as primitive as humans could figure out the unit, she was sure that Ketos could too. She wasn't, however, sure that she was that Ketonian. For all her dreams of grandeur, she still believed deep down she would never be more than an archivist. If she turned Aria over to the authorities, they could wake her, and Aria would finally realize her dreams. She pushed down the urge to do the right thing as a pang of selfish stubbornness rose in her stomach. She wasn't ready to give up her new friend yet. If the authorities took over, she would certainly never see Aria again. Sitting down at the console, she pulled up the next log.

"Good morning, Maryann. It feels silly telling you my name each day, so I'm going to assume you can count and you know who I am by now. I'm *so* excited for another day in the vast emptiness of paradise." Aria forced a smile and Maariun could detect the hint of sarcasm that came with the statement. "It's odd, you know. I've been awake"—she held up her fingers in front of her face as if counting—"twenty days since I left Earth, and it has already been a thousand years." She touched and stretched her face in the manner Maariun was accustomed to watching each time Aria woke.

"I set this last sleep cycle for five hundred years, but I've been orbiting this planet for three hundred of them. I'm not sure longer intervals are going to get me further if the ship is going to stop at every planet showing signs of life. Three hundred years circling a planet seems like an enormous waste of time. Initial indications of life were promising, but upon further inspection, there were no structures on the surface. The telescopes show bipedal life evolving, but it will be thousands of years before they're ready for contact." Aria sighed. "Maybe I'll just stay in orbit for the next five thousand years and see if they're ready when I wake up." Aria looked off the screen toward the pod. "I know there's got to be life ready for me, though. I'll be awake for five days this time. A lot more data to catalogue. Plus, I'm almost done with my book and am eager to start the next! You'll never believe what I just found out about Griz! If you've found me, the book is on the table in the kitchen. If you can figure out our language, read it, and we'll discuss it when you wake me. For now, this is me, signing out."

Over the next few months, Maariun carved out a routine. To maintain the pretense that she was putting in extra time for the team, she would forgo her breaks and focus on the department projects while at work. She was exhausted, but her commitment to Aria never wavered. She stayed in the archive late into the evening each night, forcing herself to leave with enough time to snuggle Whiskers each evening and get a few hours rest.

Tonight, Maariun tossed and turned in her bed, her mind racing with thoughts of Aria. She had listened to hundreds of logs at this point. It was clear Aria was growing weary, her hope dwindling with each passing century. Maariun noticed a weight settling in her chest. She wanted to reach through the screen to Aria, to offer her comfort, to tell her that everything would be okay, and that she would finally reach her destination. In the stasis room, she began sitting with her sleeping beauty, reading to her, chatting with her, and just gazing at her silent, peaceful face. Maariun was certain that if anyone found her there, talking to a being in stasis, they would immediately commit her to a sanity retreat. Her frustrations rose each week. Unable to break through the barriers of time and space, Maariun was trapped in her own reality, only able to join Aria through a screen.

As she lay in the darkness, Maariun's thoughts drifted back to the day she first discovered her new friend. She remembered the excitement; the thrill of finding something so extraordinary. She had felt a connection to Aria from the moment she saw her, a bond that only grew stronger over the weeks.

Maariun closed her eyes, picturing Aria's slim figure. She spent so many hours gazing down at her, she could picture her delicate nail beds, the small mole on the side of her neck, her long eyelashes that would flutter ever so slightly from time to time, indicating that at least she was dreaming. A mix of wonder and sadness filled her as she thought of Aria's smile on the screen. She could hear her voice, soft and melodic, yet tinged with a hint of loneliness. In her last log, Aria came across as dejected. She had finally given up after thousands of years hurtling through star dust. "This time I'm going to sleep, perhaps forever," she said. Maariun chose to believe that it meant she was going to sleep until someone found her, but the obvious finality sat thick in the air when she reached to turn off the camera for the last time.

As she lay in the darkness of her bedroom, a tear escaped Maariun's eye, rolling down her cheek. She wiped it away, determined to remain strong. Aria was someone she couldn't give up on. She needed to wake her.

Crisp air filled the room the next morning. Maariun opened the window during the night, hoping the fresh air would help her sleep. It hadn't. Wiping the crust from her eyes, she stretched. Whiskers sat impatiently beside her pillow, pawing the spot next to her hand. Maariun pulled him unwillingly in for a snuggle before rolling out of bed. It was the weekend, but the growing urgency to find a solution solidified as she lay awake the night before. Over the past few weeks, she tinkered with the controls using a few hints dropped by Aria as she casually mentioned the stasis in her logs, but still found no solution to wake her.

There was nothing in the ship's database outlining how the stasis pod worked. Every other facet of the ship seemed to have technical data neatly outlined, even if they read a bit like a museum display description. The slab, however, remained a mystery. Maariun searched the Biblioplex database several times using every descriptor she could think of, but Ketos had not come across this unit before. There were other stasis technologies found, and Ketonians had certainly capitalized on them, but this one remained a mystery. She was certain that this discovery alone would shoot her to the top of the archivist pool when she revealed it. She just hoped that she didn't have to turn it over with a sleeping human inside it.

There, of course, would be no way for her to hide Aria once she was awake, but if she could befriend her before Ketos got its hands on her there would be a chance to reunite after the initial buzz of a *visitor* dissipated. Ketonians often explored, but rarely received visitors themselves. She had compiled as many schematics as she could find and intended to spend the weekend cross-referencing designs to see if there were synergies with the controls. She downed her nutrient shake and headed toward the teleporter.

Whiskers sat atop the glowing circle as if in protest. He yowled at her with one sharp note, then stared up at her.

"I know, buddy, it's been tough. It shouldn't be long now. I'm close." She attempted to push him to the side gently with the toe of her shoe, but he wouldn't budge. "Come on, Whiskers, I have to go." The feline lay down, rolled onto his back, and emitted a long, drawn-out whine.

"Oh all right, you can come with me this time, but we can't make a habit of this." She scooped him up and kissed the top of his head. He immediately snuggled into the crook of her neck, and she stepped into the teleportation circle and returned to the archive. Over the last few weeks, she had chosen to use the teleportation pad directly inside the archive to avoid being seen coming and going. A door guard had casually mentioned that she was "riding the comet's tail again," and she didn't wish to, or need to, become the latest departmental neural net chatter.

Of course, it would show in the logs each time she teleported in, but she knew no one checked those unless items went missing. She hurried to the ship and closed the hatch behind her before setting Whiskers down to explore. It took only moments before the feline disappeared into the belly of the ship.

Maariun brought her holo-display into the kitchen and set it in the centre of the table. In a matter of seconds, schematics from the stasis units she found in the Biblioplex hovered around the room. She began moving them around and placing them on top of each other. The logo for ExploreTech flashed up beside one of them, and her stomach flipped for a moment. This specific stasis unit was likely the very model Saara used on her first and last mission. She closed her eyes, trying to stave off the tears welling up and refocused her energy. Seconds later, there was a crash and a yowl from the stasis room where Aria slept.

She rushed into the room to find a teacup she had left next to the console broken on the floor. Liquid glistened down the side of the machine, and a small blue arch jumped momentarily out of the console, grounding itself before dissipating. The gravity field that was holding Aria above the slab disappeared and Aria fell with a thud onto the hard, black surface. The body looked lifeless as a pale hand flopped sideways, and her head lolled to the side.

"Aria!" Maariun screamed. Her hearts pounded in her chest. She flew over to the body and resisted the urge to grab her, not wanting to contaminate the body. Aria's eyes were still closed, but as she looked closer, Maariun noticed the slightest eye flutter on the limp face. She was alive; still asleep, but alive. Once she calmed herself back down, she noticed the familiar rhythm of Aria's chest rising and falling with each breath.

"Stasis cycle interrupted. Restart stasis to preserve life or continue stasis end protocol. Life terminated in ten." An unfamiliar voice filled the room, this time coming from the unit. *What did it mean "restart stasis to preserve life"? Life terminated in ten! Ten what?!* Maariun resisted the urge to resume panic mode. She knew it would only bring unproductivity.

"Think, Maariun." She spoke aloud to herself before rushing back to the schematics. It was her plan coming here today and was her only hope of understanding the stasis unit. She flipped through the schematics more urgently. Searching for anything she could find in common. Whiskers rubbed against her leg and let out a barely audible mew, as if apologizing.

"I know, Whiskers, it's okay. You didn't . . ."

"Life terminated in nine."

"Ketos be damned!" The common thread with all the

schematics was that they emitted a powerful electromagnetic field that distorted the fabric of spacetime within its boundaries. The field slowed down the molecular activity of the object within it, effectively halting biological processes. This didn't explain, however, how to work it. Knowing that Ketonians used the machine from ExploreTech, she thought there may be more information in the database. Quickly pulling up the file, she found the relevant operation documentation.

Protocol for Ending Stasis:
1.   **Activation Sequence:** *The operator must input the designated activation code. Once input, the code triggers a series of diagnostic checks to ensure the subject is ready to re-enter the world.*
2.   **Field Reduction:** *The stasis field will gradually reduce, allowing the subject's molecular activity to accelerate.*
3.   **Life Support Termination:** *As the subject's biological functions resume, the life support systems are incrementally shut down.*
4.   **Emergence:** *Once the subject is fully awake and their vital signs are stable, it is possible to open the stasis chamber.*
   Additional Features:
•   **Emergency Override:** *A manual override system allows for immediate termination of the stasis field in case of an emergency.*
•   **Data Storage:** *The unit can store vital information about the subject, such as medical records and personal data.*
•   **Remote Monitoring:** *Operators can connect the console to a remote monitoring system to monitor the subject's condition from a distance.*

"Life terminated in eight."
Well, that was utterly useless, she thought. With the console shorted out, there was no way to enter a code, even if she knew it. There were eight buttons on the side of the machine, each with a unique symbol, which would have meant thousands of codes. She frantically scanned the unit for any clues, running her fingers across the smooth surface. She was halfway around the unit when she felt it. A barely recessed groove, invisible to the naked eye at first glance. She followed the groove with her finger, and it

returned to the starting position, forming a perfect rectangle.

"Life terminated in seven."

It must be an access panel. Perhaps there was an emergency console inside. Not that she knew what she'd do with it when she found it, but sitting here watching her new friend in imminent danger of dying, the hope for an entire species perishing in front of her, spurred her to action. If it hadn't been for her, Aria would still be patiently waiting to be found. Who knows, the stasis may have ended on its own eventually and Aria would have woken up in the archive, ecstatic to have finally reached a destination worth exploring. Maariun clawed at the groove, trying to get her fingernails to pry open the panel. Sulfuric tears stung her eyes, but try as she might, she couldn't get the panel loose. Running to the kitchen, she grabbed a long, blunt metal instrument from the drawer. It was flat, and she thought she could use it for leverage.

"Life terminated in six."

It was almost immediately clear that the tool wasn't doing anything but scratching the surface of the slab. Standing, she looked down at Aria.

"Tell me how to save you. How did you figure it out? Please, Saara!" She immediately recognized the slip. Obviously, this being from another world wasn't Saara, but over the past weeks, she unconsciously viewed them as the same. Maariun realized she had been using Aria as a proxy the whole time. She couldn't save Saara. She hadn't been there to save the love of her life, but if she could save Aria, it would make up for it. If she had worked harder, been on the mission with her, perhaps she would still have her.

"Life terminated in five."

Maariun's eyes ran up and down the now familiar figure. She didn't want to admit defeat, but it was clear this task was beyond her. She should have just kept her nose down as an archivist. It was not her place to do anything above her pay grade. Catalogue, record and file; that's what she was good at. That's all she was good for. If only her attention to detail could solve a catastrophic emergency.

As her eyes made their way back up to Aria's face, vision blurry and the scent of tears filling the air, she noticed it. A silver disc connected to a small decorative chain around Aria's neck. It must have fallen loose from her garments when she fell from stasis.

The disc was highly reflective and displayed a series of symbols scrawled on it, inlaid with the same material as the slab. That was it. Maariun lunged forward to grab it but stopped herself before jostling the body. There was no sense ending stasis, only to contaminate Aria with something her body couldn't handle. Careful not to touch anything but the object, she worked slowly to remove it from the body.

"Life terminated in four."

"Life terminated in three."

Finally, it was loose. The symbols were now clearly visible on the object. With full awareness that the console was inoperable, Maariun immediately headed to the panel. As soon as the object was close to the panel, she heard a click. The panel recessed and moved to the side, revealing a secondary console.

"Life terminated in two."

Without another thought, Maariun entered the sequence into the console, praying to Ketos that it would work, even though she knew it was preposterous to believe in a higher power controlling the outcome of anything.

"Life sustained. Stasis resumed. Stasis field will return in ten."

Maariun collapsed on the floor beside the unit. The tension in her neck, arms, and temples released at once, and she felt like a doll crashing to the floor in relief. Her hearts still beat double time, but she could feel them slowing. Standing, she gazed at Aria. After this, she knew she needed to do the right thing. She had no business trying to do a full-on analysis of an alien craft on her own. Perhaps they would still allow her to be on the team since she made the discovery. She would have to return everything to its original state, though there were some things she knew she couldn't hide, and was sure it would disqualify her from further contact. She placed the key back around Aria's neck.

Understanding that the stasis field would return soon and cleanse any contaminants, she acted on impulse. She hadn't been there to say goodbye to Saara, and she wasn't going to miss this opportunity. Bending, she placed her lips lightly on Aria's cheek. "Goodbye, Aria. I'm so glad to have met you. I wish you could have met me too. I know we would have been fast friends."

"Biometric data accepted. Stasis sequence ended. Contact made."

Maariun jumped back as Aria's eyes fluttered open.

Her eyes fluttered open and the blur of sleep wore off. Aria was surprised to be awake. When she went into stasis that last time, she honestly thought she was closing her eyes for the last time, for eternity. The face that greeted her looked shocked and oddly a bit like the librarians in the stories she read back on Earth, aside from the blue hue to her skin. Auburn hair cascaded down around the stranger's face as she looked down at Aria.

"Good morning. You must be Maryann."

The first few days after she woke, Aria and Maariun kept the news to themselves. They had a lot to learn about each other, and didn't want to share it with anyone yet. Aria explained to her that during her last stasis, she had specifically programmed the unit to wake her up only when contacted by life, rather than when life was detected. Since the pod was sealed, someone would have to open it and exchange some form of DNA or biological material to reach her. Maariun's kiss had been the last piece of the puzzle.

Maariun still spent her evenings with Aria, but this time Maariun could take part in the conversation. Aria spent her days wandering through the archive, fascinated that so many worlds yielded so many discoveries. She found out about Ketos, the explorers, and the archive, and became fascinated by how easy it was for Ketonians to identify planets with life worth visiting. Part of her wanted to join a team and find more worlds to explore, but after many human lifetimes spent sailing aimlessly through space, she thought that perhaps a nice quiet job in the archive would be more appealing, assuming the Ketonians didn't lock her up or experiment on her for the rest of her life.

After settling on a story, they introduced Aria to Ketos. Having prior experience with other lifeforms, they extended a warm welcome to her. Maariun wove the practiced tale. She was doing her regular research after hours, looking for artifacts that could help her department. Aria woke naturally at the end of her stasis cycle, finding herself in the middle of the vast archive. With no way out, she wandered around the archive until Maariun stumbled upon her.

Ketonian authorities offered an apartment and a job as an ambassador to Earth, which had rebounded a few thousand years after Aria left. Maariun, however, also offered her a room, and

Aria chose a quieter life out of public scrutiny, though her colourless complexion would draw stares no matter where she went.

"I passed!" Maariun stepped off the teleporter into the kitchen, her arms held up in triumph. Aria busied herself around the kitchen, a smile spreading across her face at the entrance.

"I had no doubts," Aria replied, lifting a pan from the counter. The cake she had prepared already displayed *congratulations* across its surface. Celebrating with cake was not a Ketonian custom, but over the past few years Aria had taught some of the best Earth customs to her new family. "Maariun Melik, explorer extraordinaire!" she cheered. "Do you know when your first mission will be?"

"I was told that it could be anytime now. My *discovery* seems to have waived the waiting period." She nodded at Aria. "I know you said you're comfortable at the archive, but please say you've reconsidered our discussion. I can't imagine heading out into the unknown without you."

Aria moved close to Maariun, taking her by the hand. Reaching down, she picked up Whiskers, who was circling their legs, looking for attention. "I know how you feel, and I've given it a lot of thought, but . . ."

Maariun's hearts sank simultaneously. She understood why Aria had no desire to continue exploring, but part of her wanted to share this new adventure with the person she had grown to love. "I know, I know . . ." she replied, accepting defeat.

"*But* . . ." Aria cut her off, placing her finger over Maariun's lips, "only if we can take Whiskers. You know he'd never forgive us."

Maariun's eyes widened. The smell of sulphur filled the room at the realization that she wouldn't have to face this daunting new journey on her own after all. Aria wrinkled her nose and pulled a hand in front of her face. Humans had salt in their tears, not sulphur. Without another word, Aria leaned in and kissed her.

BETWEEN THE HEAVENS
AND THE EMBERS

Shannon Allen

The bedraggled form limping across the polished floor five minutes before closing caught librarian Portia Telmah's attention. It was not so much the movement, but the sand left in its wake. She stepped out from her workstation, hoping to halt the advancement of any more contamination to the space station library or the delicate ancient books housed there. The daily patrons coming for digital copies of books kept her busy. As for her ancient collections, she would set up the requested material and scholars would access them by holo-conference. Both endeavours kept contamination to a minimum.

As she neared the rag-clad figure, she was surprised to recognize the deteriorated style of dress as being from Ecinev. How long had it taken this wanderer to get here from the farthest post in the system? Not to mention how unsettling that one would show up in person, the Ecinev were a deeply private race. The questions that swirled in her head quickly left as the being stumbled toward her muttering.

"Dark Lady, I bring a gift."

Portia strained to make out the words. The figure lifted something for her to take; she hastened to meet the gesture. The being fell into her arms, once again muttering "Dark Lady" before becoming a pile of sand on the floor.

Portia stood there, sand at her feet and something just below the surface of the pile. Protocol left her. Hell, was there even one for a lifeform dying and then turning to sand at your feet? Her brain raced as she tried to grab onto something as her body fought against the artificial gravity of the space station. She wobbled. Nausea tickled the back of her throat as she was thrown back to how it felt those first days after arriving from her home on Earth.

"Steady on." It was more of a command to both her body and the problem at hand. Looking around to make sure the library was indeed empty she leaned over to delicately push some of the sand aside unveiling a parcel wrapped in a type of cloth. Careful unwrapping revealed a book. Smaller than most that she had seen but the softness caressed her hands as she removed it from the wrapping. The worn corners and mottled binding begged to be looked at, but there was a more pressing matter, the poor soul about her feet. It wouldn't take long for the bio sensors to detect the anomaly and send drones to vacuum the sand up. Emotion override chip or not, she didn't think it a fitting end for someone. She needed something to put the being in.

What, what, what? Then it struck her. A book casing unit. They were airtight, the sensors wouldn't be able to scan it, and it would buy her the time to find out what the burial rights were for a Ecinev. Carefully stepping out of her shoes so she wouldn't track sand through the library, she ran to grab a casing unit.

Entering the restoration room, she grabbed the first case she found and returned to scoop up the sand. The first alarm went off. She worked quickly. She had two minutes till the second alarm and then one minute after that before the drones showed up.

Adding the book last, Portia snapped the lid shut, put her shoes on and dusted off the case just as the first drone entered the library. She dared not move. They needed to register something; she wanted it to be the small amount of sand she had been unable to pick up from the floor.

"Bio matter detected," the metallic voice announced. "Matter not Portia Telmah, head librarian. Explain."

"A life form entered the library to the point you are at now, but left before engaging in conversation."

"Matter detected on Portia Telmah."

"I touched the matter on the floor to investigate." She held out her hand, the other tightly holding the casing unit. The drone scanned her and beeped.

"Confirmed. Prepare to be decontaminated."

She remained still as the drones vacuumed her, her shoes, the casing unit, and the floor. Silently she said a prayer for both what was left of the poor soul being vacuumed up and herself. *Great stars! Stop that!* She made a mental note to get her emotion chip checked when all this was done.

"Area decontaminated. Resume activity of closing library." With a final beep, the drone was gone and Portia finally let out the breath she was holding. Tomorrow when she came back, she would deal with the contents of the casing unit, right now she just wanted to go to her suite and scream in the shower.

A sleepless night brought her back to the library long before her shift, her footsteps echoing as she made her way to her desk. Pulling out the case from her drawer, she took it to a worktable. It seemed so utilitarian for what it held. With great care she opened it, revealing the rewrapped book nestled in the sand. She hesitated—twice in as many days she would be rummaging through the remains of a someone. Her stomach lurched. *Just do it quickly*, she told herself, *and then you can close the case for good.* Slipping on disposable gloves, she carefully dusted off the small package, hoping the sensors would not go off again. That would raise more questions and a behaviour review. Both unwanted. Dusting done, she removed the gloves and laid them in the case with the sand. She closed the lid and waited.

Nothing. No alarms. No drones.

Laying the book on the desk, Portia marvelled at the details. Remnants of gold leaf clung to the embossed design. The edges worn and stained from being handled only enhanced the mottled emerald cover. She had never seen or held such a work of beauty before. It bore no title on the spine, so Portia opened the cover. The revealed page was a stark contrast with only a simple title, *Mirror*.

Turning it carefully in her hands, Portia could not find any cataloguing marks, current or historical. How odd. Every book had a catalogue number. How was she to know if it should be reported to the Galactic Council as banned or subversive literature. She put the book down and grabbed a scanner. Portia ran it over the book to see if there was a nano marker used by some planets.

Nothing.

Portia picked it up. The warmth of it seeping into her hands tempted her to explore the story within. How wonderful to feel all the little imperfections and richness of natural paper beneath her fingertips. The audible hum of the public digital systems starting up drew her attention. Soon patrons would be entering the library requiring her attention for the array of requests they would make. There was no time now for the luxury of exploring the pages, and she couldn't leave the book out. The collections room would be the perfect place to keep it because there was no public access there without permission. It would be safe there on the restoration cart.

She loved that part of the library. The quiet coolness that kept the books, the replicated wood shelves, and the light perfume in the air that only old books can give. All this was anchored between two large port windows that allowed the stars to peek in, and the restoration desk sat beneath one of them. Nowhere else on the station were ports like these, a mystery to anyone but the long-forgotten designer of the station.

Portia rounded the desk to where the cart sat. Resting upon it were two larger books, perfect for her little treasure to hide under. Just as she slipped the book under, the alarm for opening screeched. Startled, Portia toppled the cart. Everything came down, Portia, the books, and lastly, the cart. Sprawled on the floor in the dying din, her habitual "shhh" slipped out. Easing herself up off the floor, Portia surveyed the mess. The two larger books were laying off to the right while the small emerald one peeked out from under the cart. Righting the cart, she saw a few loose pages next to the open book. There was no silencing the words that fell from her mouth as she set things right. Like so much of the last two days, figuring out what to do and how to do it would have to wait, unlike the patrons at the door.

The library doors held the weight of the day as Portia closed them. Her well of patience had run dry somewhere between the third school group and the new station resident who crashed all the digital readers in the day room.

"Lights down eighty percent." With such a simple command, Portia could feel the deepening light lift the ache from her body as she made her way to her restoration desk. All day her fingers had been itching to hold the stranger's book and to see the extent of the damage caused by this morning's catastrophe.

"Desk light, restoration strength." The brightness of the lights blurred the room around her. It was just her, the book, and the loose pages. The rest of the world could wait in the shadows. As she inspected the small volume in her hands there didn't seem to be any damage. No new indents or mangled edges, no torn pages, or loose bindings. How odd. If there are loose pages they had to have come from somewhere. They were not from the other two books; they were the wrong size and held no decoration or illuminated text. They were handwritten and old but not ancient. Her cursive skills were rusty so the pages would take a bit of time to read. A pot of tea would be required.

Settling into a chair with her tea, Portia grabbed the first page to read. It was slow at first, and she fought the temptation to run a scanner over it to digitize and convert to text on a reader. It would be easier, but for some reason felt wrong. The page revealed nothing interesting. It turned out to be a retelling of the weather someone had observed on a colony planet. The other two pages were just as mundane. Why would anyone waste a scarce thing like paper on a boring subject using substandard gritty ink? Could it have been to practice a dead art form? If so, why put the loose pages in this book? Going through the book, she found nothing remarkable in the handwritten pages that would account for their inclusion. It didn't make sense and yet someone had died at her feet to give it to her. To the Dark Lady. Who in the heck was the Dark Lady? It certainly wasn't her. Portia shrugged her shoulders while tipping her head side to side to stem the flood of questions building in her brain.

"Restoration lights off." Enough, the ache of a long day was creeping over her. Tomorrow she would figure out where to shelve the book. She could feel the pull of a comfortable bed and warm blankets. Stacking the sheets to one side, she let her eyes adjust to the library's dim light before leaving.

Something moved.

"Wh . . . who's . . . there?" Silence.

"Who's there?" Nothing. "Security scan. Library. Portia Telmah, librarian, authorizing."

"Verified authorization, scanning." The nondescript voice reverberated from the station system. "One life form detected, head librarian Portia Telmah. Library doors remain locked. Do you require security assistance?"

"No further assistance required."

"Scan and response recorded. Good evening, Portia Telmah."

She giggled. The doors had been locked using her own codes. It was time for bed. Just as she passed the desk, a spot of light grew above the stack of papers and a hologram appeared. It wasn't a person. Hanging in the air was a book. A book she did not recognize. The mystery of it drew her closer. Reaching out, she could feel it and was able to take the book into her hands. This was not any hologram program she had ever seen. Carefully, she opened the cover and promptly dropped it. The title page faced her—*The Complete Works of William Shakespeare*. It was subversive! Portia had never seen a copy, but she knew what it was. It was corruption. It was free thought that brought down governments. It was the gateway to a vast range of emotions that the chip meant to subdue so that order could be kept. Every librarian knew the books in the Listing by heart. They also knew what would happen to them if they were found with anything on the Listing. Portia put distance between herself and the book. In her haste, the remaining pages were pushed across the desk and into the pool of soft starlight coming through the porthole window. Two more books appeared. Portia had a feeling they were on the Listing too.

The room spun. Air couldn't fill her lungs fast enough. What if she was caught with these? Portia shuddered at the thought of the consequences. Yanking a drawer open, she shoved the papers in and slammed it shut. The books disappeared. Tomorrow she would put the papers back in the book before shelving it in some dark back corner of the collections room so it would look like it had always been there. It wasn't catalogued and would stay that way. She had a plan as she left the library.

Only the plan interrupted her sleep. Questions ripped through her brain. So many questions. Why had the book and pages come to her? Somewhere between why and how Portia gave up trying to sleep. *This is why you get your emotion chip looked after when you notice problems,* she scolded herself. Had everything been working properly, the drones would have done what they do and none of this would be an issue now. Then the thought hit her, what if there were more? She had been told that the previous librarian had just vanished. She had heard the murmur of suspicious rumours in quiet corners of the library. That was probably why the being had come to her—because the last librarian had been taking the holographic pages. Sleep be damned, she had to know.

As the lighting switched to day cycle Portia stretched the long night from her body. She had gone through so many records, pulled so many books from the collections room, that she had lost count of how many pages she had held up to the starlight. But she had found some bound into books that were mundane works of fiction or biography, the content of the pages blending into the narratives. They hid in plain sight. The restoration records never reflected the work done in the books she found. She scanned the reading requests too. The Ecinev had always requested reading sessions in the evening. She had always put it to the shyness of their culture. Now she was not so sure.

Reluctantly, she tidied up, leaving the newest pages under the blotter on the restoration desk and the book on the cart. Hiding in plain sight had worked so far. The day would be starting soon, and she had to look respectable. She would head home. A quick shower and change of clothes would cover her growing doubts.

Returning to the library, she saw people waiting.

"Good morning, librarian Telmah." The gruff voice was attached to Zenit, head of security. A second person she vaguely remembered stood to his left. "I believe you know Aleric Streep, the head of the Galactic Council of Literature." The man nodded.

"Good morning, gentlemen."

"There was an incident in your library that we need to discuss. I have posted a notice of a late opening for anyone wishing to use the library." His fingers flew over a data pad before she could even answer.

"Of course, let me disarm the locks and we can proceed."

"I just did that."

It took all she had to walk through the doors and into the library.

Settled in the day room, Portia sat on the edge of a chair. "How may I help you, gentlemen?"

Streep leaned forward, his voice stern. "Drones were summoned to the library just before closing two-time cycles ago. In the matter retrieved, we found bio markers to your predecessor. Did you see her?"

"I never met her, but don't think so. They left before I could talk to them." The room got warmer.

"Was anything left?"

"Just the sand on the floor which set off the alarms. "

"As recorded by the drones."

Zenit handed her a data pad. "Why were you searching records last night? Odd timing, don't you think? Many of those searches came remarkably close to illegal material."

She needed time to think. "Something to drink, gentlemen?"

Both shook their heads no.

The growing doubt of what made literature illegal overwhelmed her. She felt a need to protect the pages. How much could she give them so they would go away?

"I did find a small volume the next day and didn't associate it with the visitor right away. So, I thought checking the providence would determine the proper channels for me to report it. The library has been busy. I did not want to let the matter go too long, so I worked during the night cycle."

"That's admirable, Librarian Telmah. May I have it?" Streep unfurled his long fingers, expecting compliance.

She nodded and left to retrieve it. The sacrifice. The beautiful little tome.

Streep held his hand out to receive it when she returned. "What did you find in all your searching?"

Portia looked away from his eyes, quickly sorting the details she wanted to tell. "I did not find any cataloguing information in our records. There was also a lack of nano markers. I cross-referenced the author's name, reading requests, and subject and found nothing to link this book to any records. I concluded late last night that it would need to be turned over to the Galactic Council."

"I can save you the trouble." Streep curled his hands around the book. "Was there anything else with the book, Librarian Telmah?"

"No, just the book." She knew within the hour the beautiful little book would be ash.

Zenit and Streep stood to leave. "If there is nothing else . . ." Zenit paused before continuing when she didn't reply, "We will leave you so the library can open. Thank you for your help, Librarian Telmah. We can see ourselves out."

Portia waited till they were out the doors before collapsing into the chair.

Now she needed to deal with the papers under the blotter. There was no guarantee that they believed her. They could still return with reinforcements. She shook off the thought of what they could do to her. The sooner she did something the better, and she hoped her nerves held. The next few days would have to be as normal as possible. Follow routine. Stay away from the restoration desk. Stay out of the collections room unless she had a scholar request. It would all give her time to digest what she had just set herself up for. Is this what the Ecinev had meant by Dark Lady?

When the time was right, she would bind the loose pages into a volume from the collections room just as others had done. There was a volume that needed new bindings, and it would be easy to slip the pages in with the rest. No one would question a book she had already been working on. Portia would need to be above question. In time. she would have to learn how to function as if the emotion chip still worked.

They never did come back. She grew careful in her night reads as she fell in love with the words she read. She learned of the Dark Lady in the pages of Shakespeare. The depth of emotion in other works from across the depth of space weaving into her very being. In time, pages found their way to her. Each one treasured and in need of a haven for a time when someone special came looking.

There was always a sense of satisfaction as she tapped a newly rebound book onto the shelf. Leaving the collections room, she lovingly ran her hand over the line of books leading to the door. The quiet part of her said *thank you* to the restoration case hidden behind them.

SYNAPSES

Jennifer Rahn

The look the recruiter gave me over her data holo said more than words.

"Librarian?"

"Yes."

She read from my forms: "Val Keats. Graduated with honours seven standards ago." She snapped my transcripts with her wrist as she handed them back to me. "Sorry, can't help you. Try the stock markets. Information management is all AI on the trader ships—has been for decades."

I managed to grab the pages before getting shoved out of the way. The *Majesty* was the largest trade vessel to come by Academia, and I'd thought they'd surely need a human corporate librarian. An AI algorithm would only recommend the most accessed information sources, delivering the same data on potential clients over and over again. Sometimes the more obscure files could make the difference between a prosperous or failed deal.

Try the stock markets. I had to get there first. My studies on Academia, where Liliane had deposited me, had been in preparation for resettlement on the New Worlds, and now I couldn't even get to one of them.

I dropped the transcripts as other hopefuls for the *Majesty* jostled past. I stumbled away, not seeing reasons to pick them up. My credit was negative, I hadn't eaten since yesterday, and

Liliane hadn't messaged me in months. But why would she? Out of all her eggs dispersed through the system, I was the least likely product to supply bragging rights to promote her career.

I swallowed against the dryness in my mouth as my internal self crumbled, and tried not to keep staring at where the recruiter was hiring sales staff—they were all still human. Corporations still recognised the value of their contributions.

Maybe there was another way I could get to the New Worlds. I was an information specialist, after all, finding data on possibilities is what I did best—if I could find a terminal that didn't require credit, which was unlikely for off-world searches.

I looked around as I wandered away, trying to not seem too desperate. Along the docks, there were a few other ships in port undergoing repairs or taking on supplies. None of them indicated they were hiring, and the captain who was rumoured to be an organ harvester was watching me with unnerving intensity. I pretended to check my wrist comm, then hurried off in the opposite direction as if I had suddenly received a summons to be somewhere else.

Habit directed me towards the Student Services centre. In two more standards they'd stop hearing my requests as well. I went in anyway, and against all hope, checked my soon-to-be-deleted inbox for any comms from Liliane. She'd sent me care packages before, and I could really use one now. Everything I owned was on me, had been consumed, or had been stolen.

Nothing. No care package, and still no responses to the hundreds of queries for off-world employment that I'd sent out.

I exited the building. No reason to stay there, and no reason to leave either, except to escape the feeling that I was about to crawl out of my skin. Another of those raggedy work-in-space types was loitering by the stairs. He didn't have any corporate logos on him, so he probably was a privateer. Could have been a captain judging by the tech he had strung over his shoulder.

I didn't expect him to speak to me when I passed by, since he wasn't really looking my way.

"Miss Keats? Got a spot for you on the *Scorpius*."

"Excuse me?"

"You're the librarian, right? Heard you at the lineup for the *Majesty*."

I turned and had a good look at him. There was no way this

Scorpius was a trade or tech vessel. He looked as dire as I was. I couldn't think of anything to say that wouldn't sound insulting—he couldn't pay me for that long, his ship was probably a junker, we'd end up starving together in some asteroid belt—so I kept silent, because starving on Academia was only slightly more appealing, and just maybe he did have a better offer.

"My name is Darton. We're headed out to the Boötes Void. Need someone to categorize all the data collection."

Data collection from a cosmic void? A collection of nothing from a known region of nothing? My skepticism must have shown on my face.

"We got a contract for it. Don't need to find a buyer. Equal portions split between the crew when we get paid. Should be enough to carry you for thirty-six standards."

"Oh." Here was my doorway to an illustrious career as an information peddler. Or perhaps it could lead to a position in some astronomy institute in the future. Or private investigation. Could be promising. And since it was the only offer I'd had since graduating, I said: "Yes. I'm definitely interested."

He motioned with his head that I should follow and didn't say another word as he led me to where his ship and crew were docked. Five others were working around a mid-sized vessel, none of them appearing scholarly, and the silent looks they exchanged when they saw me made a sliver of paranoia creep through my brain. The captain pointed at one of his crew.

"This is Molly. She'll show you your bunk."

"Hiya. This way."

Molly didn't wait to see if I followed. When we reached the hatch, she turned and handed me her grease-covered wrench so that she could wrestle the portal open manually.

"Don't worry. We'll fix it before we leave."

"Um. What exactly will I be doing?"

She gave me a wide-eyed look of innocence and shrugged. "Just collecting information and stuff. You know. And then send it to the client."

"You . . . don't have AI then?"

Molly snorted. "Tried that. Not what the client wants."

We had to crouch to walk through the dingy off-white passage that led inside. Multiple hand-holds were lined along the walls to assist movement in zero-g. Above and below that, black tubing and wires ran alongside. I was careful not to touch or dislodge anything, having no way to clean the grease off my hands after giving the wrench back to Molly.

"You're here." Molly shoved open a stiff shutter from an incredibly small bunk that was at eye level. "Fresh liner sheets are here." She pulled open a narrow drawer under the bunk. "It's easier to get into when we're in flight. Toilet's over here." She pulled open another narrow doorway. "That's pretty much it. We get food packets at scheduled intervals. I'll show you the work terminals now."

Another bunk shutter slid upwards as we passed. A skinny fellow covered in tats and with too-large eyes looked at me and hesitantly reached out. He shuddered and seemed like he was trying to get me to lip-read some message.

"Stuff it, Dave." Molly roughly shoved him back inside and dragged the shutter down. "Don't worry about him. He can't talk right now, but he'll be all right."

Junkie? I wondered, but didn't say anything. One or two on a crew like this was to be expected.

"Those are the workstations." Five angled screens lined a small cubicle. I finally caved and wiped my hands on my pants before I tapped the surface of a panel and looked through the apps that lit up.

"There isn't much."

Molly shrugged. "Dave managed all right. For a while."

"Okay." So, I was replacing Dave. "Mind if I code in a few new apps?"

Molly shrugged. "Sure. Make yourself comfortable. Wheels up in thirty."

Feeling much better now that I had access to a terminal, I dug through the files to see what Dave had already done. Apparently, there were . . . some sort of nodes dispersed within the void that could be arranged to form a power grid. It would be able to adapt to extreme loads equivalent to the implosion of a high-mass star. It just had to be assembled, which required organisation of information packets that consisted of . . .

I sighed in frustration. While the principle sounded extremely lucrative for a corporation with the capacity to store and distribute the energy, the gaps in the data made it seem high risk, and I was worried we'd never assemble enough of the information to get paid.

A lot of Dave's files were corrupted.

Or redacted.

Shut up, Brain. I don't need you spewing conspiracy theories.

So, what exactly is wrong with ol' Davey, then?

I took a deep breath, then refocused on trying to recover the corrupted data.

Personnel files. Every ship had to have them.

David Montgomery was an electrical tech. He'd suffered a near electrocution while working on the ship's magnetic propulsion system a few weeks back. Report signed by one Captain Darton.

See, Brain. No conspiracy.

Why was an electrical tech trying to assemble a major information database?

Maybe he was the most qualified member of the crew.

A tinny announcement sounded over the speakers: "All hands, please return your crash seats to the upright position and lock down anything you don't want smashing through the hull. *Scorpius* is outta here."

I hadn't done spaceflight for several years, but managed to adjust, without too much nausea, to the loss of gravity and unmatched inertial swings unique to magnetic propulsion. As I designed an information matrix and began inputting data, my suspicion that Dave's files had been tampered with grew. The "corrupted" data had a pattern; chunks were missing whenever I got close to piecing together the nature of the information nodes, specifically their material composition and how they were accessed. Had Dave sabotaged this when he suspected he might be replaced? It didn't make sense that someone else on the crew would have compromised the information to do the job they clearly wanted done.

I had drifted off in the crash seat by the workstation, and woke to someone patting the back of my hand. Dave was there, his face eerily lit by the dim running lights of the night cycle. He looked upset as he kept patting my hand, pointing at his opened mouth, then tapping the side of his head.

"What is it?" I asked. He immediately held a finger to his lips and shook his head, looking around nervously.

"I don't understand," I whispered, and opened a digital

keyboard on the work screen. "Can you write it?"

Dave nodded, then began typing a series of what looked like mathematical equations on the screen. He squeezed his eyes shut, spilling out tears, before shaking his head and trying again. More numbers and symbols. His agitation grew, and he began pounding his fists against his forehead. I tried to calm him by putting my hands over his and gently pulling them away. He looked at me mournfully for a few seconds before pointing into his mouth, then tapping the side of his head one more time. I nodded, just to avoid having him freak out again, even though I had no idea what he was trying to tell me. He sighed and hung his head defeatedly. I guess I hadn't convinced him of anything.

"Keats? All good here?"

I looked up and saw Darton gripping the post of the cubicle entryway.

"Davey, why're you out of your bunk?"

Dave grimaced angrily and punched the air several times. Tears were streaming down his face now.

"Rest up. That's an order." Darton grabbed Dave's sleeve and pulled him out of the cubicle. "You too, Keats."

"Okay." I unstrapped the harness of the crash seat, feeling wobbly and drained as I pulled myself toward the bunks. A silver food packet had been left for me. I climbed in, pulled the shutter down, peeled the wrapper from the food bar, and chewed slowly as I listened to Dave's muted sobs.

It took half a cycle to reach the edge of the Boötes Void. I had done as much as I could in terms of setting up a database and query system. Now I needed to fill it with something to be organised, analysed, whatever. A series of drones were embedded in the ship's hull, maybe half of them functional. Did I need authorisation to launch them? No one really talked to me, and Darton mostly left me to set things up my way. I shrugged and signalled the launch. Someone might actually give me vocal information if there was a problem.

As expected, the Void wasn't really completely voidy. The drones reported finding dust, ice, and an organisational pattern of empty space and matter filaments. I supposed I'd have to look at dark matter and energy patterns as well. Hard to believe any of this wasn't already well characterised.

Darton had activated a health-check app on my workstation a week ago, to remind me to move around every few hours, in lieu of actual crew interaction. I unstrapped and floated around. Dave was locked in his bunk, and none of the other crew members seemed to be present. Even the pilots weren't on duty.

I found Molly in the tiny medlab, cleaning out her workspace with a HEPA vacuum. Half her face was covered by a respirator.

"Hey. There's an extra food pack for you in the galley. Everyone else has already had theirs."

"What's the occasion?"

She shrugged. "Two-week bonus." She began dispensing disinfectant and wiping things down. I didn't have a respirator, so I left, wandering towards the galley more out of boredom than hunger. Off in the distance, Dave was banging on his bunk shutter and screaming incoherently.

I found the food packet floating up by the ceiling. It wasn't a firm block like the other packets and apparently contained chocolate ice cream. It tasted nothing like I expected, unless ice cream was made from mushrooms and dirt. It did have a chocolatey aftertaste.

Molly wasn't around when I floated back the other way. Since it would be a while before the drones were done their first sweep, I went to my bunk for a nap. Dave was quiet now.

I woke up with my head throbbing. It felt like parasites had invaded my brain and were reorganising the furniture. I clambered out of my bunk and went to the toilet, wanting to throw up and feeling like *something wouldn't let me* at the same time.

Get it out.

I opened my mouth wide, not sure if I wanted to reach in and pull something out, or smack myself in the head to knock whatever it was free. I began to panic. Someone grabbed my shoulders and pulled me backwards. I found myself looking up at Darton.

"Can you speak?"

My heart fluttered painfully and my eyes couldn't focus as I forced words from my mouth.

"Y-y-yes-ss. I-I-I . . ." I what? I couldn't form thought patterns the way I wanted as my brain was being reorganised.

Molly was scanning me with a handheld. "Greater connectivity between the two hemispheres and dual speech centres intact. Looks like we did need a woman. With her library skills, this might actually work."

Darton looked relieved. He held my face in his hands and turned my head so I'd look at him. "You can do this, Keats. I know you can. Organise the grid and record everything in your database."

What?!

The ice cream. Molly had lied, and nobody else (except maybe Dave) had been given that special blend.

"W-why?" I managed to tap the side of my head, like Dave had done.

"There is a biological component to the nodes. We need you to connect with it to assemble the grid. We're all counting on you, Keats."

You expect me to do ANYTHING for YOU after what you've done to ME?!

Desperation did not validate bypassing consent.

"Let Dave out. Maybe he can help her."

Help me what? What good would finishing a job for pay be now that I was probably permanently damaged?

I kept seeing flashing lights, like a migraine aura. Dave was the only person I could visually focus on when he crawled from his bunk and took my hands, watching me with sympathy and concern.

"You need to assemble the grid," said Molly, giving his shoulder a nudge. Dave very deliberately flipped her the bird before turning his attention back to me.

"Just leave them for a bit," said Darton. "We're still on schedule." He and the rest of the crew went off to whatever they were doing before.

I floated there with Dave for probably hours. I began to notice that whenever my visual cortex generated light pulses, Dave's would respond with a matching pattern.

Wait. What?

I tried to deliberately generate a patterned signal. I definitely could detect Dave's response. Well, not me—the parasites in my head could detect what the parasites in his head were signalling.

Not Parasites. Dave described them in mathematical

formulae, encoded in the flashing patterns being sent to me.

Oh!

I went to the workstation and began inputting the data, rearranging the cells to match the information being supplied to me by the Not Parasites in my head. They could link and unlink the components of their nodes as needed to transmit—not sure yet what they transmitted. It wasn't energy as described in a technical manual. I hadn't yet deciphered the equations being sent to me that described it. I input the codes and commanded the workstation processors to align them. I began to operate as an interface between the Not Parasites and the *Scorpius'* machinery.

So why am I doing this?

The thought was swept away as I was compelled to continue giving the codes structure and organisation. I could feel Dave continually supplying me with information gathered over the three cycles he had been attempting to understand the Not Parasites. He hadn't been able to arrange all the fragments, but I could.

Well, understanding them might lead to a way out of this.

As my database of organised data grew in complexity, I began to see that I was building it into something beyond information. The encoded flashing also grew in complexity, now incorporating code into wavelengths via frequency and amplitude all along the spectrum. My subconsciousness exclaimed how pretty the colours were—it was like a visual symphony. My hands flew over the digital keyboard, and I began to utter sound patterns to help speed up my coding.

The Not Parasites were becoming a network, which was responding to my inputs with mimicked patterns. Then it started to respond with complementary patterns. I was intrigued that the Not Parasites' system was becoming similar to other coordinated protists, like Dictyostelium.

Yes. Connect Us. Lead way out.

I froze. Dave and I weren't alone with some colony of microorganisms whose only worth was to be exploited to distribute energy. There was a definite third identity in our heads. One that was well evolved. One with experience.

You See Us! You not Machine. Please. Connect. Lead way out.

I turned to look at Dave, who appeared in a myriad of

scintillating colours. He stared back, then broke into a wicked grin. The message he sent to me over the Not Parasites network wasn't verbal, but along the lines of: *we-can-use-the-*Scorpuis-*like-they-were-going-to-use-us-but-let's-not-turn-anything-over-to-the-client-because-screw-those-guys-anyway.*

Indeed.

The Not Parasites had said *please.* Respect and all that. It mattered. Dave, the Not Parasites, and I were *not* disposable means to an end.

I took a deep breath and tried to focus on the entity of the Not Parasites, trying to understand what they were supposed to be as a whole. I lost my sight, but it wasn't too freaky, as a new, different kind of perception exploded in my head. The information encoding the Not Parasite network needed to be assembled on a larger scale of organisation than just the *Scorpius'* processors and my head. The physical part of the Not Parasites I had consumed as "ice cream" needed to connect to the previously mysterious nodes scattered throughout the Boötes Void.

Dave transmitted to me: *Darton had collected some of those nodes before. The client told him they'd had good lab results with them, using them as a transmission network. You and I were meant to be patsies to assemble it on a larger scale.*

Did you eat them too?

Not on purpose. I found out later that the client also told Darton some sucker needed to ingest some Not Parasites to interface with it all. They are alive, not something a machine could commune with. Obviously, this client didn't want to do it themselves. You can guess how they knew that on their end.

The Not Parasites mirrored my anger. Something . . . had happened to Them. The client had disrupted Their Network with electromagnetic bursts, wanting to claim part of it, causing a disaster that resulted in many of Them being lost in the Void. Their fragmented pieces were supposed to be easier to "manage". They needed to reconnect to the Remainder of the Network. I pushed my mind forward through Their message. They needed . . .

It took me several minutes to understand the mathematical description supplied. I had to retreat from my database and compare the information to the *Scorpius'* technical databases.

Plasma ions. Of course. There weren't many of those in the

Void.

Dave leaned back in his crash seat, tilted his head back, stretched his mouth open, and breathed out tendrils of the Not Parasites network that had been multiplying inside his body. They snaked over his face and reached towards the small viewport embedded in the *Scorpius'* hull. I felt a chill and rush of escaping atmosphere as They first broke through, then resealed the port. My own tendrils connected to Dave's, and I directed the branching according to the information structure I'd built within my database. I struggled to supply new organisational structure as the entire Network coalesced into its former . . . *glory.*

Tendrils shot out of my hands, ran through the console, and connected directly with the processors. Much faster.

I now knew the mathematical description of joy.

I registered that Darton and some of his mechanics were leaning in through the door. I disentangled myself from the Network and crash seat so I could blink my eyes free of the extra colours and interact with the crew. It took a few minutes before I could reestablish the neural connections I needed to speak.

"Are . . . you guys okay?" Darton asked. He was looking back and forth between Dave and me, his expression very worried.

"Yes. Completion required. Need access to navigation array," I managed.

"We're not leaving until the job's done," one of the mechs piped up.

"Job completion requires access to navigation array," I repeated. I began pulling myself towards the piloting controls. Small Not Parasites tendrils flickered along the edge of my sleeve, making the crew recoil and rethink trying to grab me.

"Why do you need access?" asked Darton. I smiled at him.

Nothing you need to worry about, buddy. Just like I was never told what you had planned for me.

I drifted the rest of the way to the piloting controls and the Not Parasites Network made quick work of the user ID lock. I deployed a solar collector, positioned it towards the nearest star, then engaged the magnetic propulsion system and began positioning the ship to use the engines to redirect incoming plasma ions in a stream towards the coordinates where Dave and the Not Parasites were constructing a meganode connected to the now organized smaller nodes dispersed within the Void. Dave knew his stuff when it came to setting up power grids to receive massive influx.

Darton overcame enough of his revulsion to grab my wrists.

"Whoa. What are you doing? Are you powering it up? That's not part of the contract. All we're supposed to do is assemble the grid."

I gave him an amused look as a tendril of Not Parasites shot out of my ear and punched the final commands.

You think I need my hands for this?

I now knew the mathematical description of giddy anticipation of freedom.

One of the mechs attempted to shut down nav controls as the *Scorpius* began to rotate into position. The Network snaked through the mechanical components of the pilot dash and bypassed his terminal.

Three seconds to threshold ion accumulation.

The meganode lit up in a burst of radiating colours that shot through the Void, electrifying every branch of the connected smaller nodes. The entire structure pulled together and coalesced into a waveform that shot out of the Void, towards the largest streams of plasma ions. The magnetic propulsion systems of the *Scorpius* wailed as they were bent out of shape.

Like this, Dave and I told Them, as we provided a model for a physical form. I imagined mermaids, Dave thought of dragons, and the Not Parasites added Their own dash of mathematical identity. The *Scorpius* was dragged along with the newly formed body of the Not Parasites as They rode through existing magnetic waveforms propagated by stars outside of the Void. I was nearly blinded by the auroras emanating from Their wake.

Dave gave us the coordinates of the client. Why was Darton no longer trying to prevent this? Maybe he had died. The Not Parasites were unable to find this prospect interesting as They raced towards the Remainder of their Network. I was swept up in Their thoughts. I forgot all else in the collaborative surge of information needed to Locate and Connect.

I was peripherally aware of Dave sending destruct codes to the client's machinery. He was extremely focused, whereas I felt spread out over everything. We smashed into the Remainder of the Network, along with all the organized information contained in the Original Database.

Without the connection to the *Scorpius'* processors, my mind overloaded and shut down. I think . . . I think something came out of my ears. Maybe it was red. Was that colour important?

I was registering images and sounds a few moments before I began processing them. My mind felt ripped open and empty. Weak. My body felt the same. Maybe I lay there for hours, staring upward at a sky full of dancing light: greens, reds, and blues, all writhing and blooming above me. After a few more hours, I regained the ability to process the encoded light flashes, and recognised the noises as Dave laughing as he let my head rest on his lap. He was talking to me. I guessed he could do that now that we weren't in the middle of the Not Parasites' unfiltered data rushes.

"Where?"

It was difficult to be sure I had spoken. Dave shifted to standing and pulled me to my feet. Holding my hand, he helped me stumble forward until I could see over the next rise. We were on a hill encrusted with pink and orange growths, basking in yellow light. A partially constructed city was nested in a valley below.

"From what They've picked up from the planetary transmissions, we're on New World 547. They brought us here." He pointed at the sky, where I could discern the embodiment of the Not Parasites twisting through the lights above us.

"A numbered designation? I would have expected Liliane to have given this place a name by now."

"This colony was abandoned—colonists and all. They brought us here and are supplying this world with power. We saved Them, and now They are saving us."

Some colonists were cautiously approaching us from below. They seemed uncertain, afraid. I looked at Dave. He had red encrusted around his eyes and ears. I swiped at mine too, seeing the dried flakes come away on my fingers.

One of the colonists came closer. Her uniform was ragged and torn. "Are you from Academia?" she asked. I nodded. She seemed relieved. "I thought we were cut off. How did you get here? And that power source is unlike anything I've seen before." She pointed upwards. "Our machines are working again."

"Academia *has* cut you off," I said. "But it won't matter. We don't need them."

I lifted my hand to receive the tiny snaggle of Not Parasites descending from the sky towards me. It snaked through my palm, and this time we knew each other well enough that it was a painless experience. Data began coursing through my brain as the Not Parasites began telling me about the local resources that remained untapped. If one client had known about the Network, another would also likely know, and eventually, Liliane. We needed to prepare.

"Take me to your central data storage and processing units. I have information to arrange."

WORDS OF POWER

Donna J. W. Munro

Marnie's book collection hid in spaces in the wall behind the dusty panelling and under the wide wooden planks of the floor. Her mother didn't know. If she did, she'd beat Marnie bloody and burn the books in the stove.

She'd do it that way because she'd been taught that words without limits would destroy Marnie's mind. Words with power couldn't be controlled.

According to law and tradition, they had to be destroyed. Mother believed it with all her heart and preached it every day. Books are dangerous. Books destroy families. That was her truth.

Marnie didn't believe that though.

She'd been hiding books since she had turned fourteen and had come into the Majority. She remembered her last day of school when they'd given her instructions on how to best to serve the whole. She'd been made a cleaner for the council at the traditional ceremony in front of the whole Majority, her Minority classmates looking on and her mother in back, smiling proudly.

"Marnie, here is your book. Serve the council and serve the Majority. Follow our simple way. Read only what is real and verifiable. Destroy the forbidden."

She stood before the high mentor who was decked in the black robes of her class. Marnie bowed and the mentor put the little cardboard book from the old times into her hands for the ritual. The title, *The Little Puppy Goes to Church*, caught her eye as the brazier flared up. The book in her hand was for a baby to read and the word "church" didn't make any sense, but in the long moment before the ritual started, Marnie's eyes filled with tears that she blinked back. They'd think the smoke from the brassier irritated her eyes, but only if she held the despair back.

The book wanted to be read. It wished for stubby little fingers flipping its boards and emerging teeth on its corners. The book wanted a little one to read it.

She felt that in her fingertips.

It thrummed with an energy and a need Marnie imagined was impossible but . . . possible at the same time? Longing that demanded what it couldn't get for itself.

She shook her head as images tried to grow in the meat of her mind. A puppy doing things . . . secret things. Non-dog things. She'd never seen an actual dog other than in the histories the council taught to the Minority in training. They'd been extinct since . . . Well, Marnie wasn't sure how long. That was beyond her level of knowledge, but she knew of them. What she was seeing in her mind wasn't chasing a ball or herding sheep.

Thinking about the dancing puppy trying to grow in the centre of her thoughts was dangerous in front of the Minority and the assembled representatives of the Majority. Could they tell that the book in her hand spoke to her? Marnie shook the images away and focused on the stern face of the high mentor.

"Marnie, you may now join the Majority. Burn away the past. Destroy the destroyer," the high mentor said, raising her hands and leading the others in the pledge.

"Destroy the destroyer . . ." the Majority chanted.

Marnie leaned closer to the fire, holding the book by its edges and trying not to feel the pulse of whatever called to her from those thick, stubby pages.

"Live for the Majority . . ."

Inside she felt the thrum of forbidden power vibrating through her muscles and into her mind. The book wanted to be read, understood even. Not just followed. Not like the job instruction scrolls tucked into her pockets.

"Join us now, Marnie," the high mentor said.

As much as her mind hungered for the story, she had to obey. Not obeying meant . . . Her mother didn't deserve to go through that again.

Her hands trembled and she dropped the book into the hungry fire. The thick pages delaminated and curled as the blue flame ate the cover. Marnie bit back the sadness that washed over her then and at every Majority ceremony she'd been forced to attend since.

She pledged as she had to.

She raised her hands above the flickering sparks, feeling the life leaving the tiny book, still warm in her fingertips. She'd wished then that she could run. It wasn't really *just* a wish. The urge twisted in her stomach like a biting snake spitting with anger. But her mother's gaze caught her eyes. The pride she had on her face was . . . enough. She stood straight and still, listening to the congratulations of the Majority, feeling like a monster.

The puppy and the words flashed as they and the power in them was consumed.

She started her job as a full member of the Majority in good standing, ready to rid the world of dirt and anything that would threaten the Majority. But when she cleaned the old places the council sent her to, she couldn't ignore the whispers.

She heard them on her very first day working as part of the Majority. Assigned to clean the Common House, she'd been scrubbing the wooden stairs that led up into the unused bedrooms of the third floor. Usually sealed, they were only used for visitors from other Majorities and those visits were few. The dark wood shone with her work. The wood was beautiful. So much richer than the plasticine, white walls of her and her mother's home. Nothing new used wood as a building material.

Wood had to be controlled by the Majority. Wood made paper and paper made books. But wood itself held no draw for Marnie other than a job that needed doing. Wash. Wax. Wipe.

In the quiet of her work, she started to hear the soft sounds of something dangerous floating down through the silence.

Words of Power. She knew them the minute they found her ears.

"*. . . I wanted you to see what real courage is. Instead of getting the idea that courage is a man with a gun in his hand. It's when you know you're licked before you begin. But you begin anyway and see it through no matter what.*"

The voice was soft and sweet. The man's voice was as close to her thoughts as a wish. Not that she understood all the words of the whisper . . . gun, courage, licked . . . but she felt power in them.

A knowledge that she wanted.

Even if it was a sin.

She left her bucket and rag there on the stair knowing that none of the council members would come up the steps to check on her. She was Majority. Trusted and trained to do all the right things.

If they didn't hear the whisper and she did, what did that make her?

She followed the powerful echo in her mind of that whisper up into the hall of bedrooms and toward a final door at the end. She put her hand on the knob and . . .

". . . *People generally see what they look for, and hear what they listen for.*"

Not closer to her, but louder.

She twisted the dull metal knob though it resisted turning. Maybe it was out of practice from disuse. The door popped open, letting out a breath of stale age and dust, the sort of smell that Marnie was supposed to eliminate with sprays of chemicals and swipes of her cleaner. She'd been trained to think such smells carried sickness and rot. That, like the old books that used dreams and told stories that weakened the Majority, dust and dirt would destroy them all. Destroy them the way the old world had been destroyed.

But as she walked up the creaking stair into the attic, the air was filled with a thick, delicious promise. She shivered as the ideas sparked in her mind. She wanted the strange atmosphere and the thrilling sense of wrong that crept along her skin raising goosebumps, but inside, all her training sounded alarms to flee from it, to report, to burn it, or clean it until it didn't exist anymore.

She crossed the top stair, and in the shadowy half-light, she saw the profile of an old-style fireplace made of bricks stained with soot. Her fingers itched to clean it, her training from the Minority school trying to override her curiosity.

It wasn't too late.

She could still turn back and get a council member. They would reward her if they found what she knew was hidden somewhere in that fireplace.

Not that she'd ever seen it, but she *knew*. The feeling inside her drew her as surely as any order or call of the Majority. It was deeper than that. It felt just like the pulse she'd felt from the book she'd burned.

It was a book. It had to be.

A hidden, forbidden book.

A book that wished. Or dreamed. Or supposed and was full of things forbidden after the collapse of the old human government.

The bombs and the deaths and the fires had taught them not to be "humans" anymore. Instead, they were Majority. One together. One with causes. One in thought. As a member of the Majority, she should always agree that together was better. One set of thoughts and purposes to save their lives. It's what the Majority said would save them all from greed and hate and all the old things that being full of different ideas created.

But the book's song drowned out any hesitation her training created.

The fireplace drew her. It whispered a plaintive invitation. It begged to be read.

She found it hidden behind a loose brick. The cover had colours that the sky promised when the grey clouds cleared and there were silhouettes of birds against the branches of a tree. *To Kill a Mockingbird* the cover said. And in her hands, it lit with the light of possibility. Its heart beat with a truth beyond facts she felt in her own heart. And as she turned it over in her hands and then stuffed it into her pocket, she heard the same whisper again and again.

"The one thing that doesn't abide by majority rule is a person's conscience."

She took that book home and hid it in her pillowcase until she learned how to pull a board up and leave it loose, so she could hide it under but pull it up every time she wanted to read it. How she loved Scout, and Boo, and the father, Atticus.

Marnie's father hadn't lived to see Marnie's Majority the way Atticus had for Scout because he'd joined the perverts who didn't cleave to the Majority. Maybe he had always been an enemy of the Majority. Marnie remembered when he'd witnessed hunters stumble on a secret classroom hidden in one of the old warehouses. There was a false teacher reading books from the old days to children too young for Minority school. Her father had helped the hunters clear out the books while the children and the teacher paid their debt. When he got home, he'd described the book she'd been reading. Colours that didn't make sense. A cat who wore a tall, red-striped hat. So many ridiculous, fanciful things.

The way her father had said *fanciful* sounded like he'd bitten into a piece of moulded cheese.

He spat the words out and said more about how they'd dragged the children who'd learned about the cat to carts to be taken to the edges of town where the roads cracked and buildings of metal rusted away. They'd be allowed to live there, with no instruction, hunting beetles and eating scrub weeds to survive. Life outside the Majority was a lonely, mean life, but he didn't dwell on that.

A kindness, he'd told her.

The teacher . . . Marnie plugged her ears as her father described what happened to her.

The memory her father's words about the teacher pained her. Father's words were sharp, and they cut her even though she tried not to hear how she'd been tortured to death. Execution after days of being an example of what happens when you pollute minds.

The teacher had died because of the words of power.

It was a hard lesson, and she'd learned it, but looking back, Marnie realized her father had likely read the book—a traitor himself. And if he didn't, maybe it had spoken its secrets as he'd carried it to be burned. Maybe he had the same connection to the words of power she had. How would he know about the cat wearing the striped hat and speaking nonsense otherwise?

She wished she could ask him.

He'd been killed just like the teacher.

It wasn't a month later when he'd been dragged into the square at the centre of the city. Hunters had caught him putting bricks over a pit he'd dug in the path behind their house. They'd dug up his trove of books and dragged him away. Mother had held Marnie close and marched behind the council members who surrounded father. They dragged him up to a raised platform.

They called for the pledge.

"Destroy the destroyer," the Majority screamed around them as a bag of old book fragments were spilled around Father's feet.

Marnie's mother's fingers dug into her shoulders like claws as Marnie tensed.

"Live for the Majority," the crowd yelled as the counsellors pulled her father down and tied him like a bow across the pile.

"Wait," he screamed. "Just look at them. You'll see!"

That's when they put a torch to his books.

His books.

Fifty books! Books he'd found and hidden.

Books with power.

Words that promised.

The flames had licked his skin, and he'd screamed incoherently, but her mother had held her chin and made her watch him bubble and scorch until she couldn't tell him from the ash pile the books made when they burned.

She'd been so young then, it was almost like her father became those books.

That idea had promise.

He wasn't gone.

No. He'd joined with the power of the books.

She and her mother didn't talk about what happened. They just went back to working for the Majority, living for the Majority, and never saying anything important to each other. Never remembering or judging or hoping because those things didn't work with the Majority. Those words . . . well, Marnie knew what they meant, but they were as distant as the couple of stars that twinkled between breaks in clouds as she walked home from her work at night.

Somehow, having those books made him more himself. More real and true.

She didn't really understand that until she found her second hidden treasure.

That day she'd been tasked with cleaning the collection centre. It had once been a very fine place with special windows with colours she only ever saw on the birds they raised for protein. Reds and sometimes yellow. The blue that the sky might be if only the clouds all blew away. The windows didn't exist anymore. She didn't dare ask what had happened to the them, but sometimes cleaning the new thick plastic they'd put in the frames, she found sharp shards of coloured glass caught in the window crannies she brushed with her hand broom.

She kept those in her pocket, but that wasn't a crime.

Glass wasn't a destroyer, even if it had been from the other time. They'd told her that in training, but if it was so, then why had they broken the glass in the first place?

The collection centre was wide open with tall pillars holding up the high ceiling. At each pillar, necessaries were in piles for any Majority member who needed a thing. Shoes and clothes. Take what you need, leave what you don't. Tools that weren't for Majority-given jobs, but might be helpful in other ways, waited for those who required them on long benches that had been ripped from their original positions to be used as shelves.

It was a place of great usefulness in the wide-open middle but from her high ladder cleaning windows, Marnie could see the parts that weren't open to every Majority member. Near the ceiling a shadowed area looked over the open space, though from the floor you'd never know. She could see long benches like the ones below sitting in lines and a big thing that had cylindrical tubes sticking out and running up to the ceiling. They were dulled metal, but if the sun hit them just right, Marnie saw that they shone and sparkled. When light filled the windows, Marnie could also make out painting on the wall.

And words.

As she worked, she got close enough to a plaque set in the wall. She traced her fingers in the letters, knocking loose the dust. It said, "Unity Church."

She gasped.

The puppy book she'd burned had talked about church. And unity?

The Majority talked about unity all the time. How only they had achieved it through giving up on destructive thoughts and things that confused people. They'd taught her that words of power disunited the people.

But here the word *unity* stood next to an old, abandoned concept. One so bad, the council had obliterated it from all the learning.

It made her heart race to think she knew something so forbidden.

She ran her fingers across the raised letters, feeling the cold of the metal and thrilling at the chill. Under the pressure, the wooden plaque shifted and Marnie found a hollowed-out spot hidden behind it. She reached into the dark and found a sack pushed back into the recess. The material was dark and fine against her rough fingertips. As she reached for it, she heard something inside murmur, *"Seek and ye shall find."*

She pulled out the sack and peeked in. Five books. They all spoke at the same time, the rush of their ideas a battering storm.

"Marnie, are you done up there?" an elder asked, passing beneath her ladder.

"Almost." Marnie twisted the bag of books up and dropped them into her tool bag so the elder wouldn't question her. She finished up, signed out, and was out of the building before the elder could return and see the guilt on her features.

She hurried home and pried up the panelling, letting each book linger in her fingers for a moment before she stashed them.

"Is not my word like fire, declares the Lord, and like a hammer that breaks the rock in pieces?"

The golden letters on the front said *The Holy Bible*.

The next one had a picture of a girl who looked just like Marnie had when she was a Minority. Behind her was a swirl of pattern and colour and a creature that was half-human and bird and something else that made it monstrous and beautiful. *A Wrinkle in Time*. The book whispered of pain and courage and brilliance, ideas with power. Her fingers riffled the edges of the pages and words whispered through them, soft but full of strength.

It said, *"A book, too, can be a star, explosive material, capable of stirring up fresh life endlessly, a living fire to lighten the darkness, leading out into the expanding universe."*

How it wanted her to read it.

Longed for her.

The other three books were just as eager to get into her hands. The covers depicted a woman riding on a scaled, winged beast unlike any she'd seen before. Dragonriders, each cover said. Dragons? The book whispered a bit of wisdom to encourage her to reading it. *Who wills, Can. Who tries, Does. Who loves, Lives.*

Marnie's fingers reached for them, but then she heard the front door of the dwelling open and shoved the books behind the wall panel.

The books would have to wait until the dark silent hours after midnight for her to risk opening them. Even having them tucked inside the smooth tile flooring made her heart race with excitement. The crackling potential of what they'd teach her, that was the power the elders feared. She'd be different.

Apart from them and their unity.

That was the greatest sin a person of the Majority could commit. It was a death crime.

But she couldn't stop.

Soon she had as many books as her father had collected.

Then, she had twice as many.

Books about things called monsters.

Books about gods that the old ones believed made the world.

Heroes and hobbits and so many colours.

She'd be caught someday. Marnie knew it, but the rewards of the voices in her head raised her up in a way that her work and her belonging to the Majority never did. She needed more than the life she'd been given.

When Mother opened her door and invited her to eat dinner, Marnie followed. They talked about work and nothing else. Life was grey. Gray and safe, as Mother wanted it to be for her. As the Majority made it. Soon she'd be given a husband and she'd make her own littles to grow into the Majority.

But at night, she wasn't what they planned.

Her hands shook each time she drew out the books to read, but she couldn't stop.

And when she was sent into places to clean, she couldn't help but listen for more books, full of magic and hidden inside the peeling covers.

It was one of the elders who finally caught her.

She'd been asked to clean out a farmhouse on the outskirts. It was a place no one visited, but the council wanted to make it into a place of solitude. A place to send people who'd not done what they'd been trained to do or who didn't follow the pledge close enough or who didn't seem to understand how to live for the majority.

"Marnie, we need to make sure there are no temptations inside," said the elder who'd taken her in his cart to the greyed house with windows and a sagging porch that made it look like it was smiling. "Clear out all the old things and the dust. We will paint it white soon, so that nothing will distract those who need to be reminded that the Majority is unity, understand? Your work will make it pure."

He smiled at her with the distant sort of care all members of the majority had for each other. Marnie nodded, but couldn't help remembering the words she'd found about true unity.

She'd learned from *The Lord of the Flies* that unity couldn't be legislated.

She'd learned from *I Know Why the Caged Bird Sings* that unity isn't about being the same.

She'd learned from all of her books that what the Majority had given wasn't unity at all.

Marnie nodded and went to work, wiping dust from shelves, dragging furniture out to the back of the house to be burned. The closets were full of colourful clothes and fancy fabrics that felt like the breath of a fairy, something she'd learned about from *The Brothers Grimm Book of Fairy Tales*. There was a box of jewellery tucked under a mattress with gems that glittered like those in Smaug's hoard. All of those things she could let go of because the books had given her mind places to fold them away to be loved later. But when her hand fell on the thin book with the little boy wearing a suit of dough, she gasped.

Such wonderful nonsense spilled out of the book in its eagerness to share its message.

"Milk's in the batter. Milk's in the batter. We bake cake and nothing's the matter!"

She slid down the wall and thumbed quickly through the book, absorbing the magic of *In the Night Kitchen*. The boy was an adventurer, creeping around his house, breaking rules, and finding magic. It was ridiculous and beautiful, like all the books. That was the unity she'd found. That words of power could set all their minds free.

She tucked the book into her bag and took a deep breath. She'd have to ride in the wagon next to the elder with it hidden there and the thought scared her so badly. She ought to leave this one. She ought to let it go. One little book about a naked boy running through his house at night wouldn't be such a loss, would it?

Only it would.

Words of power shouldn't be wasted. That's what her heart told her.

Words of power should be shared.

She walked to the front room of the house where the elder

waited.

"Are you done, Marnie?" he asked. There was a note in his voice that sounded like a threat. "Is there anything you need to report?"

Did he know? Marnie felt trapped suddenly like her life hung on the next set of words from her mouth. All she had to do was hand him the book and everything would be okay. He'd admire her if she handed over the book. She'd be safe to save other books from destruction if only she gave up this one.

Her hand slid into her bag and rested on the face of the book. She felt the power tingling in her fingertips and the words that whispered in her mind gave her strength. They wanted to be free.

She shook her head and started for the door . . . which closed with a click just before she could leave.

She turned and the elder was next to her with his hand out.

"I know you have a book, Marnie. Even after what happened to your father, you've been seduced by the words."

She tugged the bag close, protecting it.

"Please." The word was a prayer. A wish. But not an excuse. "Don't burn it."

The elder stared at her hard like he might just cut through her courage with his eyes.

She didn't really feel courageous. She wasn't like Micky in the bread plane or Piggy on the island or Harry fighting Voldemort. She was just Marnie, Majority cleaner. But she couldn't let him take the book.

She backed away, hoping to find a way to slip past. She'd run if she could. Find a place to hide and . . .

"Marnie, it was a test. You passed! You saved the book even when you could have traded it for your life. Listen . . ." He grabbed her shoulder and held her still, though he was gentle about it. "You aren't alone."

He released her arm and walked over to the fireplace. He pressed a brick there and the whole thing slid back. Behind it was a stairwell that led down, down, down. She followed him, feeling the chill of the air like a kiss. She still wanted to run, but something told her to be strong. Strong like Atticus and Scout. At the bottom of the stair was a strong metal door.

"What you see here is sacred, Marnie. It is our church. Our future."

He put his palm against the plate next to the door and it lit from within a brilliant yellow, brighter than anything Marnie had ever seen. Then the door clicked. The elder pulled it open and . . .

Marnie dropped to her knees as the symphony of welcoming words wrapped around her. It was a feast for her eyes and ears. Books lining shelves that reached higher than she could see and into a depth that vanished in a warm light so far back it winked like an eye. People climbed ladders on the shelves that shifted and slid, giving them access to all the books.

"Who are they?"

"They are like you and me. They are finders."

Marnie glanced at the stacks full of books, eyes as wide as her heart. "I'm a finder?"

The elder smiled and took her hand. "You are that and so much more. See, we've been saving books from the Majority for hundreds of years. This is only one of our libraries—"

"Library?" It was a word she didn't know, but it reverberated in her mouth as she said it.

"Yes, it's like a church for books and those who seek them. A place to wonder and hope and fantasize."

Marnie shook her head. So many new ideas. She dug out the book she'd saved. Micky and the chefs deserved to be here. She held it out, though she wanted to keep it. Read it again and again.

"Ah, the final test. You'd give this treasure over to us?"

"To save it," she said.

"Marnie, it's a copy. We don't just keep the books here. We print them again and again. Can you guess what we do after that?"

Marnie thought about all the books she'd found in places that had probably been cleaned before she'd come into her Majority and taken the job as a cleaner. They'd been planted there. Seeded. Placed for someone like her to find.

"You hide them," she said, excitement crawling around her heart and squeezing.

He nodded.

"We are sharers, too."

Marnie knew then she had to help. She had to let others hear the power of the stories they'd lost.

"I want to share."

"You know the risks. Your father—"

"Was he a sharer?"

The elder nodded.

"I think he'd be proud, don't you?"

The elder laughed and nodded. "He told me you'd be brave. He said you were made of the same stuff as Ramona Quimby, Pippi Longstocking, and Katniss Everdeen."

Marnie didn't know who they were but if she had a chance, she'd search the books and find out what her father thought she'd be.

"One more thing," the elder said as he walked her over to the centre of the library. The others were making their way over to greet her, smiling like she was long-lost family. The elder pointed up at the ceiling, and written there were strange words painted in bright letters that seemed to throb with a life of their own. "You need to learn our mantra. It will open the doors of any library and will bring keepers and sharers to your aid."

Libros per unity.

The others stood in a circle around her. They had different faces and clothes than her, but they all looked up at the words with the same reverence.

"What do they mean?" Marnie asked, though she already felt them in her bones.

"Unity through books," he said.

And Marnie knew it was one of the first great truths and she couldn't wait to share.

It would liberate them all.

It would make them all human again.

A whisper from a lone book called *The Grapes of Wrath* whispered through the stacks and out to them all, sweet as a song. As Marnie listened, she knew it was truth.

"And the little screaming fact that sounds through all history: repression works only to strengthen and knit the repressed."

INSCRIPTION

JR Campbell

She woke, feeling warm and well-loved, stretching luxuriously under the bedcovers. Her leg kicked out until her foot found the bed's edge. She lay alone, in a bed not her own. Opening her eyes, she scanned the room. It was, after all, a spacecraft. The sleeping quarters were not large and offered few places to hide.

Will was seated by his desk, the chair swivelled towards her. Fully dressed in his eccentrically formal style, he leaned towards her, his shaven head focused on her through steepled fingers. His posture was contemplative, somewhat befuddled, not unhappy but not as cheerful as their shared evening should have made him. A gloom had hung over him for weeks, displaced now by confusion, but depression's shadow stubbornly lingered over his long face. Part of it was just who Will was, even at his most unguarded he was thoughtful and withdrawn. His concentration was legendary. He disappeared for days when an interesting problem snagged his attention. Such focus made him great at astrophysics, but it came with a cost.

"Good morning," he said, noticing her eyes on him. "Something to eat? There's coffee on the nightstand."

Of course there was, her room was the same, but it was slightly charming to call the shelf by the bed a nightstand. An anachronism, or just a quirk? Will had been, she realized, watching her sleep as he waited for her to awaken. His expression betrayed puzzlement. His formidable intellect was focused on her. The thought was daunting.

"I'm not hungry," she answered, reaching immodestly for some coffee. She took a sip, enjoying the fluster colouring his expression as the sheets shifted. Placing the cup back on its shelf/nightstand, she rearranged the bed sheets primly and met his gaze directly. "Something on your mind, Will?"

He straightened his posture, one hand reaching out for the reader she had left on his desk. "Um," he started, shifting his words as if ordering a difficult equation. She waited, resisting the urge to arch an eyebrow. "Look, this is awkward, so I'll just ask it." He picked up her reader. "Did you just 'Mr. Darcy' me?"

It was the first time she'd heard "Mr. Darcy" used as a verb and it annoyed her. Unfortunately, Will's gaze had transitioned from focused to inquisitive, so he'd already registered her grammar annoyance, but he was serious about the question, and it hung in the air between them.

Romance didn't come naturally to Will; she was surprised he knew who Mr. Darcy was. Did he mean a love interest who, by most measures would be termed subpar, made socially acceptable by heavy literary effort? That didn't seem right. She doubted he had ever actually read the book. Her thoughts scurried as she reached for the coffee again to buy time. As she sipped, it occurred to her he meant their night together was inspired by his literary fame rather than actual attraction.

Later, she would wonder why she hadn't asked him to clarify his question, but it wasn't in her nature to let a literary reference go by her without trying to understand it on her own. After her sip, she met his gaze and replied. "That's a hell of a question to ask a librarian."

To her relief, he chuckled. His smile was so sincere, so good to see after his recent depression. "I guess it is," he admitted. But he didn't withdraw the question. Just waited. Eyes expectant and focused on her.

"Well, to be honest, I hadn't looked at it that way." She tried to choose her words carefully as she wasn't a morning person. "Now that you mention it, I can see why you'd ask, though I'm somewhat offended. I certainly don't make a habit of having sex with literary icons."

"You did just show up, no warning or anything," Will

continued. "Holding the reader, talking about the book, talking about Jo, then you cried, and I held you and, uh, you know."

"Indeed, I do." The words emerged with a tone of reckless satisfaction she wished she could pull back, but a smile tugged his lips as the words landed. When someone with Will's level of concentration was focused on pleasing you, the results were spectacular. "Look, I didn't mean to . . . Last night was not a planned seduction, if that's what you're asking." Was it her imagination, or was he disappointed? "I mean, last night was amazing. If I'd known, I mean, it's not that you're not worth seducing but I didn't, I don't, I mean—ugh!"

It took an effort to stop the words threatening to tumble from her mouth. Taking a deep breath, she closed her eyes and let the air out slowly.

"Then why did you come to my room?"

Another sip of coffee, her mind was finally starting up. She met his gaze and lined up her thoughts. "Over the last few weeks, people have noticed that you seemed depressed."

"They did?" He seemed legitimately startled by the revelation.

"There's only a hundred and eleven people on this ship, of course they noticed. We're crew, we do science, and we worry about one another. Not much else to do out here. Anyway, someone asked me if I knew what was bothering you. I didn't. They asked if I could check your media consumption, see if there was a clue there."

"That's pretty Orwellian," Will protested.

Her eyes rolled; she regretted it immediately but cut herself some slack. It was morning and she was naked. Seeing his eyes narrow, she answered. "Sorry, that's such an Earth thing to say. I grew up in a colony, class E. To be Orwellian requires a certain scale, it needs some effort from Big Brother. A class E colony is different, it's just small. My mother found out about my first menstruation before I left the washroom, someone from Supply contacted her to let her know I had used my code to unlock a hygiene product. We're stuck in a spacecraft. It's smaller than a class E colony. People notice things. Only the ship's librarian can access the media records but doing so is well within regulations, so don't get your knickers in a twist. Morale regulations, remember? Asking me was well within their rank privileges, accessing was well within mine. They were worried about you,

you big dummy. No one wants to violate your privacy but that doesn't mean they don't care. We're crew. We worry about our own."

Shifting on his chair, suffering a discomfort not physical, Will looked like he wanted to argue.

She didn't let him. "And there it was. A novel, more than a century old, a classic so outside your reading patterns I didn't need to run an analysis. The timing was bang on too, you were—what?—halfway through it when your crewmates started noticing you being distracted. I checked the publication date more out of habit than anything else."

A pause radiated out from him, but she didn't fight it. Sipping her coffee slowly, she watched him. His eyes shifted over the floor, across the wall, blinking like the little lights the computers used to show calculations in progress. It shouldn't have been endearing, but she found it so. Setting her mug on the shelf, she took pity on him.

"So, I told them you'd read something that brought you down, not to worry, I'd take care of it."

"Is that why—"

Her glare cut off his words. "Choose your next words carefully," she warned him. "I am a librarian, not a courtesan."

His eyes widened in a satisfying surprise. He hadn't meant it that way. "Is that why you read the book?"

A slight nod, a test passed. "Yes. To be honest, I'd read her work before. Not that one, there was a time when I refused to read any writer's most popular work. It was a phase; I was young and sought out the lesser-known works of famous writers."

Leaning in again, Will asked, "Was she famous?"

"Oh yes, definitely. Writer-famous, the way it was back then. Not a celebrity, someone you could pass on the street and have no idea who they were. Not Dickens famous, more a Salinger."

"I don't recognise those names."

"What I mean is: Many people knew her name and her books, but she didn't advertise herself. She rarely put herself into media, interviews or that sort of thing. There were people who wanted to talk about her work, and she'd talk, but in person rather than across networks. Make sense?"

A nod, a slow, thoughtful nod weighted with memory. His intent expression reminded her: This was much more than a book-chat to him. He'd known the writer. Cared for her and she'd cared for him. To her she was a literary icon but for him, she was a living, breathing person. It sobered her.

"Anyway, it was clearly time to read it. Honestly, I was excited to. I remembered her work and was looking forward to it. I called up her biographical info because your reaction to her novel was unusual. Her work is considered very affirming, not the sort of material likely to depress someone. I hadn't put it together, hadn't made the connection, until I started reading and . . . found you in the pages."

He opened his mouth to say something; she held up her hand to pause him. "I finished it last night. She was a hell of writer and that's a hell of ending. And then, well, I came here to check on you. To talk about the book, to make sure you were okay, but my emotions just, sort of, got away from me."

For a moment, he considered it. "There's something you're not telling me, something more." He shook his head. "You're the ship's librarian; it's a coveted post. I may not read much fiction, but I know you have. Normally you're very professional, somehow last night your emotions got away from you. Because of Jo's book? Don't get me wrong, that book affected me in ways I didn't expect. But I'm a rookie, you've read so much more than me."

"You're underestimating the book," she protested, giving voice to her inner librarian. "It's known across all the human worlds; it achieved everything a book can. I know you've been on this ship a long time, that relativity has moved time outside this ship centuries since you've come aboard, but this book is still read today, on worlds that were lifeless when it was written. I knew this book when I was a schoolgirl, everyone on my little colony read it except me. I told you it was too famous for me to bother with but that's only part of it, the other part is that I didn't want to be a cliché. The girl who loved that book and felt destined for exploration. A woman falls in love with a man destined to see wonders, who will risk his life in a smelly, tin-can ship for a chance to discover something new, and when she realizes it is his passion for wonder she loves, she decides to free him—you'd have to be made of stone not to feel that. Brilliantly written, emotionally powerful, you overestimate my callousness as a reader if you think I wasn't moved by that book!"

Will fidgeted. "I didn't mean it like that."

"And finding you, the man from the book, here on my ship? That's amazing. You do understand that every person who has served on this ship has likely read that book? If they haven't read it, they know of it."

"Not everyone," Will protested.

"Everyone!" she insisted. "My first week on this ship, just after my first transit, I went to book club and this was the book we talked of. I hadn't read it then, but I knew enough to bluff my way through. Even on this ship, with all the books from human history to choose from, it's always read."

To her surprise, Will's eyes filled with tears. "Jo would be so proud. She wanted to be a writer so much."

It wasn't graceful, if she still held her coffee she'd have spilled it, but she hurriedly wrapped the bedsheet around herself and was embracing him. She knew the author as a literary icon; it was surreal to think Will had known her before she'd published anything.

"It's all right," she told him. "I know of her, well, her writing career. What happened to her after you joined the Exploration Service. She lived a happy life, she married twice, had three children. Two sons, one daughter. One of her sons was named to the Nancy Pearl chair with the Restored Library of Congress, but she insisted she didn't have a favourite."

Sniffling, Will chuckled again. "That sounds so much like her. How did she die?"

"Elderly, beloved, surrounded by her children. A short illness, she opted out of treatment. I'm sorry." Then, because she couldn't think of anything else to say, she added the unofficial motto of the Exploration Service, "Relativity is a bitch."

"That it is," Will agreed. "I'm mourning over a woman who has been dead for centuries."

"A ridiculous thing for an astrophysicist to say," she chided him. "It hasn't been centuries for you, and you know it. You're mourning someone you cared about. Nothing strange about that."

Will wiped his eyes.

"If you want to know anything about her later life, I've read a great deal about her. Before I knew you were in her most famous book. That's why I came here last night, I wanted you to know how accomplished she was, how happy her life was. I thought it would make you feel better but then, well, you distracted me."

"Thank you," Will said. "I might take you up on that offer. I've a million questions about her life. It's just, right now, I need to process a bit."

"Take all the time you need," she assured him. "But there's something else I should tell you. Well, two things."

He looked at her expectantly.

"The first is this: She never gave you up. Everyone asked, interviewers, biographers, if your character was based on someone she had known. It would have been easy for her to tell them about you, sensible even, but she never gave them your name. I can only imagine she knew you were out here somewhere and didn't want to complicate things for you. She told everyone your character was based on a few people she had known or, sometimes, she said she'd simply imagined someone like you. That's what she told her biographers. She cared for you right up until the end."

Will nodded but she saw the skepticism on his face.

She tilted his chin, so his eyes met hers. "I know, you're thinking I don't have enough evidence to support that assertion. But I do. Hand me my reader."

She released his chin, and he reached for the reader. Tucking her bedsheet in place, she opened it. "You were right before, when you said there was something else. Why I was emotional and hurried to see you. When she published the book, she made a big deal of offering the download to the Exploratory Service free of the usual fees. Everyone figured it was a publicity thing, given her book's subject, but it was more than that. I found a hidden file in the manuscript. It had a password: your name. When I opened it, there were two pages. Both were the title page of the first edition but with different inscriptions."

"I don't understand," Will said.

"She signed a book for you," she explained, handing him the reader.

"She signed—" Will started to repeat her words but his eyes fell to the reader. There he read the words written centuries before in the universe, decades ago for the traveller. "To Will. You'll know much of this is fiction but, alone in the universe, you'll know the feelings were real. I enjoyed reliving those cherished times, pinning them to the page. My life has been joyful, I have no regrets, hope your path has been as wonderful. Love Always, Jo."

His head bent over the reader; he gasped as the tears fell over the screen. Still wrapped in the sheet, she held him as the emotional wave washed over him and left him again. Wiping his eyes, he looked up at her. "Two pages?" he asked, and before she could answer, he'd swiped to the previous inscription.

The same title page, the same blue ink, the same handwriting. "To the librarian who found him. Thank you! Writing this I have no way of knowing if this book will ever find its way to him, or if it does if he'll be alone when he reads it. He has always been broody, and I worry that, if he finds it, he'll need someone to talk to. Go to him. Tell him I've lived a glorious and happy life. As a favour to me, make sure he is well. I'd hate to think something I wrote might harm a man I once loved."

A signature below. When he finished reading, Will looked up and met her gaze.

"And that's why I hurried here last night," she confessed. "With no idea what to say, no plan at all, just a need to make sure you were well. Not to visit a literary idol, I wasn't thinking of you as a Mr. Darcy. It felt like a friend reached out and asked me for a favour. I suppose you could say we were both unsettled by the same book, two emotionally perturbed individuals who collided and, well, you know. I don't know what comes next, except for this: I'll be making myself a hard copy of this book with the inscription in it. I would be happy to make one for you too. I am the ship's librarian, after all, and—believe it or not—this sort of thing is permitted."

"I'd like that," Will said, gently freeing himself from her embrace.

"As for us," she shrugged, handing him a tissue she recovered from his desk. "We'll work things out. Whatever happens, I've no regrets."

Will nodded, his face composed into his customary scowl of concentration. "I should go; they'll be waiting for me in the lab."

"Of course," she agreed, relieved she'd be able to get dressed with his attention elsewhere.

He moved to the door, opened it, paused. "I think there's some sort of show on deck C, if you'd like to join me there, I'd like that."

"I'll be there," she answered. Of course she would, the presentation was an old-style film from the library. She knew Will would hate the film, there's no way he had chosen it, she was surprised there was room in his memory for the event. Will nodded and grinned, his expression free of the shadow he'd worn for these last weeks, before disappearing behind the closing doors.

THE SPACE LIBRARIANS' CODE

Lisa Timpf

U h—hello?" A brown-haired young man with a sweat-stained Engine Tech's uniform clinging to his upper body strolled up to the Alliance Star Ship *Bonavista's* main circulation counter.

Hertha Risley, the *Bonavista's* Chief Librarian, popped up from behind the desk and grinned when she recognized her visitor. "Hi, Maarten. Looking for book six in the Techman series?"

Maarten shuffled his feet and offered a goofy grin. "Yeah. You said you might receive it around now?"

Hertha frowned. "I expected to. But the latest traspo-packet from the publisher didn't arrive. Do you know anything about a glitch with the communication systems?"

Maarten rubbed his right hand over his chin, as though assessing the degree of stubble accumulated since morning.

He didn't have stubble to worry about, when he started here, Hertha thought. She looked at her crewmate with the fondness born of familiarity.

"I don't think it's the pulse-mail." Maarten shook his head. "No. Can't be. I got a message packet from my parents yesterday."

"Huh. Well, could be the publisher's behind in their shipments. I'll make a note to let you know when it comes in, how's that? You'll get first crack at it."

"Aw, I'm sure you're busy with other stuff."

"Never too busy for customers." Hertha pointed at the

document affixed to the green-tinged wall. "Space librarians' code, remember? My core mission is to ensure access to information for all. Regardless whether it's for business or pleasure."

Maarten's answering smile boosted Hertha's spirits. They needed a boost. She'd been following the news. The change in leadership of the Galactic Alliance, governed by a mix of space-faring species, worried her. A new party had swept into power. They'd pledge to fight the challenging economic climate with austerity and centralized control. She'd read enough history to know what the seeds of tyranny looked like.

The change might affect the *Bonavista's* assignments, but it wouldn't reach down to the library level, would it? She paced through the customer area, past the sim-booths where users could experience movies or books first-hand. Past the audio chairs where readers who wanted to get away from the bunk-rooms could relax while listening to books on their headsets.

She checked the MasterMynd, a giant hard drive housing electronic copies of all the books and manuals available for loan. Nothing but green lights on the control panel.

Hertha released a pent breath she hadn't realized she'd been holding.

See? Nothing to worry about.

Later in the day, the ship's walls deepened in colour toward a dusky smoke-blue. Hertha stretched. Soon, Arlice would arrive to relieve her for the night shift.

She'd already downloaded the weekly backup copy of the MasterMynd's data and transported the tape to the secure storage in the Information Technology lab. Everything was ready for changeover.

As usual, Arlice strolled in ten minutes before the start of his shift. He offered a quiet greeting, and Hertha replied in kind.

Today, Arlice had opted for the short-sleeved version of the blue-green librarians' uniform. Watching the play of muscles along his bare arms, Hertha smiled. *That reminds me. I'd better hit the gym after shift.*

Someone cleared their throat, and Hertha jumped. She'd been so focussed on Arlice that she hadn't noticed the newcomer.

Security Chief Mimi Vincent, five-foot-five of coiled-spring tension, stood in front of the circulation desk.

From the look on Mimi's face, this wasn't a social visit. The greeting she'd been about to offer died on Hertha's lips.

What did I do now?

Hertha had never fallen into Mimi's bad graces, but the Security Chief's presence sent Hertha searching her memory for past misdeeds. Perhaps some involuntary transgression . . .

"We've received new orders." Mimi rapped the words out, her tone businesslike.

Okay, definitely not a social visit.

"We've been ordered to rendezvous with a ship from the Alliance." Mimi's mouth puckered as she said "ordered", as though she'd tasted something unpleasant. "One of their agents has been dispatched to shut down the library."

"Our library?" Arlice voiced a dismay that Hertha shared.

"Not just our library." Mimi's voice softened. "All the libraries. It seems some of those at the top think humanity is getting too big for their britches—and that books are one of the things that give us ideas."

Hertha placed her hands on the desk, willing her mind to stop spinning, stop leaping from one catastrophic vision to the next. "They'll arrive—when?"

"Rendezvous is tomorrow. Our orders"—again, Mimi accompanied the word with a mouth-pucker—"are to place you in custody immediately."

Hertha's eyes darted to the door, then back to Mimi. She'd never be able to outrun the security chief. But Arlice might, if she provided a distraction.

And go where? This is a space ship, remember?

A life pod—

"You okay in there, Chief?" Security Lieutenant Chip Ashton poked his head through the entry-way. *She brought backup.*

Mimi shot him a grin. "It's all good." She waved Chip back to his post, then turned toward Hertha and Arlice. "Are you going to come quietly, or do I need cuffs?"

"Quietly," Hertha said. Arlice shifted his weight as though he might offer a different reply. Hertha shot him a warning look. "We'll need to shut down the system. Given your—orders—I don't imagine they'd want open access to the electronic files."

"Proceed." Mimi wandered through the circulation area as

they worked, avoiding their gaze as though by intent. Communicating by eye movement and gesture, Hertha directed Arlice to power down the access terminals while she gathered a few things she thought they might need.

After making sure that Mimi's attention was elsewhere, she dared to whisper a message in her co-worker's ear. "Put the MasterMynd in sleep mode, not off."

Arlice nodded.

When they were ready, they joined Mimi, who stood in front of the poster displaying the Space Librarians' Code.

A stab of pain arced through Hertha's chest as she glanced at the document. *I won't give up yet.* She flung the promise grimly, silently toward the poster, then slung the strap of her day-bag over her shoulder. "Ready whenever you are."

Bold words, but Hertha felt anything *but* ready as she followed Arlice and the Security Chief out of the room.

As Hertha watched the technician sent by the Alliance wipe the MasterMynd's memory banks, she offered a brief, silent prayer to whatever higher powers might be listening.

Please don't let him remember the backups.

While she and Arlice cooled their heels in the cells, Hertha had tried to imagine best-case scenarios. Maybe the tech sent by the Alliance would be a sympathetic one. Maybe he'd just go through the motions, allowing them to keep some, if not all, of the collection she'd added to so laboriously over the years, pruning and shaping with the meticulous care of a bonsai expert.

But this morning, after Mimi had escorted the two librarians to their workplace to witness the disintegration of all they'd worked so hard to build, Hertha had to abandon those hopes. The Alliance tech undertook his task with enthusiasm, his fingers flying over the keyboard, his eyes bright and alert. He showed no sign of reluctance. Rather, he approached the job with the zeal of someone who thought they were doing right by the universe.

You're human, too. How could you? She beamed that thought at him, but daren't voice it aloud. The tech had his background. His reasons. Perhaps he truly did believe that humanity had extended their reach. Perhaps he was from one of those wealthy families whose power would be expanded and whose pockets would be padded by a new, totalitarian regime.

Whatever the case, it was clear he wouldn't be swayed from his task.

She could only hope he was incompetent. But this hope, too, was quickly dashed.

"You're allowed to keep the technical manuals, of course. As well as all training geared at hard skills." The tech didn't bother turning his head to see their reaction.

Damn! I wish I thought of hiding some novels in those sections!

But clearly, another librarian had. Hertha could see, by peering over the tech's shoulder, what he was working at. He'd deployed an algorithm that checked the titles and sampled the contents of books in the library's education and technical sections, making sure they hadn't tried to pull a fast one.

This guy knew his stuff. Unfortunately.

Feeling muzzy, Hertha allowed her mind to wander. Where did books go when the last copy was destroyed? Did they vanish into the ether? Was there a plane on which they still existed, like pale ghosts robbed of power? Or were they sucked into some voracious black hole, an anti-consciousness, never to reappear?

Hertha's vision blurred as she pondered these notions. But the Space Librarians' Code demanded professionalism. And she was still a librarian, as long as a single book remained in existence. She wiped away the gathering tears and straightened her back.

At length, the Alliance tech pushed back his chair and stood. "Done," he said.

He checked a small device in his hands, and grinned. "Bio-stats suggest relief on your part." He took a step closer to Hertha, who blushed. She'd wondered why the tech had insisted they be present. She should have guessed he'd access the biostat system, to monitor their reactions. Just to make sure he didn't miss anything.

"Don't worry," the tech said. "I didn't forget about the backups."

He slapped her on the shoulder, and turned to go. Headed for IT, no doubt.

At the door, he turned back to address Mimi. "I'm done with these two. I'll take one of them with me. Prepare for transport."

"Transport?" Hertha had never heard surprise in Mimi's voice. The Security Chief prided herself on being prepared for anything. But surprise is precisely what Hertha had detected.

"You won't need two librarians, with the book-stock so depleted. In fact, I doubt you need even one, but my orders are clear. They are labour, to be redeployed. Pick one. It doesn't matter to me."

"It does to me." Captain Conway Kerry stood in the door, seeming to fill that opening by dint, not of his physical size, but his presence. "I need them both. Arlice will staff the Library. I have an opening in Hydroponics, and this one has a green thumb." He jerked his own thumb toward Hertha, at the same time giving her a brief, brows-lowered look that vanished so quickly she wondered if she'd seen it.

It was his *don't argue* look. Hertha didn't know what he was playing at, but she knew better than to second-guess.

"I do have a green thumb," she said. *Just not the way you think.* Her throat ached as she thought of her bonsai analogy. She allowed her shoulders to slump, hoping this sign of dejection would satisfy the Alliance envoy.

For a moment, she thought he was going to protest.

But stronger entities than he had wilted beneath the captain's gaze. "Fine," he grunted. And left the library.

The Alliance tech did some additional sweeps which, mercifully, did not require Hertha's presence. He departed the *Bonavista* by the time the ship's walls were tuned to the light green of early afternoon the next day. The colour usually lifted Hertha's spirits. Today, it reminded her so much of home it made her heart yearn for the Earth she'd left behind so many years ago.

At the sound of approaching footsteps, she turned.

She leapt from her chair. "Captain Kerry."

"We need to discuss your new assignment. Follow me." The captain's expression offered no hint of warmth. Hertha had hoped he had something up his sleeve.

Now that hope evaporated. Maybe the *Bonavista* really did need new hands in hydroponics. Well, she'd always prided herself on her flexibility.

Hertha took one last look around at the library, impressing on her mind a memory of What Once Was. Then she followed the captain.

Though she desperately wanted to know where she was going, Hertha was too proud to ask. And so she matched the captain's brisk strides, almost trotting to catch up.

Perhaps the indignity was on purpose.

She shook her head. That was unfair. The captain had always been forthright in his dealings. There was something else going on here.

A door slid shut, leaving Hertha and the captain in a room with unchanging metallic grey walls. Hertha raised her eyebrows. "A Safe Room?"

"Yes. Until Security finishes their sweep, to check for any listening devices the Alliance may have left behind, it seemed best to go where there's no possibility of anyone overhearing. I wanted this meeting offline."

Hertha raised her eyebrows. *That seems like a lot of fuss for a reassignment discussion.*

She thought back to her time in the cells. How frightened she'd been. How lonely, despite the steadying presence of Arlice. And the Captain had stood by while all this happened . . .

She clenched her fists, then forced herself to open them. Arguing with the Captain was never a wise move, but he did value a forthright approach. "You brought me here to tell me about an assignment in hydroponics?" Even as she spoke the words, she realized how ridiculous they sounded. "You'll have to excuse me. I'm having trouble processing right now."

That much was the truth. Since that night in the cells, her mind had felt stuffed. Over-stuffed, in fact.

"Well?" The captain's eyes gleamed as he took a seat, gesturing to Hertha to do the same.

"Well, what?" The words slipped out before Hertha could stop them. As damage control, she added, "Sir."

"Please tell me that you used the time Mimi gave you to good effect."

Though she willed herself to remain calm, Hertha could feel her heart rate rising. "When Mimi turned her back on us, that was on *your* advice? Why?"

"I'm familiar with the Space Librarians' Code."

"The Space Librarians' Code." Hertha rolled the words on her tongue, thinking of the familiar content she'd memorized and pledged allegiance to, so many years ago. She closed her eyes and scrolled through the list while the captain waited.

Her eyes flew open. "Librarians and other information workers reject the restriction and/or denial of access to ideas and information through censorship by states, governments . . ." She studied the captain with a new appreciation. "You were counting on us doing something."

"I had to follow orders and have you locked up. I knew the Alliance would have access to the camera feed." The captain leaned forward. "But I *could* buy you some time. Please tell me you did something with that."

"Perhaps not enough." Hertha thought back to the night in the cells. She and Arlice had quietly used the memory expansion packs she'd slipped into her day-bag to upload all the information they could from the library's memory banks. Because the MasterMynd had been in sleep mode, and not powered off, they'd been able to connect and access the collection.

By mutual agreement, they hadn't bothered with the tech manuals and training documents, figuring those would be safe. Aside from that, they'd uploaded samplings of everything they could. Mythology. Poetry. Philosophy. Fiction. All of the things that made humans, human. All of the things that contributed to their dreams.

The sensation of uploading so much information into her expanded brain had been the mental equivalent of participating in a hot dog eating contest. It was one she never wanted to repeat.

"We used expansion packs to upload what we could. But it was like taking a bucketful of water from an ocean. It wasn't enough. It wasn't nearly enough."

Hertha rocked back in her chair, thinking of all of the lost books. All of the books they failed to retrieve. Even now, their ghosts haunted her memory.

"It's a start." The captain nodded approval, then toggled a remote, opening a door that led to a larger safe room. He gestured. "This isn't on any blueprints, in case the Alliance comes sniffing. It's your new library, if you'll accept it." He lowered his voice. "We don't know when or if they'll be back, but we need to be ready, in case. We'll have to keep the existing library area going, as a pretense. But once you and Arlice download what's in your heads, we can store it here. Allow people to access it, here."

"You would risk that?" Hertha's eyes met the captain's.

"If we don't preserve past knowledge, we risk losing ourselves. That's a greater loss, don't you think?"

A month later, Hertha was working in the Safe Room/Library when Maarten entered.

"It's not here," she said, replying to the question she assumed he was asking. "I don't think it's coming."

Maarten shrugged. "I have the other volumes to remember. I just wish—"

"I know," Hertha said. "I wish, too."

"Do you think libraries—open libraries—will come back, one day?"

His voice was so full of yearning, Hertha longed to give him assurance. But she'd told herself a long time ago not to make promises she couldn't keep. "All I can say is that the pendulum always swings back. It has all through history."

"How long will it take?"

"I don't know the answer to that."

"I don't suppose you saved any of the Techman novels?"

Hertha sighed. "No. I'm sorry."

"It's not for me." Maarten cocked his head. "I have an eidetic memory. Did I ever mention that?"

Hertha straightened. She sensed a glimmering of hope, for the first time in weeks. "You did not."

"I'm not so great with typing, but if I did an audio recording of the books as I remember them, would that help?"

"It would," Hertha said. Already, her mind was skipping ahead to other possibilities. "Do any of your shipmates have the same capability?"

"They might."

"We'll have to get the word out then."

After Maarten left, Hertha bustled around the Safe Room, feeling more optimistic than she had in weeks.

Back in the cells, she'd thought it all rested on her and Arlice. She'd been wrong.

Already, crew members had come forward to offer their personal copies of certain books for the library, and now this. It showed how much the shipboard community valued them.

The Alliance, in their arrogance, had assumed sweeping a few computer chips clean would solve what they saw as a problem. Instead, they'd illustrated the fragility of relying on one place, on one system, to store humanity's knowledge.

And they'd forgotten the most important place where the library lives—in peoples' minds and hearts.

Hertha thought of the vast web of librarians scattered across the galaxy, finding their own solutions to the Alliance's actions. Maybe some had taken the same steps as she and Arlice. Maybe others had found their own, innovative solutions.

They'd have to be careful, for sure, in who they approached. But next time they docked at one of the Stations for resupply, she'd make some inquiries.

The walls of the Safe Room remained unforgivingly grey. Her catalogue, for now, was significantly depleted from the bounty it once held. But she had glimpsed a more promising future, one in which she was able to offer a respectable array of reading material. She'd do everything in her power to make that future a reality.

The Space Librarians' Code demanded no less.

Notes: The Space Librarians' Code draws from the CFLA-FCAB Code of Ethics, published by the Canadian Federation of Library Associations.

IS ANYBODY OUT THERE?

Rhonda Parrish and E.C. Bell

The voice woke me again.

I hadn't managed to sleep through to my alarms since I'd arrived on the *Joey Moss* space station two cycles ago. Frankly, I had no patience for this bullshit. Sleep was the only time my knees didn't ache and I needed my eight hours.

Ached. There was a hell of a word choice, I thought as I sat up in my bunk and swung my legs over the edge. I took a deep breath in before attempting to stand because even in the low gravity atmosphere *Moss* provided that "ache" often hurt so bad for the first couple steps of the day that the pain made my head spin. There were surgeries they could do, of course, but I had never been comfortable with the idea of billions of nanobots running around in my body.

"I've never heard of an engineer who avoided wet tech before," the station's Director-General had said at my job interview.

I'd refrained from telling him the about all the risks people with wet tech opened themselves up to—just last week one of my clients had his nanos hacked and had to pay a ransom to get control of his body back before I could secure his system for him. It was a perpetual game of finding and patching exploits that I wasn't interested in playing. "I don't need to incorporate tech into my body to know how it works," I'd said.

And I'd gotten the job.

The job itself—trying to fortify the station's systems against entropy and chaos—was also a perpetual game of finding and patching issues, but as a bonus it got me into a lower gravity situation to reduce the pain in my knees.

Once the meds kicked in, the "ache" was bearable and I could go about my day. I picked up my tablet and switched it on.

All the other people on the ship were nano-enabled and able to access systems and each other via implants in their bodies or overlays in their eyes. I, however, had to get by with an earpiece for communications and the tablet for interacting with the systems themselves.

It didn't slow me down, though. I could work just as fast as the people who were directly connected to things—it was a skill I was especially proud of.

As I logged into the system and scanned all the issues that had come up while I'd been sleeping, I sighed. It was worse than the night before.

Shit like this made me feel like my whole life was dedicated to trying to pull out of a death spiral even while my descent—the whole universe's descent—just kept speeding up.

Once upon a time all these systems would have done everything they needed to automatically. Everything was automated and while there were occasional hiccups, for the most part things did what they were supposed to do.

Then, twenty years ago, some Red Hat hackers unleashed a vicious AI on the universe. Ingeniously, they buried it in the systems that linked all space craft and stations with each other as well as the bases on Earth, Mars, and Abradus. By the time they activated it, it was already spread through the universe. That AI, colloquially called "Hatred", ravaged all systems, overwriting any text documents it found with gibberish. "Word salad" my professor had called it back when I was first learning about it.

With the loss of so much information—so many textbooks and instruction manuals—maintaining systems had become a nightmarish job. And not just at the software level, either—when no one knows how to manufacture materials, replacing parts that break down is also a nightmare. Some things we can recreate with 3D printers and replicators, but some more complicated pieces were becoming increasingly impossible to get a hold of.

People were scrambling to find workarounds and develop new systems and computers, new programming, and giving them the time they needed to do that without space stations crashing, ships' life supports shutting down, or people dying was my job. Bandage up the wounds as well as I could for as long as I could while they laboured away in the background.

It was exhausting and getting harder and harder every single day. I wasn't going to be able to do it much longer.

Still. I'd best get at it for today.

Yesterday evening—right during dinner rush—all the food replicators went offline. Completely offline. I've dealt with more than my fair share of tech crises, but there's not a lot that compares to having a whole space station worth of hangry crew.

Someone found a supply of ancient protein bars and handed those out while I worked, and good thing too. It took me hours to get the replicators back online, and then hours more before I could figure out how to get them to dispense anything other than green slime. That "anything" just happened to be oatmeal, which I fucking hate, but at least it was food. Ish. I mean, at least it was something that other people (with no sense of taste) considered food.

I figured it would buy me some time to catch a few Zs and then be up and working on fixing the rest of the systems before lunch.

Alas, the voice had other ideas.

I hadn't slept for more than two hours when it woke me.

This time I was able to catch some of the words and hang onto them as I struggled up toward consciousness—probably because I had only recently gone to sleep. I could be mistaken, I was very tired after all, but I'm pretty sure they said, "Is anyone out there?"

"Hello?" I said and then hearing the frog in my voice, cleared my throat and tried again, a bit louder. "Hello?"

"Hello?" someone said back. But it was a male voice that answered from the other side of the wall, not the female voice that had woken me.

"Hello?" I said, this time directing it toward the male voice.

"Do you mind?" he said, groggily. "Some of us are trying to get some sleep."

I gave the wall the finger.

I dragged myself out of bed, gritted my teeth, and stood. The "aches" were even worse today—they always were when I didn't get enough sleep. I dragged myself the two steps to my medicine cabinet, dry swallowed my pills, and got ready to start the day.

After six hours of trying to make the replicator actually replicate something other than oatmeal, I realized the problem was bad shielding. Something was on the same frequency as the replicator, and each time it received a signal the faulty shielding on the replicator meant that it also got the signal. However, since the signal was just gibberish to it—word salad, one might say— the replicator didn't know how to process it, but its attempts to do so interrupted all its other processes. Then, when it finally gave up on processing the nonsense it defaulted back to replicating the easiest (because of its complete lack of texture and flavour) and most bland thing ever. Oatmeal.

I patched up the shielding—another Band-aid solution, but it should allow the replicator to do its job long enough for me to track down where the rogue signal was coming from.

That's when I realized that was also likely the origin of the voice that kept waking me—a rogue signal picked up by my earcell. If I was right, the reason I heard it at the same time every day was because that was when the *Moss*'s orbit took it over the signal's origin point on Earth. It would also explain why I was the only person who ever heard it—no one else used ear pieces like these anymore.

I went through the rest of my day distracted by the possibilities—I had thought Earth was empty. Ten years ago, the news said it had been stripped of everything useful, including people, and then left to regenerate however it could. But if there was a signal coming from down there the news must have been wrong.

What could it mean?

I clocked out early to make up for the long day I'd worked yesterday, and after gagging down a bowl of oatmeal I went to my room and set my alarm back an hour. This time when we passed over the place where the voice came from, I wanted to be awake to hear it.

Lisbeth sat in front of the mishmash of radio equipment she'd cobbled together and flipped the *on* switch, and a light glowed green. Looked like it was working.

"Is anybody out there?" she said. "I want to tell you a story."

"To be honest, I'm not sure where to start. If you're human, you should already know this. And if you're not. Well, if you're not, I better start at the beginning . . .

"Once upon a time, we humans lived in relative harmony on Earth. We did it for thousands of years, until something terrible happened—we figured we could make it better with technology. So we did. We made it better. And better. And better. Until it barely worked for anyone or anything anymore.

"Instead of fixing what we broke, we decided to try again, somewhere else. The tech bros aimed for Mars, and managed to cobble something together that worked for a few of them, just as long as the big long lifeline, composed of a series of space stations, kept them attached to Mother Earth. Then, they found Abradus, and tried there. Can't begin to tell you how happy they all were when they found someplace new to pillage. They figured that eventually they could cut the lifeline and let Earth die, while they lived.

"In case you can't tell, I'm not too high on the tech bros and the progress for the sake of progress scenario they played out over and over again. And you can probably also guess just how hard I laughed when Hatred hit, and it looked like it was going to bring down everything the tech bros had worked so hard to build. All of it.

"System after system bricked and people couldn't quite remember how to do—well—anything to fix it. That's when I bought my first gun. To protect the library where I'd worked forever, it seemed.

"I'd seen the writing on the wall, years before Hatred, and started saving hard copies of everything, and I mean *everything*. From the complete Terry Pratchett collection to the *Use and Care Guide* for a John Deere 6R 175.

"It drove my boss crazy, but I insisted it would to be worth it.

"'Someone will need this someday,' I said. 'You'll see.'

"He just shrugged and decided to ignore me. So, I continued to collect every bit of printed text I could find and store it down in the bowels of the library where I worked.

"When Hatred hit, I stayed with my collection over nights to keep out the looters, but it soon became apparent that I'd have to stay on a more permanent basis.

"My boss was actually happy when I offered to stay full time. 'Just don't let anyone know,' he whispered. 'It'll look like we don't think the Party can get this under control. They could cut our funding.'

"Three months later, I was all moved in—even brought my cat Jones. Told my boss I needed her to keep the mouse population down, but really, she was something to talk to at night when I was alone. Then the funding was indeed cut—it wasn't my fault, honestly—and when everyone was gone, I decided to stay and guard the books.

"Physical books. In shelves. All the stories—or as many as I could get my hands on—that the human race had to tell.

"Someone had to.

"That's why Jones Number 3 and I are still here. That's why I taught myself how to send my message out. No. Not out. Up.

"I don't know if there's anyone left here on Earth. It's been a long time since I've seen a human. Alive, anyhow. And, to be honest, I don't know if anyone is left on any of the space stations, either. I don't know how there could be. Not after Hatred.

"But maybe, just maybe there's someone out there to talk to. To tell the stories to.

"The wolves were back yesterday. They tried to break into the library. At night, after I'd let the bats out of their dayroom. I could hear them outside, scrabbling at the barricaded back doors.

"When the motion-sensitive lights came on and the automatic announcement boomed out, 'Extreme force will be used if the door is damaged!' they gave up and went away, but it wasn't as quickly as I'd hoped.

"I'm afraid that one of these days, they'll finally figure out how to break in. And then, they better be ready for bloodshed, because I'm not giving this place up without a fight.

"The information I have in this library is priceless, and I will defend it with extreme prejudice. They better be ready for that. "I just hope I am."

"System after system bricked and people couldn't quite remember how to do—well—anything to fix it. That's when I bought my first gun. To protect the library where I'd worked forever, it seemed . . ." I heard the voice say.

I didn't know for certain what had come before that sentence in her story—that was where the signal had started in my earpiece—but I could guess. There was only one thing in modern history that had bricked system after system and that was

Hatred. It was called Hatred because that was what had spawned its creation and, ironically perhaps, it was also an anagram for Red Hat. But it fit for another reason too—not only had it been born of hatred, it inspired it in people.

She clearly had some capital *F* feelings about what humanity had done to the Earth, and I couldn't say I blamed her—especially since we'd apparently left her down there alone with her library, her cat, her bats, and a bunch of scavengers—but also because she was right. We had fucked the planet over. There was no getting around that.

There was also no getting around the fact she was sitting on a hoard of information that was more valuable than any of the resources the "Tech Bros" had stripped off the planet before leaving it for dead.

"One of these days, they will finally break in. And then, they better be ready for bloodshed, because—" the voice cut off.

Because what? I wanted to shout. But I didn't—my grumpy neighbour was sleeping, don't you know?

I picked up my tablet and fired a message off to the Director-General, highest level of urgency, requesting a face-to-face. Then I looked over the growing number of jobs I had to do—including figuring out what was on the same frequency as the replicators—and limped off to get started. With a little more hope in my step than the night before though. If that woman was still down there with all her books, if we could find her and get in to talk with her . . . well. Not only could we save her from her lonely existence with just a cat and a bunch of bug-eating bats for company, but she might be able to save us. If she had user manuals for tractors that had been obsolete before I'd been born, surely, she'd have the sort of textbooks and resources that we needed, too. Not just to repair all our tech to keep us going, but to aid in the rebuilding as well.

Just this morning there had been a story on my tablet about how the crops on Abradus were all failing. Apparently growing food wasn't nearly as simple as "put seed in ground, water, harvest", and all the required knowledge about food production and preservation was dying along with the people who held it. There were teams dedicated to trying to learn as much from those who'd been around before Hatred as they could, but progress was slow. That library could, quite literally, save humanity.

If only we could find and access it.

Or at least send her a message.

"Is anybody out there?

"I started rearranging the stacks today. Mostly to clean up guano—the bats had made it to the third floor without my knowledge, and it was a hell of a mess. But I'd also decided to reorganize, and get everything put in its proper place, once and for all. The wheels kind of fell off the whole organizational principle of this place back when the world was deconstructing, and I hadn't gotten around to cleaning up, but now that I'm attempting contact, it feels like the right time to pull it together. It's probably going to take me years to do this by myself, but that's all right. It should be fun. And if you ever respond—"

"Can you read me?"

Lisbeth blinked rapidly several times, and stared at the motley collection of radio equipment sitting on the desk in front of her. That voice, that human voice, had come from the speakers.

"What the fuck?" she whispered, her heart pounding in her chest. She felt too afraid to move. It had been years since she'd heard another living human. Years.

"Isn't this what you wanted?" she finally muttered to herself.

"Hello?" the voice said again. "Can you read me?"

She took in a deep shuddering breath, and let it out. "Yes," she finally said. "I can hear you."

"Holy shit, that's fantastic!" the voice cried. "We weren't sure this would work."

"Looks like it has," Lisbeth said.

There was a moment's silence as Lisbeth tried to think of something else to say. She figured the woman at the other end was doing the same thing.

"Where are you?" Lisbeth finally asked.

"I was going to ask you the same thing!" the woman replied. "I started hearing your transmission a few days ago—"

"I just got the equipment up and running," Lisbeth said. "I wasn't sure whether it was actually working or not." She shook her head. "Looks like it is. Where are you?"

"The *Joey Moss*," the woman replied. "In low orbit over Earth."

"I've heard of it," Lisbeth said. "I wasn't sure you were still there."

"Yes, we're still here," the woman replied, and chuckled. "What, did you think we left?"

"I wasn't sure," Lisbeth replied.

"Well, we are," the woman said. "Did you say you have information there?"

"You mean books?" Lisbeth asked stiffly.

"Right," the woman replied, and laughed. "Books. Who would have thought?"

Lisbeth didn't respond, because she honestly couldn't think of a thing to say. She was beginning to feel like making contact was a mistake.

"We might be able to help each other," the woman continued. "It sounds like you have a problem down there. You said scavengers are trying to get into your bunker—"

"Library," Lisbeth said stiffly. "I'm in a library."

"Oh," the woman replied. "Library. Sorry."

"That's all right," Lisbeth replied. "It does look like a bit of a bunker, truth be told. But it's a library."

"And that's why you have books," the woman said.

"Yep," Lisbeth replied. "Exactly."

"So, you got a favourite?" the other woman asked.

"A favourite what?" Lisbeth asked. "A favourite book?"

"Yeah. You must have at least one." The woman was clearly just making small talk—even twenty years removed from civilization, Lisbeth recognized that tone of voice, but she didn't care. It was a chance to talk about books.

"*The Hitchhiker's Guide to the Galaxy*," she replied. "By Douglas Adams. Ever heard of him?"

The silence stretched. "Can't say that I have," the woman finally said.

"Oh." Lisbeth felt a small pang, even though she knew Adams hadn't been everyone's cup of tea. Then she felt a bigger pang. "Do you read?" she asked.

"I did," the woman replied. "But it's been a while."

"Oh," Lisbeth said.

"Ever since Hatred," the woman continued. "All the books are gone up here. I miss it. Reading for pleasure." She paused, as though considering. "You ever hear of Eden Robinson? She wrote—"

"*Son of a Trickster*," Lisbeth said. "Yes. I know her work."

"I loved those books," the woman said. "I cried when I realized I'd never be able to read them again." She laughed awkwardly.

"I've got that book," Lisbeth said. "In fact, I've got everything she wrote."

"Oh my god," the woman replied. "Are you serious? Maybe when we come down to get you—"

"What?" Why would that woman think that she would want to go with her to the space station? She'd kept herself safe for years.

"—And we can digitize all your information—well, we should be able to do that soon, because our techs have been working on an answer to Hatred, and they think they're close—"

"What?" Lisbeth had difficulty keeping the outrage from her voice. This woman was talking about her abandoning the library, and the books.

"We'll save you, and save the information you've gathered," the woman said. "We really need that information you say you have. It's a win-win."

"Thanks," Lisbeth said, her voice shaking with rage. "But no thanks."

"What?" the woman sounded dumbfounded, like she couldn't believe anyone would not want to live up there with them. "Did you understand what I said? We can save you—"

"I don't need saving!" Lisbeth snarled, and then gasped when she heard her own voice booming "Extreme force will be used if the door is damaged" at the back of the library.

The wolves were back. Them, or something worse.

"Gotta go," she said, and grabbed her gun.

"Are you all right?" the woman cried.

"Fucked if I know," Lisbeth muttered, and headed out to protect the library.

I was pretty sure she muttered something after all the commotion happened, but I couldn't make it out—our connection was tenuous at best. But just before it broke—our station moving out of range her of library—I definitely heard a gunshot.

It wasn't a sound I'd ever heard in reality—not a lot of combustion weapons out in space—but I'd watched enough movies to know what it was.

"Fuck," I said.

Technically, we just needed this woman's library—even if it was apparently infested with bats? What was up with that—but I'm not a complete asshole. I didn't want her to be hurt either.

"And besides," I was saying ten minutes later, as I paced around the Director-General's office. "We don't know what the invaders are going to do if they get in. What if they are burning the exact book I need right now?"

"Okay," he said. "Okay. But I can't spare any crew on this crapshoot. Do you know how to fly a shuttle?"

Every kid tall enough to see the screens while sitting on the seat could fly a shuttle.

"Of course."

"Take a shuttle and go check it out, but make it fast. There is a problem with the climate control in the Central ring. Everyone is sweating pools in there. It's like a jungle. It's horrible."

"I'll get some of my people on it," I said. I wasn't the only engineer on board, just the best one.

"Do that. But also, hurry."

And so, I hurried. I rushed to the shuttle bay as fast as my broken knees would carry me, and before you could say "faulty shielding" I was on my way down to Earth.

It was a strange feeling.

I had been born on Mars, and though I'd read tons about Earth, I'd never been any closer to it than the window of the *Moss*. And now, as I watched Earth resolve from a blue and green ball, into continents and oceans, and then specific forests, and the ruins of cities, it struck me just how much damage we must have done, even before Hatred, that people would chose to leave this lush planet to live on Mars, or even Abradus.

Then the gravity dug its claws into me, and the agony in my knees was brilliant and white. It nearly made me swoon . . . but I held onto consciousness and steered toward where my calculations on the Station had told me I should find the library.

And there it was. Sort of.

It had clearly once been a large building, but part of it had crumbled in on itself. A giant sign, etched into stone and barely legible through the plants that had pushed through concrete and asphalt to crawl over top of it said "Libr". I could only assume that "ary" was carved into the similarly shaped chunk of stone that was laying on the ground beside it completely obscured with growth.

If these had once been the front doors, they were no longer—everything was crumbled. And, actually it looked intentional. As though someone had attempted to barricade the building . . . though it was impossible to tell if it had been done from the inside or the outside at this point—it was all just rubble.

I landed the shuttle on what had once been the street. It didn't land smoothly, having to crush bushes and vines beneath its weight rather than settle nicely on the middle of a landing pad, but it landed well enough.

When I stepped out of it, I was aware of three things immediately. The first was the pain in my knees. Gravity was not my friend. The second was the way the sun shone down to warm me and the air moved against my skin. Perhaps Abradus had this—breezes and sunshine that one could enjoy out in the open—but Mars and the *Joey Moss* certainly did not. I stopped moving and closed my eyes to better enjoy the sensations. It was magical. It might even be worth enduring the pain in my knees for. Maybe.

The third thing was how everything smelled. Fresh and clean and . . . green. Mars smelled like dust—no matter what we did, it smelled like dust. And the station smelled like metal and stale food and people. This smelled like none of those things.

And it was quiet.

Not silent. I could hear birds, and things rustling in the wind, but everywhere I'd ever been before, my entire life, there was always, always, always, the sound of machinery. Machinery to clean our air so we could breathe it. Machinery to keep the station in orbit so we didn't crash. It was omnipresent. I didn't usually notice it. But now I was keenly aware of it because of its absence.

"Wow," I said. And even my voice sounded different than it had in those other places. Smaller, somehow. Less resonant.

No wonder Lisbeth wanted to stay here in her library. I was starting to see the appeal.

Of course, I didn't have to deal with scavengers up in space and she did.

That reminder set my feet in motion, and I moved as fast as my knees would carry me, circling the library and trying to find a way in.

If the scavengers could, so could I.

It was the absence of vegetation that eventually revealed the way to me. The only place I didn't see things growing proved to be a narrow passageway through the rubble toward what must have once been a loading dock. It was wide enough for a person, but only one at a time.

"That would make breaking in hard," I thought. And then. "Go big or go home."

I stepped into the passageway and felt my way forward in the dim light. Suddenly a booming voice, a familiar voice, shouted, "Extreme force will be used if the door is damaged!"

Lisbeth heard the alarm sound, again.

"What the fuck?" she yelled, and pelted her way to the loading dock. This was the second attack today. She'd scared the wolves away, but she'd had to use a bullet to scare them off. That wasn't going to work forever. She was afraid she might actually have to point her gun at whatever was trying to break in and pull the trigger. And then what?

She missed the days when the city had been empty. When everyone had run away from the various pandemics that had run through the area—actually, every area. All the areas. Because there was no way to get away from them.

All she'd been left with then was the dead. Mostly inside buildings, because the fools all thought the buildings would save them. She hated going to the hospitals when she needed supplies. The smell was still horrendous, and clung to her like a greasy film.

"Animal or human?" she muttered as she wound through the stacks. "Who's trying to break in now?"

She rounded the corner that led to the loading dock, and pulled the gun. Walked silently to the entryway. And then she waited.

Someone fumbled through the opening, cursing softly when they got caught on the sharp chunks of metal poking out everywhere. Those sharp bits were entirely done on purpose, to slow them down, and keep them from coming in en masse.

Human, then, she thought, and shuddered. The humans had finally come back.

"Holy shit!" the person gasped. Lisbeth cocked the gun, and waited. Wishing they'd just go away, but knowing they wouldn't.

Humans never just leave. Not until they use up everything.

Then the person yelled, "Lisbeth! Lisbeth, it's Samar from the *Joey Moss.* I heard gunshots, and—ow! Fuck!—I've come down to make sure you're all right."

Lisbeth stared at the small opening through which the woman would eventually enter her domain. The voice sounded like the one she'd heard on her makeshift radio. Could it really be her?

"What's my favourite book?" she asked.

"What?" Samar called, and then squealed when she cut herself, one more time. "It's *The Hitchhiker*, or something. I don't really remember. Are you all right?"

"Yeah," Lisbeth said. It did sound like the woman from the space station and she had mentioned the right book—which was sitting on Lisbeth's desk at this very moment—so now it was up to Lisbeth. Should she let the woman in?

"Oh, why the hell not," Lisbeth said. "Get down on your stomach. Crawl in."

She cut herself a few more times getting down, first on her hands and knees, and then onto her stomach. She grunted and gasped, working her way through the last ten feet of the trap. And then she was inside, and the alarm finally shut down.

She lay on the floor for a moment, trying to catch her breath.

"You all right?" Lisbeth asked.

"Just give me a sec," she said, pulling herself to her knees and groaning. She had deep brown skin and nearly black hair. Originally, it had been in a ponytail, but the "doorway" had snagged and pulled it so that pieces stuck out in all directions. She was wearing a boring navy-blue jumpsuit—probably standard issue.

"How bad did you hurt yourself?" Lisbeth asked, and took a tentative step forward, lowering the gun. "The barbs are only supposed to slow you down, not kill you."

"It's not the cuts," she said. "It's my knees. My joints are bad. Just give me second."

She slowly stood, but did not look well at all, and Lisbeth reached out a tentative hand. "Need some help?"

She shook her head and then laughed. "I'm here to help you, remember?"

"So you said." Lisbeth gestured behind her, in the general direction of the library proper. "Want to come in? I mean, since you're here."

"Okay," she said. Samar smiled, and Lisbeth tried smiling back. It had been years—years—since she'd smiled at another person. Samar didn't look afraid, so Lisbeth guessed she'd pulled it off.

"Want some tea?" she asked.

"Tea?" Samar looked confused.

"It's a hot drink," Lisbeth replied. "You don't have tea up there?"

"Yes," she said, then shook her head. "But we use the replicators. How do you still have tea down here?"

"Gathering," Lisbeth said. "I gather."

She didn't bother telling Samar about all the books she'd read to find out what plants she could use without poisoning herself. That was a story for another day.

"Tea sounds nice," Samar replied, and hobbled forward a few steps. Then she grabbed Lisbeth's arm to keep herself upright.

They walked through the doorway, onto the main floor, and Samar gasped.

Lisbeth didn't blame her. The main floor of the library was beautiful—or had been, once. Warm wood everywhere. Wooden shelves held the books, and wooden tables graced the area where the guests had sat—back when there were guests. Even wooden floors underfoot, that only creaked in a couple of spots, which was a minor miracle. Off to the left, a staircase led up to the second floor, which held the original reference section. The windows—the ones Lisbeth hadn't blocked—glowed with the early evening sunset.

"How many books do you have here?" Samar asked.

"Ten million seven hundred and seventy-six thousand and fourteen," Lisbeth replied. And when she smiled this time, it was genuine. "Not including periodicals, pamphlets and manuals, movies and music. They're upstairs."

"Can I see it?" Samar asked. "The upstairs?"

"In a bit," Lisbeth said. "After you rest."

Lisbeth led Samar through the stacks to the back offices, where Lisbeth and the cat lived. The area looked more like a workshop than a place where a human being lived. Still, it was comfortable.

"Sit," Lisbeth said. She pushed Jones Number 3 from the couch and gestured for Samar to take his place. "I'll bring you the tea. Spruce bud all right?"

"Whatever," Samar said. She stared at Jones as he jumped back up on the couch and settled beside her. She touched his fur, smiled, and petted him gently. Lisbeth could hear the reprobate purring from across the room.

"Kick him off if he bothers you," she said.

"No," Samar replied. "This is nice."

Lisbeth had made the tea sometime before the first attack, so was able to quickly pour two mugs full. She carried them over to the couch, and handed Samar a cup before sitting down at the opposite end. Jones stared at Lisbeth with half closed lids, still purring loudly.

"That cat is taunting me," she said, and took a sip of the tea. Grimaced, and shook her head. "That's pretty strong," she said. "Want some fresh?"

"No," Samar said. "It tastes wonderful." And then she downed the whole cup, and leaned back, sighing contentedly.

"Good to hear," Lisbeth said. "Now, tell me why you're here. Really."

The tea tasted fresher than anything I'd ever had before, and I didn't know if that was because it was the only thing I'd had in decades that hadn't been replicated, or just because of the nature of the tea itself. Either way, it was incredibly invigorating.

"Now," Lisbeth said. "Tell me why you're here. Really."

Weird. My reasons for coming here and been front of mind and urgent right up until I sank into her couch. It was far softer than anything on the *Joey Moss*—even softer than my bed—and it, combined with her cat, had evaporated all the urgency from my mind.

Now, with her sitting beside me on the sofa, looking at me super intently, it all came back. She looked a bit older than me, and rather like what I would have imagined an "earthbound librarian" would look like. She was wearing several, layered long skirts, a frayed cardigan, and bright blue cowboy boots. Her steel grey hair was pulled into a huge bun on the top of her head—so huge that if she let it out, I bet her hair would fall past her waist—with an actual wooden #2 pencil jammed into it.

"Ahem," she said, and I realized I hadn't answered her question.

"I really *did* think you needed saving," I said, leaning forward and setting the mug down on the coffee table right beside a stack of books.

"Really," I repeated when she just looked at me dubiously. "But I can see that I was wrong. Looks like you have everything under control."

"You were, and I do," she said with a decisive nod.

But I *had* heard the sound of people trying to break in, I could feel the chill in the air, and see how thin she was—not emaciated by any means, but not as well-fed as anyone on the *Joey Moss* or Mars would have been, and so I continued. "But I still think that we could help each other."

"I—" she started. She wanted to argue with me, I could see it on her face, but something stopped her. I don't know what it was, but it involved a glance at her cat. I reached out to stroke him again, where he was pressed up against my side.

"Firstly, I need to change the frequency you're transmitting on just in case it's the reason everyone on the *Moss* is being subjected to the horror that is oatmeal." At her confused expression, I shook my head in an "I'll explain later" kind of way, and rushed on. "But also, we—all of humanity—need the information you have saved down here."

"You certainly don't expect me to just hand it all over to you, do you? I've been guarding this for half my life, I'm not just going to—"

"Of course not," I hastened to reassure her. "I would never ask that. But you saved it to be used, right? And we could really use it."

"What did you have in mind?"

"Loan it to me—just some of it, a bit at a time. I will take a selection of books up to the *Moss* with me, and in a cycle when I bring them back, I will bring you supplies. More food. Blankets. Cat food—*bat* food, if that's what you need." She started to say something, and I held up a finger and kept going. "And security. That's actually my specialty. I can make something safer for you than the system you're using. It might work now, but if someone is really determined, it won't keep them out long."

"Not human," she said.

"What?"

"The invaders aren't human. But more security would be nice.

In fact, all of it might be nice."

"For me too," I assured her. "Not only because it will help me keep the *Moss* in orbit where it belongs, and something more than oatmeal coming out of the replicators, but also because this"—I gestured to the cat—"this is pretty special. We don't have anything like this up there."

"No pets?"

"No room for pets."

"Oh," she said. "Well, that settles it, I guess. It would be inhumane of me to keep you from being able to visit with Jones Number 3 here."

"It really would," I said, with a grin. "Now, please tell me you've got a section about electrical shielding in here somewhere, and that I don't have to brave the bats for it."

"The bats only come out at night," she said. "And they're just here to eat the bugs that would otherwise eat the books." She smiled. "You'll be safe."

"All the same."

"I understand," she said with a laugh, just like we were old friends even though we'd only met. "Give your knees a rest, though. I'll get some books for you before you go." She stood. "And if you want, I'll lend you *Son of a Trickster*. If you want."

My favourite book.

"And another mug of this tea?" I asked, pushing my luck and my manners just a wee bit.

"And another mug of the tea," she agreed.

ALL THAT GLITTERS

Liz Westbrook-Trenholm

Would this be the one? Tanis still asked herself that question before entering a fresh site. She didn't hope. That would be foolish after all the dark hulks she floated through out here in the Belt. This one had gravity, at least. She whistled up her head-light critter. Even on a site where the initializers got some systems running, the peripheral areas were often as dark as they were cold. She stepped inside.

She startled as light flashed on, pouring from white circles in the ceiling. Kudos to the initializers. Whistling down her bio-light, she gazed about her. She stood in a sphere huge even by ancient space station standards. It was filled with work carrels, data ports, and—Tanis caught her breath. No. Couldn't be.

She closed and opened her eyes. Still there. Books, three-dimensional, static units displaying print, colours, and designs spread in glorious profligacy over plant pulp surfaces. They were sealed in clear cubes mounted on conveyor belts. They filled every cube. They looked—fresh.

This was no dead asteroid mine-hab where she'd find, at best, frayed depictions of large humans in unlikely physical congress or manuals in broken ancient dialects that she had to decipher.

This was—had to be—an exemplar of the Bright Age before the Great Dark, cherished, protected by some Ancient with legendary foresight. She'd dreamed of this, studied for seven rotations to be a librarian with a space archaeology specialization, and took what her fellows considered a dead-end mission in the pale hope of finding a pristine site. Now they were sifting through the pickings still drifting in the Earth-Mars belt and she was at a site that would demonstrate to all the system the majesty, the magnificence of the Bright Age giants.

She fluttered along the book units, running her fingers longingly over their smooth surfaces. Where were the controls to open them? The initializing team had promised systems were active on the ancient station before heading off with the Team Director and the top researchers on another priority. That didn't mean they'd checked *what* they'd turned on, or how it worked. They'd been in a hurry. Tanis smiled to herself. If they'd only known what they were leaving behind.

She spied a central work carrel on a raised dais at one end of the aisle that faced the rest of the room. It was furnished with a large, padded chair positioned before one of the large, shiny screens the Ancients favoured, only its back visible to the room. Maybe she'd find controls centralized there.

She slipped around to the front of the screen and startled back with a cry. Before her on the screen loomed a face and shoulders, heavy-boned, adorned with black head and facial hair, eyes with deep brown irises edged in gold, a long narrow proboscis and full lips parted as if in mid-speech. She sank back into the sumptuous chair to gaze at that face. Classic Ancient of the giantism era. The wisdom, the strength, the knowledge in those eyes! She had found not only the library. She had found the Librarian.

She had no idea how long she sat, joyful shock ricocheting off myriad questions. How was the image so fresh and immediate? What momentous words had he begun to say? Could the tech still work? It had to be hundreds of rotations old. Could she activate the image, hear the voice of an Ancient? She knew, looking at him, that he was key to unfurling the ancient knowledge around her.

She examined the silent controls, metal, or plastic, rather than anything that could be coaxed awake with a whistle or a stroke. She'd worked at inflexible toggles before, but her confidence failed her. Surely a control system in so sophisticated a site would be more complex, responsive, even delicate. What if she pressed a wrong toggle and lost it all? She needed help.

She nudged her comms critter. "Find Tech Twins. I need

them." No response. No signal, even. Anxiety flickered. Silence was never good when it came to the twins. The whiz duo were smart but tended to use their hands before their heads. They needed managing.

Whispering farewell to the Giant Librarian, she left to search them out.

She all but ran over Fern Lentil, their small team's small overseer, in the corridor.

Tanis's "I need the twins" collided with FL's "Have you seen the twins?" to which FL added, "Does the air smell funny to you?" As usual when stressed, which was often, her voice squeaked.

Tanis shrugged. "I've found the most amazing collection, FL. This will make and break careers and reputations."

"What?" FL squeaked.

Tanis skirted around FL's diminutive form into the main corridor. "I'll check the lab hab. Maybe Scientist has seen them." He had a name but preferred the honorific. He loved his work. Before she could approach the scientist's hatch, it zipped open and his bald head with its satellite ears zeroed in on them. "Twins! Get them! They've got to recalibrate my gas analyzer. I'm getting readings like I've never seen before. Twins!"

"We can't find them either," Tanis and FL said.

Scientist's body stumbled after his head. "How? It's not that big a station, is it?"

Tanis thought of The Librarian's laughing, wise eyes and said, "The initializers got the power on, but I think they missed a few details."

FL said, "The Director has tasked us with undertaking a review of the artefact to map out its networks and their interconnections. The Initializers left us with such necessaries as are needed."

"Needed necessaries are always useful." Scientist's head twisted around on his spindly neck, amused by himself. "First I heard of it."

"I was going to call a meeting."

Tanis had had enough. "Galley," she said. "They might be recalibrating the Cater again."

"Oh no," said FL. The twins liked adventurous recipes. "They really need organic integration."

Tanis cast her a bland look. It seemed FL had been studying

Introduction to Organic Team Management, again.

FL gulped. "I guess that's my job, now the Director's left us while the rest go off prospecting." She swallowed what looked to be imminent tears. Tanis and Scientist didn't wait for her to work through it.

At the galley, the Cater hummed inoffensively, ready to offer up standard balanced sustenance choices. Behind it, square lockers, or doors rose in rows, each one labelled in ancient script and adorned with a protruding knob. The work surface was littered with unfamiliar chunks which were only identifiable as food because bites had been taken from each of them. The Cater hadn't produced those.

FL said, "This looks strange, even for the Twins."

"Hah!" declared the Scientist and pushed, pulled, and twisted a knob.

"Wait—" Tanis and FL cried.

Something whirred.

The drawer opened, revealing a steaming tray bearing a puffy object draped in viscous pink. It emitted sweet, toasty aromas. It smelt like holiday food, even if it didn't resemble it. Tanis wondered what Vac-day the Librarian might have celebrated with a thing like that.

Seizing the object, Scientist sank his teeth into it, spluttered "Ah!" with a spray of crumbs and gusto. "Sweetness and, uh, huh." He shrugged and twisted another knob.

The object that emerged was a deep brown, sizzled, and smelt something like unlaundered underwear and unwashed body. They looked at it, congealing.

"Even the twins wouldn't—" FL said. And then, "Scientist, maybe you shouldn't—shouldn't we be—?" Catching Tanis's expression, she shut her mouth. Her eyes took on the glazed expression of one reading an internal feed.

"Defining and isolating integration priorities," she announced.

Right heading of *Introduction to Organic Team Management*, Tanis thought. Hopefully, she'd get to *Actioning Integrated Objectives* before too long. Tanis wondered where she might find some necessary necessities that would let her operate the library controls or break into the collection. She really needed the Twins.

Exiting the Galley, she noticed a trail of crumbs. The Twins had found something worthy of more than a single bite. The fragments led her along the main corridor past the lab and the library, where she repressed the urge to check on the Librarian. Twins, she reminded herself.

She followed the corridor to unfamiliar territory, to a junction. Right? Left? Straight ahead? The cloying remembrance of the sizzling brown food and the whirl of excitement was making her feel fuzzy, poorly focused. She'd felt that way in early morning tutorials after an all-night shift on composting critter quality control. She gathered herself and examined where she was. A familiar piece of equipment-critter chirped to itself at the turn into one of the smaller junctions.

"Hah!" Scientist cried, whooshing up behind her. "Air scrubber!" He pushed past her to the critter hunkered on its perch displaying scrolling yellow numerals on its face screen.

"You see?" Scientist rapped the display cover with his knuckles. "As I said! I told you, didn't I? I said, 'Anomalous substance! Find the Twins!' Didn't I?!"

Moving to give him gesticulating space, Tanis's foot nudged an object on the floor. A tech critter lay unmoving against the base of the machine. Tanis picked it up, recognizing it as one of the bio-clones whose designed DNA gave it the ability to sample and analyze novel substances. They were essential in unfamiliar environments, being robust and able to recover from sampling even substances toxic to most Earth life. It was warm and pliable, but unresponsive.

"Oh no," murmured FL. "Is it dead?"

"Seems to be sleeping," Tanis replied.

"Gassed by over-sampling!" Scientist said. The enthusiasm faded from his expression as he registered what he'd just said.

They all gazed at the critter, its display window shuttered, and its sampling proboscis coiled. Scientist reached out a knobby finger and stroked the velvet of its round body. "You're a bit too good at isolating molecules, aren't you, little fella?" He glanced at the others' staring faces. "The gas comprises only a few molecules per ten thousand."

Tanis gestured at the air scrubber. "Why has the scrub-critter's numerals gone from yellow to orange?"

Scientist peered at the display and hunched his shoulders.

"The unknown gas is creeping up on the oxygen-nitrogen mix. It seems to be—competitive."

"I have a headache," FL said. "We have to find the Twins."

"Why would the Ancients let something like this into the air?" Tanis asked. "Is it an accident? A pollutant? Could it be what made them abandon this station?"

FL said, "This is all very interesting, but we need the Twins to help us figure out this tech and stop it." She rubbed the bridge of her nose.

"Did they abandon it?" Scientist asked. "The station is in very good shape for an abandoned site that's, what, a thousand rotations old?"

"You're saying they're still here somewhere, a thousand rotations after the Great Black?" Tanis rubbed her temples. The Librarian had looked very fresh and alive in his image. But it was an image. Wasn't it? "I'm having trouble thinking straight."

FL squeaked, "We're being poisoned by mystery gas and now we're being hunted by ghosts?"

"No, no. An academic discussion—"

FL shouted. "We have to find the twins! *Now!*" Into their shocked silence, she added, "Follow me!" She turned on her heel and collapsed.

"She is smaller than us! More affected!" How could Scientist always sound excited?

"And the gas levels are rising, so we're next?"

Scientist nodded.

"Necessary necessities?"

He nodded again. She noticed, irrelevantly, that his ears flapped a little.

By unspoken agreement, they separated. Scientist headed down a side corridor, Tanis toward the main airlock into the station where the crew first penetrated the structure. It was the most likely place they would leave equipment.

Her feet pounded as she ran, echoing inside her skull. She sensed the dead metal under the muffling surface of artificial fabric, her passing echoing off the hard, unnatural walls. She was seized with a sense of peril, of being a hunted intruder in an alien place of bones. She thought of the Librarian and wondered if protecting his domain involved poisoning intruders. Air whispered through painted grills, bearing poison into her lungs with her every breath.

The corridor seemed endless, but at last she staggered into the vestibule opening off the main airlock. Heaps of sleeping equipment lay banked against its walls, comforting in its familiar irregularity, warmth, alive-ness. *Necessary necessities.*

She popped her lips, one-two-three, a landed fish gasping for air. One breather and then another cheeped from within the stack. As she dove toward them, other equipment woke enough to scuttle aside to give her access. Even as she reached out a hand, a breather ran up her arm and clamped its belly over her face, its claws wrapping tight around the back of her head. The critter poured clean, optimal air mix into her lungs, its bellows pumping. It could do this for hours before it needed a feed and sleep. She fell to her knees and took breath after breath. The breather's hard, lichen-based shell was impervious to any intrusion, from toxins to hard space. She was safe. She hoped.

No time to consider, she repeated her pop-pop-pop. It resonated through her breather's shell, calling more breathers. When she had as many breathers as would fit clamped to each arm she rose and ran.

The return trip took mere moments, where the other had seemed an endless nightmare. She fell on her knees beside FL and a breather leapt to her face. Tanis waited just long enough to see her tiny young manager's eyes flutter open, widen, and then crinkle with joy. She started babbling about messages or instructions, a jumbled tumble of words that made no sense.

"Rest, FL," Tanis said. "I'll go look for the others."

She left FL calling reassurances that everything was fine, fine. Maybe it was. Tanis hustled down the corridor the Scientist had taken; she was haunted by foreboding.

The corridor seemed to lead to a maze of possible exits. She tried a couple, but they led to dim spheres lined with silent machinery. She shivered at the hard lines. How hard and unrelenting the Ancients' structures were. She'd never paused to wonder about it. She'd focused on analytical discussion of fragments of data retrieved by Techs, without thinking about the structures that had housed them, long silenced by the Great Blackout. Did containers define content?

Thinking of techs raised her worry about the Twins, and Scientist. Where were they? Was she even in the right corridor?

As she swept her eyes across her surroundings, she spied a crumb on the floor. She slowed, searching. Another. Had the Twins filled their pockets with ancient food stuffs? A laugh burbled up through her fears. So like them.

As she moved, she thought she detected a faint sound, an insect-like murmuring. She wished she'd thought to find and bring a search critter. She could really have used its eyes-on-wings, right now. She followed the hum down a branch curving into a cul-de-sac off the main corridor. It ended in an open hatch.

Slowing, she approached it with caution. Inside was a dimly lit space packed with humming equipment. All of it was made of gleaming metal, glass, and plastic, yet it seemed to breathe. Repressing her unease, Tanis edged along the margins of the crowded room, peering between ranks of machines, dead, yet speaking muted sounds. She shuddered.

She found all three of them sprawled at the base of one of the machines. In moments, the breathers had detached from her arms and leapt to their faces. The Twins leaned on each other, dark curls seeming shared as if their heads were joined which, metaphorically, Tanis supposed they were. When Scientist's breather attached, it pinned back his ears so that he resembled a meerkat.

She peered at the structure they leaned on, but could make nothing of its smooth surface, feeds, and valves, all inscrutably machined, utterly lacking in control interfaces, toggles or anything that made sense to her. There must've been a reason they'd ended up here. She would have to wait for them to wake and explain things.

They woke, eventually. There was no explaining. All three perched on the floor, cheery, chatty, and incomprehensible. At some point, FL found them.

She exclaimed, "There you are, Twins. We've been looking for you." She dropped to the floor with them and added her voice to the cacophony.

Tanis was crouching on the floor, her face buried on her up-drawn knees, arms flung around her head when she heard a Twin say, ". . . figured this had to be the source."

The other added, "It's connected to everything but no controls to be found."

"Then I forget."

"Me too."

"You passed out," FL squeaked enthusiastically. "Me too,"

"Remarkable experience," Scientist added.

As Tanis leapt up to stand over them, he said, "How about you, Tanis? Did you pass out too?"

"I got the breathers," she said, faintly.

They fell silent. Then in unison they all sighed, "Oooooh!" as if achieving some leap of enlightenment unparalleled in their existence. It appeared they were not quite back to themselves. Tanis tried, anyway.

"Twins, we found your portable scrubber and—"

"That didn't work."

"No. Had hopes."

"But no."

Tanis persevered. "We also found your comatose analyzer."

"Poor little thing."

"Probably happy, though."

"Happy, yes. And comatose."

"Could you tell us what it found?" Tanis insisted.

"A gas."

"Very complex molecular structure."

"Self-replicating—almost alive."

"Ha-ha, I was going to say almost alive too."

Tanis ground her teeth. "We know that, but what does it do?" And before they could speak added, "Besides making us comatose and happy."

"Not you, obviously."

The other twin snorted and nodded.

"I need your answer." Two cherubic faces gazed up at her, heavily lashed eyes wide. She realized she was looming, her fists clenched. She forced herself to relax. "Please."

They extruded a back-and-forth explanation that seemed to say that the gas was impervious to scrubbing and that the more oxygen-nitrogen mix the Twins had encouraged out of the Initializers' critters, the larger the volume of the mysterious gas became.

"It's going to put all our critters to sleep pretty soon."

"We think it's what keeps the station in such perfect shape."

"Stasis."

"Could be. Preservative?"

"Could be."

In unison, "We don't know."

Tanis found her mind shrinking to a panicked nugget trying to hide in her skull. From far off, she heard her voice sounding quite reasonable, considering.

"Even our breathers will become non-functional?"

"Not them. They're tough."

"Impervious."

"But all the other critters are going to sleep," Tanis reiterated, as if, perhaps, she'd heard wrong the first time.

"That's kind of sweet," FL said.

Tanis ground her teeth. "And the rest of the team won't be back for nearly a quarter rotation. And we have limited breathers. So, eventually, we'll all be drugged into unconsciousness. And so will any other humans who enter the station."

"Our Cater will go to sleep?" FL asked. "We'll have to eat that food that tastes like body odour?"

Scientist broke in. "And sweetness and . . . something. This sounds serious to me! Does this sound serious?"

Flooding with relief, Tanis said, "Yes, Scientist. This is very, very serious. Very, very, very . . ."

FL said, "Don't cry. The Twins will figure something out. You'll figure something out, won't you, Twins?"

For once, neither Twin had a thing to say.

Fear, despair, a sense of failure, loss, grief: Tanis had a full menu of awful feelings to draw on. Age of Light, indeed. Age of cruelly illuminated inertia. Death without release.

The thought of the Librarian, his wise, wonderful face frozen. She was to be trapped as he was, forever . . .

"The library," she said. "Twins, you need to help me wake it up. We need to search it. The Ancients on this station must have left records for us to find."

"Or," said the Twins, "you could just ask them."

A silence fell, filled with staring.

The Twins led them along a convoluted route, sprinkled with crumbs, which, Tanis realized, were the Twins' dumb-bio substitute for a locator critter.

They entered an airlock, a tight, uncomfortable space that emphasized the hiss of their breathers and odour of their stressed bodies.

"We smell like Ancient food!" Scientist said, genially.

They spilled into a dimly lit sphere, the floor, walls, and ceiling unadorned and formed from hard white panels. The space was filled with sarcophagi, each cradled within a moulded white plinth. Symbols adorned the sides of each sarcophagus.

"They're in there," said a Twin.

"Show you," said the other. He traced around a whorl with his fingertip and light rose in the lid of the sarcophagus closest to the hatch. Scientist leapt forward to look, meerkat straight and alert with interest. FL peeked from behind him, on tiptoe. Tanis hung back, overcome by reluctance.

Scientist examined the symbols on the side of the casket, his enthusiasm entirely restored. "You think you can wake them?!"

The Twins pointed to the symbols. "These are straightforward Ancient logic."

"Algorithms that outline the parameters they want and ignore all the complexities."

"They were quite simple thinkers, really."

"Probably why they made everything so lifeless and hard edged."

"Holding off nature's matrices and variables, instead of allying to them."

Their matter-of-fact dismissal of the great Age of Light gave her the courage to step forward and look. Blood rushed to her head as she recognized The Librarian, eyes closed, face relaxed in repose within the flow of black hair swirling over the headrest and his shoulders. His mouth was quirked in a slight smile. He was really big.

"Or maybe they just wanted to make it easy for someone to wake them up," said a Twin, and began touching buttons.

"Shouldn't we—?" FL and Tanis chorused.

The sarcophagus lid retracted from the face of the sleeping Giant. They all waited. He continued to sleep.

"The gas."

"Have we got any more breathers?"

Tanis lifted her arms where two pairs of breather-critters still clung.

As soon as they sensed the unconscious figure, they leapt. One clamped onto the Librarian's face while the others scuttled at random, seeking more emergencies. The Twins popped two of them back, and the third returned to its familiar perch on Tanis's arm.

Time passed, and still the Librarian lay, inert, neither alive nor dead.

Discussion arose, the Scientist proposing a range of stimuli, some alarming, the Twins speculating as to whether thousand-year-old Giants could still be viable, and FL suggesting they wait and see and, besides, there was still the issue of the gas. In fact, she said THE GAS!!! in a squeaky scream oddly amplified by her breather. The Scientist admitted his ears were getting sore. The Twins went back to considering the problem.

Tanis remained, gazing on that sleeping face, her mind wondering and wandering over what lay within that mighty head. She began worrying about speaking with him, wondering if her Ancient was up to it. She tried a couple of phrases of greeting and her embedded translator critter responded. So, it wasn't put to sleep, feeding off her oxygen supply. That'd help.

What should she say? "Welcome to the—" What was the age she lived in called anyway? Would the giant consider this a fallen or a dark age, with all the minerals and energy sources his kind had relied on depleted? Could he recognize the richness of the interconnections among all Earthly existence, humans but one curious, seeking, creative part of the whole? Maybe she shouldn't try. Maybe just welcome him on his terms and let him figure out the rest. For example:

"Welcome, Giant of the Age of Light."

"What?" A deep, sleepy rumble issued from the sarcophagus. The Giant sat up.

He peered around, shook his head, and felt his face, finding the breather clamped there. His eyes widened, he caught sight of Tanis and screamed. He scrabbled at the breather which obligingly jumped off and back onto Tanis's arm.

As he fumbled at the symbols on the side of his sarcophagus, the others reassembled around him. A Twin touched a series of symbols, and the sarcophagus split open to reveal a body clothed in slightly sparkling white tunic and leggings. The Giant leapt to his feet, moaned, and fell back onto the couch, his eyelids sagging.

"Gas," said the Twins in unison.

A breather leapt to the rescue on the Giant's face. The Giant screamed and scrabbled again. Twins, Scientist, and squeaking FL blended into a symphony of cacophony.

Tanis laid her hands over the Giant's frantic fingers.

"Breather," she said distinctly. Her translator repeated it in Ancient. She hoped. "Air. Oxygen, Nitrogen."

The Giant stilled, although he continued to gasp and whimper. His eyes were fixed on hers, such warm, brown and gold eyes, if a bit wide and frantic at the moment.

Tanis popped to her breather, which hopped off onto her arm. She immediately felt the effects of the gas filtering into the edges of her consciousness. She popped again, and the breather brought her welcome relief.

The Giant's enormous head tilted to one side.

"You haven't turned off the ????" The translator repeated the string of syllables he had produced with no translation. The Giant swung his bare feet over the edge of his couch, walked to a panel among the many on the wall, slid it open to reveal a console, and pressed a series of symbols on it.

A breeze swept through the sphere, accompanied by loud hissing. Somewhere in the distance, a soft, repetitive tone began to ring, like the ding-dong of a bell-bird in a forest.

Minutes passed. The dings ceased. The Giant peeled the Breather off his face, and it leapt nimbly onto his arm. The Giant shuddered and recoiled. Tanis popped it back to her own arm and released her own. The air was breathable, cool, sterile without scents of life, but definitely clean of the cloying gas.

They formed a tableau, the semi-circle of Tanis, FL, the Twins, and Scientist gazing at the Giant perched on the edge of his couch. Tanis waited for his first real words, the statement from a past age bringing ancient wisdom to her own, or doom. Perhaps it would be doom, words of destruction—

The Giant spoke. The translator said, "They sent hobbits?"

"That stuff you drink is disgusting, you know."

"Coffee? It's life blood, elixir of the gods. FL and Scientist are fans."

"As if they need stimulating."

"What's that, sludge?"

"Balanced, delicious sludge. Let's go, Ancient. We have work to do."

"Zak! Ancient makes me feel—ancient. Wait, I'm getting a doughnut."

"Ooh, get me one too. You *are* ancient, all focused on cultural artefacts even older than you are."

"Those films are classics, definitive of their time!"

"Calling us Hobbits."

"Well, you are all kinda small. And you're into that whole earth; every worm's tunnel connects with all being stuff."

"*You* are gigantic *and* obsessed with repetitive visual artefacts featuring unconvincing monsters with anatomically impractical snapping tongues."

"You have to get why the breathers freaked me out. I expected an implanted alien-ette to slide down my gullet."

"At least you were able to clarify the cause of the Great Black. Solar flares!"

"Well, on top of economic and climate collapse."

"We need to expand on that in the paper, I think. The interconnectedness will resonate."

"Sure. Rub it in."

"C'mon, you ancient old giant Zak. That paper won't write itself." Tanis led the way out of the galley.

"We had AIs that could do that, you know."

"I've analyzed the rescued fragments."

"Say no more."

Tanis swallowed her bite of doughnut. "Two Earth-spins to the presentation and we still don't have a title. How about: *The Ancient Speaks: Lessons from the Anthropocene.*"

"Enough with the Ancient! How about *Past into Present: Integration of Living Cultures.*"

"Integration! We're not integrating. We're observing and learning from yours, but integration would be unwise if not impossible."

"I'd say our integration is going fine." Zak kissed the top of Tanis's head.

"Oh, you."

Carrying their morning drinks, Tanis and Zak entered the library together.

TETROMINOES AND SEEKERS

Trisha Jenn Loehr

Dolen: I need a favour.

Woman of Wisdom: I sincerely hope you don't actually think I'm the right person to ask.

Dolen: Believe me, doll. You're the absolute best person to ask. The only one I'd trust, in fact.

Woman of Wisdom: Funny, you and trust don't really go together in my mind.

I was pushing my luck sending a comm to Kiandra. But she really was the only person I could trust with this—and the only person I could think of who had the brains and resources to help me do this.

Because I sure as hell can't do it on my own.

And I'm not sure I really want to.

I shove my techpad into my back pocket and glance around the chaos of Gantium Station Nine's massive docking bay. The hangar is four levels high, the outer gunmetal grey walls lined with viewports to either open space or walkways connecting residents and visitors to services and sleeping chambers. Gantium is one of the busiest ports the Denison Galaxy. It operates seventeen commercial ports out of this hangar and houses over twelve-hundred residents and guests at any one time. There's always stuff happening here. Some of it good. Some of it not so good.

And as much as I love it here, I'm ready to be able to explore other parts of the galaxy, to go planet side rather than simply going between various port stations making rich folks richer.

I want to do more.

I give the burnt orange hull of the *Ionia* two quick taps. A promise.

I have two days. Two feckin' days.

And if I can pull this off, then I'll no longer be a grunt on somebody else's ship. I'll be captain of my own feckin' ship. And a damn pretty one she is.

With quick steps, I merge into the mass of crew members, mechanics, medics, and other folks going to and fro between ships, cargo holds, and the lifts to the upper levels of the massive space station. As a Terran who grew up on a planet populated mainly with other Terrans who complained about Krenlins, Garniums, Q'rsh, and Jomalians doing things differently than they'd do it, I love seeing folks from all over the galaxy in one place, sharing space, food, and ideas.

And I want to see more of it.

On my own terms.

"I don't read those made-up stories. I like to learn when I read." Chet's voice assaults my ears the moment the airlock doors slide open into Gantium Station Nine's Information and Research Sanctum. Of course, on the most important day of my life, he *would* show up and put everything at risk and not even realize it. Nothing good ever happens when he's around, which is just one more reason why I'm determined to get myself onto a different (and solo) shipping route.

As I step through the airlock, *her* retort is polite but cold. I can't help but smile. When she speaks to me that way, it's with an amused lilt to her voice—a hint of warmth left over from when she liked me. But right now, that lilt is nowhere to be heard.

"We serve all kinds of patrons here. Including those who are intelligent enough to enjoy a wide range of reading interests, from fiction to non-fiction to technical manuals and other resources."

The only thing chillier than the silence in the room is the darkness of space outside the small viewports on this isolated corner of the space station. I grin and roll my shoulders back, then I break the quiet in a way that I hope earns some karma units for me in Kiandra's books. The stars know I need them.

"I've learned a lot from reading stories, Chetanuson. Like how to know when a lady is not interested in a feck's advances." I stride past a couple of research pods toward the most annoying Terran I've ever met with as much of a saunter as I can muster—channelling the swagger of the cowboys in the retro romance novels Kiandra got me hooked on that first time I came here.

I give Kiandra's scowl a wink hello and lean my hip against the curved counter that separates her workspace from the public area of the Sanctum. Her scowl only increases my swagger. Even with such an angry expression on her face, I still think she's the most beautiful creature I've ever seen. She dislikes me (fairly, I do admit) but she despises my older brother. I fold my arms across my chest and turn to face said dear brother and smirk at the red-faced glower on the grunt's face.

"And, if you're really trying to impress the person who provided all those stories to me . . . may I suggest you try a different tack?"

The heat coming off Chet rivals a Q'rsh laser gun, and it only makes me want to laugh more. My entrance into the Sanctum is going better than I expected. I look a whole lot better standing next to Chet than I do on my own.

"Neither of you are worth my energy," Chet mumbles. With that weak comeback, he thumps toward the door. As soon as the airlock hisses closed, I laugh and turn fully to face Kiandra.

Unlike the heat in Chet's eyes, the heat in Kiandra's burns as it rakes up and down my body. Her gaze settles on my belt buckle where a Terran cowboy on a bucking bronc is memorialized in antique pewter.

"You playing dress up now?" She lifts her eyes to mine and raises a brow.

I'll go along with this, try to warm her up a bit more since shooing Chet wasn't enough for her to appreciate my presence. Again, that's fair, considering.

"Found it in a junk shop on Vanian on our last pickup there. They had a bunch of those antique paper books from Terra that we like too. I'm happy to lend them to you if you want some new reading material."

Her eyes flash with something. Longing maybe? But she shakes her head and starts tapping at a holoscreen behind her workstation and consulting a handheld techpad. "As I made clear in my comm, Dolen, *I'm* not the person *you* should be asking for help."

I stride around to the side of the counter closer to her and tuck my hands in my pockets like Rhett on the cover of *Ranches and Wenches*. From Kiandra's posture, I immediately realize that is not the kind of guy she'd want, which she promptly confirms.

"I'm not interested in the kind of chaos you leave behind." She focuses her gaze on the holoscreen, tapping on file names.

She's probably organizing lists containing information around a specific topic. That night we met all those years ago in NetZen, she'd explained over a couple of pints of Furkian ale how part of her job as a curator was to compile information from sources throughout Gantium Nine's knowledge network. When the higher ups or the rich folk needed info, they didn't gather it themselves. They hired grunts to do all the work. As a curator, she's just a fancier kind of grunt. An expert in her craft, but still a grunt in the view of those above us. Not technically better than me but definitely lives a way more sophisticated and appreciated life. Even if she is stuck on this station, doing the same thing every single day.

The later the night got, the more she'd said . . . and rather than dwell on what I did that next morning and the ramifications of it, I try to redirect the conversation. "Look, Kiandra," I pause, hoping she'll look at me. When she does, albeit with an annoyed tilt to her head, I continue. "I know I've been a brute." I pause again, trying to figure out which words to use, how to say what I need to in a way that doesn't come out totally wrong.

"Want to expand on that statement, Crew Member Dolen?" Her words are like ice—she knows how much I want to be a captain and not just a grunt. But there's fire in her eyes. So much anger that I look away and study the hold we're in.

The Research and Information Sanctum is tucked away on a lower deck of the station and only has a limited number of small viewports to the stars. Single and double-occupancy research pods are scattered around the hold to afford quiet and privacy to anyone, no matter their race or level, to conduct informational searches in Gantium Nine's database. It's a neat and tidy place if you like that kind of thing. But I know it's not where she wants to be. There's a whole galaxy outside of this room, this station.

I hiss a breath out. We're more similar than different, she and I. We're both explorers, seekers. I want to explore every planet I can find. She wants to explore all the information out there: the books, the media, the databases. The stories, the tools, and the tales. To seek it out, collect it, and bring it back here to share with anyone and everyone who wants and needs it.

"No? I didn't think so." Her words pull me from my revelatory thoughts. Kiandra shakes her head and turns back to her holoscreen. "Now if you'll please follow your brother out, I have work to do."

"There's a ship. I can get it—with your help. And you could come with me. Wherever we want to go." Feck! What the feck did I just blurt at her. My breath stops in my throat. That was not the eloquent speech I was planning . . . thinking . . . hoping for. Feck.

Kiandra slowly turns to me, her wavy dark brown hair swaying ever so slightly. I want to touch it. I grip the counter in front of me instead.

She just stares at me, a stoic expression on her face, unreadable.

I stare back. I probably look like a fool. Nothing like the cowboy I pretended to be when I walked in. I swallow again, audibly.

The airlock hisses and a massive blue Jomalian walks in. From the corner of my eye, I see its three eyes briefly widen at our standoff and then flick away as it scurries—I didn't know something that big could scurry—to a research pod. The pod door clicks shut, the sound painfully loud in the awkward silence hovering between Kiandra and me.

She raises an eyebrow.

I lean crossed arms on the counter in an attempt to seem a little less freaked out, a little more casual. But really to get just a tiny bit closer to her . . . and try to be a little more eloquent this time round. Maybe . . . just maybe . . .

"How many other knowledge keepers are here?" I ask the question quietly. I know she could get in trouble for having a conversation like this. It's a touchy subject. Like anything between her and me, and for people in her position. Curators are expected to be happy, just like any grunt is. None of us are expected or encouraged to move up in the world, in our industries, into new roles.

But I know she wants to. Or at least she used to.

So maybe I can save a little face here and help us both.

She puts her techpad down so gently, I barely hear the click of it settling onto the metal counter. She watches me, and this time her eyes are softer. Still critical but questioning rather than straight out condemning me.

A pull of longing fills my gut. I miss those eyes.

"Twelve," she whispers the word.

"And how many have been promoted to knowledge seekers?" I whisper too.

"Three."

"If you help me get this ship, I will be at your disposal to seek and gather information, resources, whatever this place needs." My voice is too eager, I know it. She knows it too, by the look on her face.

"I've heard that promise before, Dolen."

"You did." She thinks I'm saying all of this for me, and not her. That the ship is for me alone. That inviting her is for me too . . . and her wants are secondary. "Ki . . ."

She shakes her head again. And the way her shoulders droop hits me like a gut punch. I really fecked up back then. And I've regretted it every day since. Sure, my techpad is loaded with digital books that she's found in Gantium's database and helped me transfer to my device, but those transactions have been stale each and every time for the last two years. She's been cool towards me since that damn Morning After.

"These stories," I pull up my library on my techpad and toss it on the counter between us. The screen is filled with filenames of every single Terran cowboy romance novel she introduced me to and more. I pull a compact paper book from the back pocket of my jeans (another junk shop find that go perfectly with my belt buckle) and drop it on top. "You introduced me to them. I loved them then because they were fun. They were adventures. The cowboys had confidence that I could only dream of having—I wanted to be the cowboy in space." I gesture at my clothes that I've carefully curated to fit that style. "So, I tried become that." I pause and swallow. I stare deep into her eyes and will her to believe me. "And maybe I did and maybe I didn't. But that was the wrong choice."

She studies me. I will my body to stay still. I will myself not to twitch under her scrutiny. She doesn't trust me. And she's right not to. I screwed up. I made her big promises, and then, when it came time to make them happen, I listened to guys like my brother instead of the guys like Cade and West in the books Kiandra hooked me on. Those guys, they'd be honest, real. Feck, they'd let her see them cry about how they'd messed up. And then they'd do better.

Now it's my chance to do better.

"These stories are about so much more though," I continue. "All stories are. The surface is the adventure. The swagger." Her eyebrow rises and a derisive laugh bursts from my chest. "It took me a while, but I get it now. These stories are about earning redemption too.

"I'm tired of lugging loads of copper to port station after port station. I want to *be* more." I grab my techpad again and tap on a filename, pulling up the cover and turning it to her. "I want to help people like Red." I switch to a different book cover. "I want to make a difference like Beau." Again, I switch to another. "And like Ford, I want to do those things without making a bunch of money for somebody else."

I swipe out of the digital reader protocol and into the photo protocol to pull up an image of the *Ionia*. I drop the techpad back on the counter and hold my hands palms up. I've got everything to lose here. I may as well just lay it all on the table, go all in.

"That little beauty is available. And if I can prove, using math and stuff, that I can fit Jung-Shi's entire shipment of fancy protein bars in it, he'll pay me enough up front to buy her and contract me for his next eight shipments. He ships out every four weeks. Which means in between, I can go where I want, do what I want, take on whatever other jobs either pay what we need or make a difference." I pause and swallow. Will she believe me? "And those weeks could be yours, Ki. To go seek knowledge and gather information to bring back here for whoever needs it. Stories or histories, or feck—more tech guides if that's what you want. Whatever information you want, I'll help you find it. All we need is this ship."

"What makes you think I want that?" Her voice is low. Disappointed, almost.

I lean closer, looking deep into her hazel eyes. "We spent thirteen hours drinking ale then soda then tea and talking about our favourite books and stories and characters. And every single one of them had something in common: they went after what they wanted. They did the work. They refused to just do what was expected of them. They refused to stay stagnant because it was easier. That's what I'm trying to do. And every time I walk in here, I see you looking out that viewport at the stars and the ships passing by." I rest my fingers on hers where they're clamped on the edge of the counter. "What you do here is important, but I know it's not what you want to be doing. You want to be out there. Seeking the knowledge, not just sharing it on a space station."

I hold her gaze and I let the heat rise where our fingers touch. It's wonderful and painful at the same time. Being near her, touching her . . . it's life-giving.

She pulls her hand away and the cold of the metal counter under my fingers feels like death. My chest tightens.

"What model is that ship and how many protein snacks are you needing to move?" She steps around the counter and walks with long steps to a dual-capacity research pod at the far end of the Sanctum.

I stare after her, confused by her words and distracted by her ass in the tight black skirt of her Sanctum uniform.

"You implied you had a tight timeline." She stands in front of the pod entrance and tilts her head at me.

I grab my techpad and run a hand through my hair. That's a tight space for two people. I slide along the bench seat to the not-so-far end and Kiandra perches on the edge with barely enough space for the door to click closed beside her.

Maybe I haven't failed after all.

Kiandra's fingers fly across the research pod's holoscreen, typing on the keyboard and dragging and dropping files and text from one place to another. She's got a digikey in one slot and some other cable plugged in on the other side of the holoscreen.

She's finding information and doing calculations that boggle my mind. I didn't even really know where to start on this. But she immediately pulled up a maintenance manual for the *Ionia* and found not only its cargo capacity—in both space and weight limit, which I already had—but also every single measurement of every hold. And then she found a file somewhere that specified all the details about how Jung-Shi's protein bars are packaged in all the measurement units you could ever want.

"I'm not a mathematician, Dolen, and this is all a little tricky. But . . ." She blinks and taps quickly a few more times, then says, "Using search terms related to your problem, and your love of twentieth century Terra, maybe this will help you understand."

The holoscreen fills with brightly coloured shapes. They're combinations of squares in different configurations; each configuration is a set of purple, red, blue, green, or yellow. Upbeat music plays and the pieces fall slowly, a few pixels at a time, from the top of the black screen to the bottom where they stack on top of each other.

I watch, confused, and utterly fascinated as the combinations of four squares slowly drop. And then with quick taps of her fingers, Kiandra makes them shift sideways and rotate. She manipulates them so they fall into place, fitting perfectly together. And with a flash, a row of blocks disappears.

"It's a game, Dolen. What they called a 'computer game.'" Kiandra quirks an eyebrow at my expression. Is she making fun of me? "The little blocks are called tetrominoes and you need to make them all fit together in the space allotted."

"I'm on a deadline, Ki. Why are you looking up old games?"

Kiandra waves a hand at the game still playing on the holoscreen, the stack of coloured blocks now nearly to the top of the black rectangle. "This is *Tetris*. It demonstrates a two-dimensional version of what you need to solve: the bin-packing problem." The words GAME OVER flash in white across the fully stacked rainbow of blocks.

"Ki—" The buzz of my comm is shrill. I grab my techpad and glance at the screen. I feel all the blood leave my face. There's only one reason why Jung-Shi would be contacting me before our deadline.

I quickly tap the notification to see the entire message.

Jung-Shi: Got another interested transporter. They got a bigger ship. But bigger ship means higher fuel costs and shared shipments. You get me proof you can fit it all in that little orange cutter and our deal's still on. They're shifting out in two days. You've got one.

My breath catches. My deadline was already tight. Now it's even tighter, like a pair of wet jeans. Uncomfortable and restricting. Still functional . . . for a short time. A very short time. Feck.

"Something's wrong." Kiandra's voice breaks into my panicking thoughts. I lift my gaze to hers and see actual, real concern there.

"Just a little hiccup, doll. Deadline's been shortened." I use my cowboy voice to try to hide the panic, shove it back down.

She narrows her eyes, assesses me.

I swallow and try to shove a different feeling down. I like her eyes on me too much. "Time to stop playing games. You got any real solutions for me?"

A while later, I'm exhausted from trying to wrap my mind around the slew of articles and academic texts Kiandra found about the whole bin packing problem thing and how theorists analyzed various methods of developing the concept for two-dimensional problems and then used it for actual factual three-dimensional mathematical optimization, specifically for packing various sizes and shapes of objects into standard-sized containers. Most of the stuff is really high level, but even the textbook that Kiandra says is from a high school curriculum—for kids!—is confusing to me.

"So, these are the measurements of your hold," Kiandra says in an astoundingly patient voice, pointing at numbers on her own techpad, "and if the small protein bars are packed into these cases with these measurements and the large protein bars in these and those are loaded onto these pallets with these measurements," she taps another set of numbers. "You'll be able to fit one-point-five times as much as Jung-Shi wants in each shipment. And even better, both container types are reusable, saving him money with every shipment."

My mind is spinning; my stomach is roiling. She's done it. She's figured it out, written it all out, and made it so clear. The *Tetris* thing makes sense now. She was priming me for the more complicated information. And instead of making me tie it all together and do all the math, she's done that too. She's making my pitch to Jung-Shi possible.

And she's done it in only a matter of hours.

"This is . . ." I can't even find the words. I've been trying to figure out how to get my own ship for years. I've been searching for ways to be bigger, tougher, more impressive. And I've accomplished nothing.

"You broke my heart when you left." The non-sequitur hits me like a punch. I rear back and my head knocks into the wall where it curves into the dome above us. My chest heaves with a deep, frantic breath. "I wanted the world you promised me: Adventure; something beyond this little hold on this never-changing hunk of metal." She waves her hands, palms up. "And then you left without me."

"I . . . I did." I can't even defend myself. I can't be anything but honest here because that's exactly what I did. I was a pompous youngling wanting to make a name for myself. That's probably why I fell in love with those novels. They were exactly what I thought I wanted.

She gives me a sad smile. "You did."

"So why are you helping me today? Making this easy for me?"

Her expression softens, just a bit, but her eyes stay sad. "Because even though you left then, you kept coming back, asking to learn. Even just a little bit." She holds eye contact and my body screams at me to lean forward, to close the inches between us and see if her lips still taste the same. I press my back against the wall behind me. "My job is to know what information people need and when they need it. And to give them the time they need to understand it."

The research pod door clicks open, and she steps out. Before I can follow her, I hear the whoosh of a comm sending and the ding of my own device alerting me to a new message.

"Good luck," she whispers and leaves.

I grab my techpad from the bench beside me, sweating that it's more bad news. She's sent me the whole file; all the info I need to get the *Ionia* and that contract.

I inhale that fresh scent of recycled oxygen and relax into my high-backed chair. With a slow exhale, I examine the cockpit around me. Even inside, the *Ionia* is orange. She's retro in the best way. She's on the smaller side, but sturdy and compatible with any upgrade I could want. And she's got a full hold: I've got Jung-Shi's shipment and a contract for a three-crate shipment of specialty tequila.

As soon as the biometrics were rekeyed to me, I sent a photo to Kiandra with my shift out schedule. She didn't respond.

I check all my inputs about the route—I've got two drop-offs of protein bars before the tequila pickup. My launch dock is 7B and scheduled for twelve minutes from now.

My spatial awareness sensors beep, a flare of red flashes from my dash signifying that something is blocking the *Ionia's* nose. I look through the canopy and my stomach leaps. She's dressed in tight jeans and a dark green leather jacket with a Knowledge Seeker badge sewn onto the left shoulder.

I tap the external comm and with a grin say, "Time to shift out." Together.

THROUGH TIME AND CALAMITY
Nico Martinez Nocito

There were three possible paths when facing the application to Aibrani, the cosmos' premier academy for chronicling not what is, but what used to be.

The most popular path, and the easiest, was to not even try.

Marin frowned down at their stack of paper, its deckled edges rough against the side of their hand. The sheets were thick and strong, left to dry for three full days for maximum durability. Still, they doubted it could resist every volatile condition the universe could throw at it.

They took a deep breath, then lit a candle. The flame sputtered to life upon the damp wick, and Marin cupped one hand around it, shielding it from the breeze snaking through the broken siding.

Then they tore a corner off one sheet and held it in the centre of the flame.

At first, the paper didn't react. The words they'd scrawled across the scrap still stood out stark against the grey background: *this is a test*. Then the letter *e* blackened and collapsed. The edges of the paper started to fray. Black ash crawled up from the borders to absorb the entire sheet. Flames neared Marin's fingertips, and they released it abruptly. The scrap landed, smouldering, on the sheet rock that served as their desk.

The writing had been rendered utterly illegible.

Marin exhaled slowly and crossed their eighty-first and final idea off their mental list.

There were two possible paths for those who decided to pursue admission to Aibrani. The most popular was the submission of an essay, proving through simple wordsmithery that you deserved to take your place among the most venerated guardians of cosmic knowledge.

Marin couldn't shake the memory of the moment they'd received the notification letter. The holographic notification had materialized in the corner of their glasses, and they'd fully taken them off and wiped them on the hem of their shirt, as if the triangular logo was just a dust triggered blur. When the message had refused to disappear, they'd gone to their old, half-rusted computer and opened the missive.

Marin Ategas, we regret to inform you . . .

That was all they'd managed to read before the words had blurred for real this time, and their face had gone wet with tears.

The rejection letter concluded the same way as every other Aibrani rejection that Marin had seen on the countless forums and blogs they'd scanned while searching for advice on how to get accepted.

If you would still like to pursue admission to Aibrani, please respond within fifty-two days to the following challenge: Determine what will preserve knowledge through time and calamity.

For those who completed the essay prompt, there was an approximately three percent chance of selection, according to officially reported statistics.

In the seven hundred years since Aibrani's founding, no one from Mars had solved the alternate challenge.

Marin let their head fall to rest on the cold stone desk. Years of dedication, and nothing. No other school for librarians would even consider an orphan living on the outskirts of the Martian capital, their credentials limited solely to their own ingenuity. Particularly not when that same ingenuity had failed them on the application.

Clearly, Marin couldn't defeat whatever the universe threw at them. But then, what could? Maybe the challenge was just another lie, elongating rejected dreams that would never come true.

And yet . . . what if that was the answer?

After all, what *did* last forever? Not stars, not paper. Not even Aibrani, despite its stellar reputation. And yet Marin's belief, their drive, had endured even after their rejection. Through time, and through calamity.

A small *beep* caught their attention. They glanced up. An alert had appeared on their computer, set fifty-two days ago:

Challenge closes in ten minutes.

They clicked open Aibrani's portal. Their hands were shaking so much that they struggled to delete the lengthy essay they'd written on hypothetical substances and replace it with five brief characters.

Marin hit submit.

The letters shone reflected back in their glasses, almost mocking them for their naïveté in believing the answer could be so very simple.

Hope.

After all, what did it take, truly, to be a librarian for the cosmos? Understanding. Belief. Commonality. An understanding of what brought everyone together.

A triangle materialized in the corner of their glasses.

Marin blinked. They rubbed at their glasses again, as if this time, it would get rid of what had to be a mirage.

Marin Ategas, we are pleased to inform you that you have been accepted into Aibrani as our newest librarian-in-training.

FIFTH BOOK FROM THE SUN

R. Overwater

I figured recruitment would be difficult this far into the desert. Manned outposts were few and far between. Deployment numbers would be under quota. It made sense, then, that the patrol stopping us had only three men, no sergeant in command. The highest-ranking guy, a corporal, stood by the wing of a tan-camouflaged air-trans, interrogating Jeanette. Behind the air-trans, a terrified family, who'd mistakenly agreed to split the rental cost of a mobile land-plat, huddled on the edge of its cargo bed.

We were two days out from New Reno, the Great Basin Suborbital Elevator still two more away. I was surprised we hadn't been stopped earlier.

Jeanette lowered her hands from above her head. Whatever story she told must have worked. The corporal turned and strode through the sagebrush toward us. The sun threw up a shimmering vapor-mirage behind him and the blue sky absorbed it with dead silence. Energy-proof armour is miserably hot, unwearable when it's forty-degrees Celsius, and he sweated profusely.

"Don't look at her," he commanded the two men beside me. "She might be one of them." He pointed his pistol in my direction. "What's the story with this guy?" His question gave everyone a perfect excuse to stare unapologetically at my scuffed, hairless metal skull. I was careful not to meet their eyes.

"Says he's hitching a ride to the camp," the PFC closest to me said. Likely, he was the pilot. His hands were uncalloused and he wasn't sunburnt. Tattoos covered his arms. The other two still bore patches of bare skin, indicating they had less free time and money than he did. "Another old-timer, should have taken the relocation chit when he had the chance."

"Oh?" said the corporal. He pulled a scanner from his belt. "C'mon. Let's see it." I held my palm up and he scanned the mylar sheet where creased skin used to be. When he touched the line where the scars on my forehead gave way to steel, I kept my cool, willing myself not to react.

"I heard about these. Field hospitals don't worry about a guy's good looks, do they?" The corporal's scanner beeped, and he glanced down. "Huh." He looked at his men. "He didn't take a relocation chit because he never earned one. Dishonourable discharge." The PFC beside the pilot put one hand on his pistol. The corporal studied his scanner again. "But," he continued, "that was after a *fifteen-year* rotation in the Djibouti Republic."

"Jeezus Gawd," said the pilot. "You might have been lucky. My uncle told me anyone who didn't get mustered out after Djibouti finished their career in dead-end postings like this." The pilot gestured towards the miles of unbroken, ankle-high scrub between us and the mountains. All three men laughed. The corporal holstered his pistol.

"I heard that a guy could line up for unsecured elevator spots," I said.

"Yeah, but competition is stiff," said the corporal. "Every time Surveillance One passes over, the camp is a little bigger. And Upward Dynamics is running the intake process. They're corrupt as hell."

I smiled and rubbed my thumb and forefinger together. "Good. Corrupt staff are easier." I angled my chin toward Jeanette. "What's *her* story?"

He leaned in. "HQ says the new elevator is a prime Librarian target. I'm thinking maybe we found one."

The pilot spat in the dirt. "God damned brain-polluters. They all should have been shot the day the Information Act came in."

"Damn straight." The corporal looked over at the family gathered on the mobile land-plat. "Them over there? They don't know shit. Just your basic migrants, gambling on a chance that ain't never gonna come."

"I was C-1 on our suppression team," I said. "If that woman *is* a Librarian, don't let on that you know. Maybe she won't resist at first."

"You don't have to tell me," the corporal said. "One time, we arrested this old—" His head exploded in a cloud of red mist. My ears rang from the thunder-snap as hot air rushed away from an energy discharge. Two more snaps. By the time I wiped the contents of the corporal's skull from my eyes, the other men were dead at my feet.

I could barely see the pistol in Jeanette's hand; it was so small. She tucked it back into her sleeve and glared at me. "Well? Are you just going to stand there?"

I had to admit, I hadn't really earned my pay so far. I picked up the dead corporal's pistol. Our migrant family cowered behind one of the transport's hover-struts. Aiming the pistol, I shouted, "You over there! Do you want to live?"

That night, while Jeanette busied herself securing our camp— instead of trusting a 30-year stealth commando to do it—I thought about the poor bastards lying dead beside their burning air-trans. They'd been told the camp was a hotbed of Librarian activity. Elevator camps were a hotbed of *everything* activity. Robbers, smugglers, drug peddlers, fake insurance salespeople, converters exchanging company scrip at five percent. Every crooked opportunist imaginable. Librarians, maybe not as often. But at this camp, they'd be there.

This new elevator was the first one connected to our continent. Before, if you needed to get onto one, you went down to the equator because of "geostationary orbit," and other stuff I didn't understand.

I looked it up on InfoOfficial. The North American United Republic led all things technological. I was curious what they'd learned by studying spider silk and would have read more. But that was the beauty of InfoOfficial. It didn't cram your head full of useless information a practical man didn't need.

What I *did* understand was that Librarians no longer had to smuggle illegal information off the continent before they could sneak it onto a space elevator. If I was them, I thought, this would be a game-changer.

I waited until after we'd sealed our cover, so our body heat wouldn't be detected by drone infra-ware. Then I pushed for more info. She was cautious but shared more than I expected.

"Now that you're complicit in an executable crime, I should come clean with you." She removed her boot and sock, showing me the sole of her foot. On it was a simple black tattoo of a stern lady with ancient eyeglasses, tilting her head and holding one finger to her lips to make the "shhh" sign. "I'm a senior commander in the Free Thought and Knowledge Archive Defense Group. You probably suspected that."

"A Librarian! I did not know that," I lied. "But you paid for armed escort, and you will pay me, right?" She nodded. This was where I needed to be convincing. "What I don't understand is how you're gonna meet the other half of your bargain and get me up that elevator and onto a transport ship."

"I'll tell you what you need to know when you need to know it."

"You aren't so different from the military," I joked.

"We're a *lot* different. You don't have what it takes to be a Librarian." She reached into the satchel that hung from her shoulder every minute of the day. Producing a bundle of old rags, she set it on the thermo-block plastic floor between us and unravelled it. It was old and obsolete, and I was genuinely surprised.

"A military-grade data core!" I said. It was about the size of a baby. Deep scratches marked every inch of the white, non-conductive coating. The connection ports showed years of atmospheric corrosion. It could only have come from something old and gigantic, like a naval destroyer or one of the first Mars landing ships. Not something that would go missing without being noticed. "How did you get your hands on *that*?"

She wrapped it up and stuffed it back into her satchel. "That," she said, "you will never learn." She pointed at me. "What matters is that you'll never get off this planet if it doesn't reach its destination."

I'm not stupid. It was easy to guess the data core's destination. Another thing guaranteeing Librarian activity at the Elevator was the grand experiment currently floating in Jupiter's atmosphere. The future of human knowledge-storage, broadcasting to all outposts and the Kuiper asteroid mines where hardscrabble communities thirsted for information and education. This early in the project, security would be poorly coordinated. Now was the time to infiltrate.

"Where exactly *is* the destination?" I pressed.

She lay down and turned her back to me. "We have a few days of hard walking ahead. Get some sleep."

Jeanette knew that, for me, true sleep was an impossibility. And had been ever since the day I was airlifted out of a combat zone with a temporary skull crammed with nano-junk. Every night, a parade of dead bodies awaited me when I closed my eyes, their images jumbled among bursts of white light and the constant, electric squeal of feedback. The brain, I was told, has a thing called an amygdala. Mine, they said, was finished. And the chip attached to it had been tweaked at free clinics so often, it could no longer be operated upon. Every night, the light got brighter, the din louder, the corpses more vivid. I needed to get into a real hospital, the kind they had on planetary transport ships. And soon.

It was better to hike at night. But daytime temperatures in the Great Basin were hotter than body temperature, making it hard for infra-ware to distinguish between us and other objects. The sun beat down through the empty sky. I sweated gallons. Fortunately, we had more than enough water. That was Jeanette's doing.

She'd pushed me aside when I gave the family on our transport two days' water and food. Levelling her pistol at them, she scooped most of it back, leaving only a half-day's worth. She threw the rest onto the land-plat's porta-skid with our stolen loot, flicked the skid into hover mode, and began pulling it back in the direction we came. The mother was crying when we left.

I didn't speak up until they were out of sight and smoke from the burning air-trans was just a thin whisp. "Jeezus," I said. "We could have left them a little better off than that."

Jeanette scowled. "We're a couple of ruthless thieves. We took their possessions and stripped that air-trans because we're robbers. That's who everyone will be looking for. Real robbers."

The mountains were still distant in the shimmering haze. As I walked behind Jeanette and dragged the porta-skid towards them, a picture began to form. Yesterday, even though I was

clearly in her field of fire, she didn't hesitate to shoot in my
direction, killing three patrol officers with rapid-fire accuracy.
And she knew an awful lot for someone from a profession whose
chief job was sorting and hiding books.

"Most of the robbers working the Basin Elevator are in the
Nevada Gang," she said as she rolled up our thermo-cover before
we embarked.

"Stupid sounding name," I said, lashing the last of our
overnight gear to the skid.

Her look was half pity, half contempt. "Before the NAUR, long
before this was militia territory, before First Government even,
this place was called Nevada." She threw the thermo-cover at me.
I caught it. "Anyways, the gang works in-to-out, to increase their
haul. They catch people in the more concentrated ring
approaching the camp when they're exhausted. Then they keep
moving out. By the time the victims reach camp and complain,
the thieves are far away and getting farther, robbing as they go.
They sell their loot, sneak back into the camp disguised as
elevator-hopefuls, and start working their way out again."

"So that's why we wasted a day heading in the wrong
direction."

"And why we didn't hide our tracks. We'll be on rockier
ground soon and what little trace we leave after that hopefully
won't get noticed." Now she was being condescending. Nevada,
who'd ever heard of that? But I *did* know advanced stealth and
tracker avoidance.

The rest of the day, she didn't speak. Only our scuffling boots
broke the silence. My mouth was dust-dry, and my shoulder
ached from turns at towing the skid. If the combined toil of
carrying a 30-kilogram memory core and pulling the skid took
anything out of Jeanette, it didn't show in the way she trudged
ahead. She marched with the determined air of a combat vet.

"You were a lot nicer to me when you worked at the free
veteran's clinic," I said as we spread out the thermo-cover for the
night's rest.

"That job calls for nice people," she said. "This one, mean
people."

"So, that's why you picked me."

She snorted. "I saw all your records. You're not mean.
Ignorant. But not mean." She walked over to the skid and broke

out two meal kits. "They put you into military school at age six. I shudder to think how many innocent people you've killed since then. But they made you into what you are and that's not your fault." She pointed at my skull and the filter where my eye used to be.

"Those chips in your head were supposed to be field dressing. You've spent the rest of your life hoping some free clinic will keep them working so you don't crap your pants when you smell lemons or develop thirteen personalities or whatever is going to happen when they eventually break down."

"Now *you're* being mean." I opened the shelter, and we crawled inside. "One good thing about low-tech fixes, I can get any doctor, anywhere, to service them."

She brightened. "Yes. That proved to be a good thing." She handed me a meal kit. "I know why you received a dishonourable discharge."

"A real veteran outreach volunteer wouldn't know that."

"Who cares? It wasn't fair."

I pulled the tab on the meal kit's heat pack. "Thirty years of service. The whole time you're expected to make calls on the fly. They said it was the woman who was ferrying intelligence off base. But it wasn't. It was her husband."

The meal kit pipped, and I handed it to her. I motioned for her to give me the cold one. "When I brought him in, they took him away and no one said anything. So, I put her on an air-trans. The next day I was charged."

"Good way to cover up their mistake." Jeanette peeled the meal kit's lid off and reached in with three fingers. "She still remembers you."

I didn't ask her how. But I could see how carefully I'd been sized up. "Were you ever an actual veteran counsellor?"

She chewed and swallowed. "I really was."

"You're a lot of things," I said.

"I am a lot of things." She scooped the last bit of protein out of the pack and licked her fingers. "The most important thing I've ever been is custodian of this. It was my mother's job before me." She tapped the satchel beside her. "When I met you, I knew you could help me get this thing up that elevator and onto a ship."

I nodded and chewed. That core and I were going up. With or without Jeanette.

Things were still going according to plan in the late afternoon. Jeanette was ahead of me again and we were making good time. On her orders, I'd buried the skid and our stolen loot. "They're looking for robbers with a bunch of clearly identifiable items," she said. "Now we're just migrants who own nothing but what's on our backs."

My entire career had been point-and-kill. It was increasingly obvious that my deception skills were below hers.

Her back stiffened and then she was flat on her belly. "Get down!" I had my face in the sand before she'd finished uttering the words.

I'd missed seeing it. The bright sunlight hurt my good eye, so I'd kept it closed, relying on the optic filter that replaced my other eye. But it can't differentiate fine detail. Then I saw it.

The watery waver of hot desert air was such a constant out here, it was a more prominent backdrop than the mountains. But unlike the telltale glimmer of a multi-cam invisibility system, the wavy motion you see rises. This was horizontal. The scrub we could see through it was extra-distorted. Then it was gone.

"Did you see that?" Jeanette whispered.

"I did," I whispered back. Who, I wondered, has access to that kind of tech out here? Not robbers. I wormed my way closer to her, stopping by her feet. "If it was NAUR, thinking that was *us* at the air-trans, they'd have shot us dead already."

Jeanette shook her head, no. Then she stopped. "Yeah. They probably would."

"Stay still," I whispered. "I got something." Lying as flat as I could, I shrugged my pack off and reached into a side pocket.

Meat exploded from a hole in Jeanette's right boot with a loud crack. She shrieked. Her body jolted and I was afraid she'd sit up, exposing herself. Instead, she rolled sideways, blood spilling from the hole in her boot. She stopped behind a patch of knee-high sagebrush.

If you listen to the air surrounding an energy discharge, you can roughly gauge your distance. I hoped I was right. I only had one signal-buster and might need it if things went sideways at the camp. But nothing interferes with stealth-gear like the lumpy, silver ball in my palm and I couldn't use it if I was dead.

I sat upright, took my best guess at the shooter's position, pitched it, and ducked back down. I pulled my pistol from my belt.

Ahead, near a patch of scattered rocks, the air distorted and rippled with colour. The distortion faded and a man crouched behind a low thicket of greasewood. He wore the same uniform as the patrol officers we'd killed.

I sat up and busted off two quick shots, one deliberately at his shoulder, one into his lower abdomen. He fell over, screaming. Falling prone again, I dropped my pistol and detached my rifle from the pack. The man howled and shouted for help.

"Put him out of his misery." Jeanette's voice was fraught with pain and well above a whisper. I shook my head. *No.* I pointed at my eyes, pointed ahead and she took the cue. The man continued screaming.

It seemed like forever. Blood pooled around Jeanette's boot. If I didn't dress the wound soon, it would be beyond anything I could fix out here. Finally, she whispered, "There!" To the man's left, I saw a telltale ripple. To the right, another. I waited for the two to converge on the injured man's position, banking on their compassion for a wounded buddy.

I switched the rifle to auto. Rising to one knee, I sprayed a volley of shots just above the wounded man, starting at the left and working to the right. The air kaleidoscoped and another body appeared, slumped down on his face beside my first victim. I could have sworn there were two targets by the wounded man, but I concentrated on laying down a wide field of fire, low at first, and elevated my aim in careful increments to catch anyone still approaching in the distance. Sure enough, the sky undulated several metres back. A man emerged, clutching his chest. He collapsed and stopped moving.

Another dance of distorted hues coalesced beside my first target. Invisi-gear I hadn't damaged as badly as its owner, belatedly failing. A woman lay there, motionless, clutching the hand of my first victim. That guy was silent now, riddled by my second flurry of shots. The lifeless quiet of the desert returned.

"Are you okay?" I kept my voice low. Jeanette's face was the ashen complexion of a cinder block. She nodded. I began crawling through the sand toward her, but she thrust out her palm. *Wait.* "Make sure you got all of them," she said.

"This black-market medi-kit is so old it dates back to First Government," I joked. "No pain inhibitor unit, sorry. You'll have to settle for good old micunambalone." I pulled the cover off a single-use ampule. It bristled with rows of tiny needles, resembling an old-fashioned hairbrush. "Lie still," I said.

Jeanette shifted her gaze from the ceiling of our plastic shelter and locked eyes with me. "*No*. No drugs. I need to stay sharp."

"Okay." I slapped it down hard on her bare ankle. She gasped and glared. "Your head will be clear in the morning," I said.

"It's only mid-afternoon. What if they find us before then?"

"I buried the bodies already." I pulled every hemo- and platelet-replacement pack out of the kit and slapped them one-by-one onto her leg. "And this shelter will kill our heat signature. We're safe."

The drugs kicked in quickly, and within an hour she was eating. Micunambalone was powerful stuff. Her pupils were wide, and I could see the mild euphoria.

She chewed silently at first, just staring at me. "So, what's your game plan when you get all the way out there?" she said at last. "Live your final days as a broken-down asteroid miner?"

"Naw," I said. "Guys like me get pilot and patrol jobs. Military experience commands a good salary. And no one out there gives a crap about your service record."

"Working for one of the big mining corporations."

"Yeah. Why not?"

She thumbed the top off a water flask. "Do you know what indentured servitude is?"

For her, this was downright chatty. The drugs must really be working. "I sure as hell know what servitude means," I said. "'Indentured' means you can't quit, right?"

"Something like that." She stared at me again for a long time. I pretended it wasn't unsettling. For a moment she looked . . . I wasn't sure. Disappointed, maybe. "Have you ever heard of a thing called the Triangle Shirtwaist Factory Fire?" I shook my head. "The Pullman Strike? The Ford Hunger March?" Again, I shook my head.

She sighed. "What about Ludlow, Colorado? McGill, Nevada? Matewan, West Virginia?"

Annoyed, I grabbed my handi-source and pulled up

InfoOfficial. "Towns during the First Government. Doesn't say where."

"Does InfoOfficial say anything about a book called *The Jungle*? Upton Sinclair? Harriet Jacobs? Friedrich Engels?"

I could tell she already knew, but I looked anyways. Nothing. In the most robust database ever created. "How do I know you're not making all this up?"

"There's no way you could." She squirmed onto her side and faced away.

A different aura hung over her now, something I struggled to associate with the woman who'd helped me navigate the free clinic system and stay alive. *Defeat.* Even as she healed and lived to fight another day.

I don't know why but, this time, I didn't feel like enduring her rigid silence. I tried a different tack. "What about you? After this. Smuggle another one of those data-cores somewhere?"

She didn't look back at me. "No. This is my last mission."

"Oh. Really?"

"You know Librarians weren't always an armed resistance, right?"

"People raised in military school study history too, you know. It wasn't until the Information Act that your disruption became violent."

"It wasn't disruption. It used to be an everyday job where people got up and went to work, same as everyone else. Most of them actually loathed conflict. Libraries were repositories of all information, bursting with vast quantities of great stories, presenting an unlimited variety of human perspectives."

"That sounds like official Librarian indoctrination script."

I heard her chuckle. "It is. You know what natural selection is, right?"

I did my best to sound insulted. "Darwin. Survival of the fittest."

"More or less. A wide, varied gene pool births a range of individuals, increasing the chances that some will possess a unique combination of traits that best position the species for survival. The less mutation and variety, the less likely someone has the right combination of attributes to suit the unforeseen challenges of nature."

"You told me, the other night, I was ignorant. Not stupid."

"You're not stupid. I'm sorry." She sounded sorry. "Anyway, ideas and stories are like that too. The more ideas and historical facts we must reflect upon, the more choices we have for determining how to thrive. And InfoOfficial, I assure you, does *not* offer all the choices."

"Did you know they routinely identify Librarian sympathizers by their philosophical mumbo-jumbo?"

She sighed again. "You asked about my plans. I want to quit sleeping with a pistol. I want to get the information we're protecting off this planet so it can't be wiped from human memory. I want to live long enough to quit worrying about prison. Or worse."

Flickers of decomposing families half-buried in beach sand. Brain-splitting bursts of light. Squalls of white noise. The thunder of rail guns. Snippets of the national anthem rising over a military funeral. Electric shocks shooting down my neck from somewhere above my jaw. Random moments of disorienting, terrifying blackness, adrift in a void where I could think—but hear, smell, taste, feel, and see nothing.

That's what constituted "sleep" that night. A few more days like this and I wouldn't have what it takes to walk out of the desert alive. *The Nevada Desert*, a voice in my head said. It started getting like this about a month after I began treatment at the free clinic. When I complained, they said it was getting worse only because I hadn't already died from catastrophic chip failure.

Luckily, it only took two more days to reach the camp. If it was a hard slog for me, it was doubly so for Jeanette. Her skin was the colour of the ground we trekked across. Her limp grew progressively worse. It was a testament to the quality of the medi-kit that she could walk at all. She spoke less than ever. "A little to the right and that tattoo would be gone," I said, trying to engage.

"That would have been fine by me."

Not by me. They needed proof that it was her when we arrived.

Aside from a small exchange as I prepared her food that night, she said nothing again until the last afternoon. I nervously scanned the horizon for trouble. I'd wrapped a rag around my head to prevent its metallic glint from catching the eye of any robbers working the camp. For the first time, I led our little party, and I looked back to see how she was doing. Her gaze was infinitely distant, looking beyond anything in the here and now. A bemused smile crossed her face.

"What?" I asked.

"I was just thinking, if my plan works, future generations might think of Jupiter more as a giant book than a planet. Other planets too someday, maybe."

"Fifth book from the sun," I said.

"You make weak jokes."

"You barely know what a joke is," I countered.

"There was a song a couple hundred years ago with a similar title."

"By someone in your illegal library."

"Only about half his stuff. Some of it's still accessible. He was very creative. Despite being ex-military."

I think this was the one time we both smiled simultaneously. I handed her my last water container and made her drink half. She gulped it down and squared her shoulders. I don't recall us saying another word to each other.

About three hours from the camp, we passed the land-plat we'd abandoned. It lay on its side like a scavenged animal carcass, stripped to its chassis. The cab windows were smashed out, fringed by black scorch marks. Patches of warped steel marked the doors where energy discharges struck at close range. I never learned what happened to the family we'd left it with.

Jeanette glanced at me; guilt written across her face. I could imagine what she felt. In the last hour, a similar feeling had anchored itself deep in my gut. Not exactly guilt. *Shame.*

The dry, scentless, desert air receded as we stumbled into camp. Whiffs of smoke and the damp reek of unbathed humanity invaded my nostrils. The quiet of the last few days was obliterated by the din of shouting hawkers, people pleading, soldiers bellowing, corporate chaperones blowing whistles. Beneath it all, the steady hum of the elevator, ferrying away the lucky few.

Jeanette nodded toward a woman in an Upward Dynamics jacket, indicating that I should offer her the bribe concealed in my pocket. Instead, I raised my arm and summoned a soldier.

He shouldered his way through the crowd, and I showed him my palm and the screen on my handi-source. He looked at Jeanette, tapped the jaw shield of his helmet and spoke tersely into its mic. In less than a minute, a cohort of guards surrounded us, led by the base commander himself. He took my handi-source from the guard, read it, and looked back at me. His eyes lingered over my skull. "Wow," he said. "You've been through the shit, old-timer."

I grinned. I was one of their own again and it felt good. "Sir," I said. "You don't wanna know."

He grinned back. "Do you have it?"

"Right there, under her arm."

He drew his sidearm. The guards levelled their rifles at Jeanette. Her eyes boiled with contempt. The commander snatched her satchel and pushed her toward the closest guards. "Detain her." He kneeled, carefully removing the prize from its wrappings. "I'll be damned," he said. "When they briefed me, I could hardly believe it."

He slid the data core back into the satchel, stood, and slapped me on the shoulder. "We don't get much recognition out here, old buddy. We're all going to come out of this looking good."

He pointed at two guards. "Restrain her and put her in her own cell." He waved at the rest of the unit. "Lock this up in the armoury and guard it with your lives. I cannot overstate this thing's value. I will personally shoot any person who takes their eyes off it."

The manacles they clasped around Jeanette's wrists were newer, more tech than the ones I wore at my court martial. Two soldiers, each holding an arm, led her into the thick of the crowd. She disappeared without looking back at me. I wish she had.

It was reassuring that they led me straight to the elevator, bypassing the lineups and ushering me underneath the inner guard tower. I didn't look down during the ride up. The platform commander was waiting for me when I disembarked. Five soldiers stood behind her, rifles at the ready.

She saluted as I stepped out of the capsule. "Welcome to Suborbital Platform NA One. I am Major Violette Tinibu."

I saluted back and set down my dusty pack, struggling to appear balanced in the platform's microgravity. My gear looked extra-meagre and ratty in the sterile, white landing bay.

The major stepped forward and thrust out a tattoo-covered hand. I shook it. "Let me be the first to congratulate you on a significant win."

"Thank you," I said. But my eyes were on all the rifles pointed my way. She noticed. "I'm sorry. You must realize we're obligated to follow stringent security protocols up here."

I didn't doubt it. And with the pressure smothering me the last few days now dissipating, all I could really think about was how spent I was. Suddenly, I yearned to sit in a proper chair. "Understood," I said. "Where do we go from here?"

"Well, please forgive us but we're bound to follow a few more protocols before we can get you settled. Number one is a full medical examination and brief quarantine."

I'd seen more than one TrueSpeak broadcast covering outpost outbreaks. "Of course," I said.

The guards never took their rifles off me all the way to the medical bay. I walked ahead of them, behind the major. Everyone's demeanour was all business. The major squeezed my shoulder as we entered the bay. "Once we're sure you're stable, we'll get you scheduled for upgrades and cosmetics by the Jupiter medical team."

"Jupiter? I have a job waiting at the Kuiper belt. Right?"

"The Jupiter team has the best facility," said the major. "The NAUR liaison who recruited you at the clinic advised us that your hardware condition was more precarious than you knew."

I started to speak but stopped. I was a civilian at that point, technically, but when had the brass ever worried about risking a soldier's death in the name of an objective? Anything that might have dissuaded me from taking their offer, they would never have told me. And the gamble had worked out for everyone. Everyone except Jeanette and the Librarians.

"Lie here," said a man in a matte white bodysuit. He pointed to a grey, contoured bed beneath an intimidating chandelier of steel appendages and dangling flex-tubes. A similarly clad woman slapped a magnetic clamp on my skull as soon as I was prone. She ran a long cable from it to a console on the other side of the room. An unpleasant tingle cascaded through my body. "I can't move my arms or legs," I said.

The woman kept her eyes on the console. "For your safety."

The major drew her sidearm. "Guard detail, clear the room," she ordered. The guards lowered their weapons and filed out of the bay. The hatch swung shut and the major punched a code into the pad on its doorframe. Steel bolts clanked into place. "We're clear," she said. "Open him up."

The man in the bodysuit reached above me and pulled down a cable with a long, thick needle at its end. From the corner of my good eye, I saw him push it into me, somewhere behind my upper jaw. I felt nothing. He walked to a console beside the woman's and addressed the major. "Give us a minute."

I tried to speak but my face was slack and unresponsive. My ears sizzled with the white noise that had dominated my nights, and I could barely make out their voices.

"What have we got?" asked the major.

"Just a second," said the man.

"Got something," said the woman.

The major sounded pleased. "Give it to me."

"Phillips County Library," she said. "There's more."

"Keep it coming."

"Wyoming State Library."

"Safe at last," said the major.

"Brumberg Public. Athens-Clarke County." The technician's voice grew more excited. "San Diego Central . . . jackpot!"

The major pressed her palms together.

"Library of Congress, one week after the Act!"

"Before the purge!" said the major.

"Lots more. Small towns mostly."

The man adjusted something on his console. "About thirty minutes to copy it all."

"He's not going anywhere," said the major. "I've got a couple of questions still. And I'll take responsibility for the last bit. You don't have to be here for it."

"Oh, thank you," said the woman.

"Bless you, Major," said the man.

The major punched a code into the hatch frame and swung the door open. The technicians exited. The man glanced back, his expression somewhere between distressed and wistful.

A guard leaned in before the hatch could close. "Major, there's been a development down at the base. The captain wants you to check in." The hatch slammed shut and I heard the bolts clank again.

I fought to pull some semblance of thought from the buzz inside my skull. Jeanette had been wrong: I *was* stupid.

No wonder that first patrol had no commanding officer. He or she knew they'd find a Librarian and knew better than to be around when she resisted. They knew I'd have to back her up until I got her to the camp. And all the command between that officer and Major Violette Tinibu, every layer above her, were even bigger dupes than me. The guards watching that data core could lie down and take a nap.

I closed my eyes and saw Jeanette's cold expression as she snatched our supplies back from the crying mother at the land-plat. I wasn't leaving this room alive. If I did, I'd be shown an airlock somewhere between here and Jupiter.

When I reopened my eyes, the major was studying her handi-source. She clipped it to her belt, walked over to me, and fiddled with the cable behind my ear. Sensation drifted across my upper torso. My legs remained dead. She drew closer, face to face. "What's she like?"

"Huh?" I said, my face and brain still shedding the numbness.

"Admiral Jeanette Myowicz. You had the honour of spending more time with her than all of us put together."

"She was a tougher, more disciplined soldier than this whole base combined."

"I can't argue that. No one wanted her to take this mission. She insisted because she picked you herself."

"What's the new development down at the base?" I asked.

"A fire in the detention centre. Six detainees escaped."

"Let me guess. You've only managed to recapture five," I said.

"Four, technically. There was a gang leader the guards were itching to shoot as soon as they had the chance."

"Did he lead something called the Nevada Gang?"

She looked impressed. "Yes! I hate to condone it, but I worked pretty hard to become a major in the NAUR Forces. Gotta stick with the program, maintain appearances."

"Let me guess what your program has in store for me."

The mirth drained from her eyes. "Everyone agrees you're getting screwed. But you can't grasp what's at stake here."

"The true story of McGill, Nevada," I said. "The legacy of Harriet Jacobs."

The major's expression warmed by a tenth of a degree. "You definitely spent time with the Admiral."

"I was promised I could be a patrol commander."

"I know."

"I could visit every outpost and asteroid mine in the system, get routine exams because of quarantine protocols, and no one would think twice." I wrestled against the weight of my dead legs and propped myself up on one elbow. Tilting my head, I put a finger to my lips and made the "shhh" sign.

The major stepped back against a bulkhead and studied me for several minutes. She exhaled. A few more minutes passed. "Maybe the admiral was right," she said.

My stomach growled and I lay there wondering if I'd disappear with a full belly at least. The major approached me again and clasped her hands, knuckles outward.

"Huh?" I said. Then I looked closer. The outlines of the major's hand tattoos merged to imply a new outline: A woman in glasses, finger to her lips.

"Do you know," asked the major, "that we could have pushed a button at any moment and you'd have dropped dead?"

"Then you still can. Anytime."

"We still might."

"You'll never have to." I wasn't lying.

"You'll get private quarters. This is the last time we'll ever speak."

That night, there was no feedback, no blitz of noise and light. When I awoke, the time displayed on the wall was a shocking ten hours later. I hadn't seen any dead bodies. There was only a fleeting recollection that, somewhere in the darkness, I'd seen Jeanette. And she was right.

I didn't have what it takes to be a Librarian. But maybe I have what it takes to be a library.

THE THRIVING GREEN

Kayla Whittle

They said if you had a question no one could answer, you had to go into the walls. The *Gateway*, Mara's home, bulged with walkways and public spaces and rumours. Even on a ship large enough to house thousands over several lifetimes, boredom threatened. The stars in the viewscreens rarely changed. The course never altered. Everything around Mara had been built and designed long before her time; it would land, end, and become something new long after her.

She liked that, knowing her place and purpose out in the depths of the universe. The unknown felt like someone turned off the life support systems in her living pod, leaving her cold and broken.

Mara's lungs tightened, heavy as twin socket wrenches, when her automated plant life systems failed for the third time. A few years back, when she'd first been assigned her own living pod after graduating her schooling modules, the greenery had been gifted to her. Research said having a living specimen to return to after a long shift optimized happiness and provided an easy, peaceful sense of responsibility to any *Gateway* resident. Her maintenance manager had sent her home after her first half-day shift with the greenery and a new soreness in her joints. All that was needed after a day's repair work was to ensure the automated light and watering systems operated at maximum efficiency.

The light had failed to turn on again after her latest sleeping cycle. Her greenery looked parched, so Mara reset the system. She pinged it with her handheld, but received no response from diagnostics. With the heel of her palm, she smacked the plant life setup, hard. Twice. Shouted at it, expected and received no results.

It was her third system to shut down and short out in as many weeks. If she brought it with her to the repair shop, she knew her manager would ping the gardening unit. They'd requisition her little plant life to keep it safe from her and her clearly incompatible living space.

Sitting on the edge of her cot, Mara stared up at the singular bulb filling her pod with simulated morning light. The grey walls and standard eggshell ceiling pressed in close around her. On her shelving unit, a few holophotos ran through timed displays in electric blues and greens. They were the only pops of colour, besides her greenery.

Mara loved the green. She loved how vividly emerald and spiky the tiny stalks were, how they swayed gently in the false breeze created by the air filtration system.

The gardening unit held some notoriety for its reluctance to allow any back into its graces after some reported or perceived slight to their plants. It could take years to beg and pay her way into purchasing her own greenery again. No artificial replacement could bring Mara the same satisfaction.

Her handheld, useless, buzzed against her palm. Any information inside suggested ways to fix her systems that she'd used and tried and failed at, several times over. Most information pages were covered in pop-ups severely recommending a trip to the repair shop. She poked at her screen, and when another webpage with the shop's pod number and ping code popped up, Mara closed her handheld entirely. She worried that ignoring the suggestion too many times would alert the system into ordering her a home visit.

The thought of her coworkers with their oily boots and judgmental sneers stomping around her pod before stomping out with her greenery made her clench her jaw tight. Aching teeth felt better than the bleak imagery in her head.

Mara looked again at her blank, grey walls. She'd never been within them before.

One last place for her to look for answers. One more shot at fixing her plant life system and rescuing her greenery without anyone else needing to know it'd been endangered.

It seemed frivolous to ignore protocol and the old warnings of her parents, all for the sake of a small piece of greenery. Venturing into the walls wasn't illegal; getting out was the problem.

Her modulemates had pressed ears and fingertips to chilled panels in main hallways, listening to the hum and thump of working machinery. They told each other the noise was the souls of the lost, fumbling their way toward forgotten exits after seeking answers from those who dwelt within the ship's innards.

Mara stood, hunching over her bright stalks in their little tray. They seemed stiffer, already. It wouldn't be long before it all browned. The thought sent her heart racing faster than any talk with her manager, any lecture on the greater good inspired by *Gateway*'s journey.

It was decided then.

She waited until most in her quadrant had settled for another sleep cycle. A short hall a shorter walk from her pod held the panel she wanted. An odd bump distorted the seam at one side, leaving enough space for her to squeeze in a few fingertips.

When Mara pressed her hand against the metal, too cold and too smooth, it reminded her of the projections of endless, unchanging stars that filled the halls of her home. Showing a journey distant and inevitable, nothing like her patch of greenery. Mara didn't know how much longer it could survive without any simulated light or auto-watering. All her knowledge of steel and wiring and basic mechanics fell short and useless, faced with a living problem.

Fingers straining, Mara pried open the panel and crawled within the wall.

Metal groaned and the panel snapped shut behind her. Mara drew her heels closer to her core, blinking in the sudden darkness. Coils pricked and pipes warmed her skin. Something caught and tugged at her shirt hem. She couldn't see her hand in front of her face, let alone the panel she'd squirmed through. The interior lay darker than her pod in night mode, bleaker than *Gateway* itself during emergency drills.

Freeing her handheld from her pocket, Mara tapped the screen to life. Light flared around her, valiantly fighting the dark.

She opened her shipmap and pinned her location, thinking of the future, retracing her steps back to her greenery.

Exhaling, cradled by the *Gateway*'s guts, Mara turned her handheld light outward. Multi-coloured wiring and dull piping illuminated in the dense, rarely touched depths.

Stories of what waited beyond the walls never provided much detail beyond saying to go in deep. Then deeper, deeper still, until someone waited with the answers you sought. Mara turned her heels toward the panelling and wriggled between twin coils of wire. They slithered across her skin. She imagined sparks of power escaping, improperly insulated, leaping to her, singeing her hair.

The wiring allowed her to pass into an empty space where she followed the path of a rattling pipe. Elbows tucked in close, sliding forward on her knees, she moved onward and inward. Whenever her light fixed on what might have been another wall, another way out, Mara turned away.

The space grew tighter, hot with the endless churn of working machinery. Sweat dripped, stinging Mara's eyes. Her hands ached as she felt her way forward over irregular ground and her arm shook, protesting, as she held her device out to light her way. When her muscles ached and temples throbbed, she thought of her greenery. She imagined soft little stalks beneath her hands instead of wiring in shades of yellow and blue and red. Pushing forward, Mara startled when something softer crumbled beneath her weight.

Contorting in the enclosed space, Mara picked up the . . . thing. Wrinkled, scrunched up until she unravelled it, smoothed it against a nearby pipe. It felt delicate and wrong against her skin. Writing filled the rectangle, irregular and untyped. Like the handwriting modules, brought out of the handheld somehow. Mara touched the words—fleeting, unimportant words, a transmission report from years back. Unable to bring herself to crumble the rectangle again, she left it pressed between coils in her wake.

More appeared. Some smoothed over by other, unseen hands. Some piecemeal, scattered among the hum and chatter of electronics. Scraps of words in her hands, Mara paused, listening. She heard nothing beyond the irregular thump and churn of machinery. No handheld pings, no trailing voices, no shipboard announcements. She wondered where she sat within the depths of *Gateway*.

Setting her scraps aside, Mara checked the shipmap. Her screen fizzed, flickering with irregular yellow and black spots. For one throat-drying moment, the handheld went dark, washing the circuitry and metal blank with the interior's void.

She tapped her screen again, heartbeat drowning out working machinery. Light returned. Her handheld steadied. Mara didn't dare to touch the shipmap icon again. She moved onward, and inward, and whenever she thought of the location she'd pinned, her broken panel exit, she pressed her tongue between her teeth and bit down, hard.

When the voices started, Mara mistook them for the clatter of technology until she recognized the far-off cadence of conversation. Then she saw the light and felt how the metal had softened beneath her hands and knees. Tumbling out of the coils and into brightness, Mara looked upward and saw a woman tangled within the wiring.

"Welcome," the woman said. "I'll be with you in just a moment."

It was difficult to determine if the woman was stuck, melded into the ship's interior, or if she knew the depths so intimately, she could lounge among wiring as if it held her as an extension of itself. Vivid, rubber-wrapped threads curled around her limbs and obscured part of her face.

A man sat by her feet. He wore the pressed, pristine uniform of a swap shop worker, someone who collected and traded in antiques. Mara rarely encountered any of them, as her family no longer held any heirlooms to barter. A mechanist like her wouldn't be able to afford old junk, anyway. Just a bit of greenery.

The woman disappeared among the pipes and machinery, too quickly for Mara to see if she walked or crawled or ended up swallowed whole by the interior. The man sat, silent and surrounded by piles of words. On their individual rectangles, in shreds, in hard receptables tucked between tubes. Mara reached for one of those, peeling back the thick cover.

"Careful," the man said quietly.

Mara left space for air between her skin and the typed print. It felt fragile and timely, like it waited, tucked away among metal, for the right resident to crawl in and find it.

"Here you are," the woman said.

Mara flinched but kept her grip gentle around the words. The woman's return had been silent, the noise of slithering hidden beneath the whine and press of mechanics. A small hand reached for the man, handing him a little white square.

"I'll return it by the end of the week," the man promised. He nodded to the woman, and then to Mara, before burrowing among wiring and pipes, disappearing from the light.

"How can I help you?" the woman asked.

Iron in her mouth, hair prickling on her arms, Mara drew closer. The woman's wire-coated face lit eerily from below, blue, and green lighting nestled among circuitry. When she smiled, soft lines surrounded her eyes. Mara didn't recognize her jumpsuit, plain and grey, unobtrusive. The human parts of her blended with shadow.

"If I have a question, you'll find the answer for me?"

"I always try," the woman said. "My directory and book collection hold a lot of information, but I can't promise this ship holds the answers to everything."

Book collection. Mara's hands flexed around the receptacle she still held before setting it down on the word-strewn floor.

She knew about books, of course. Novels, stories, and texts meant to accompany her modules. Books as they once were, off ship, had sometimes been a physical thing to hold.

"So," the woman startled Mara. "What question do you have for me?"

"It's my greenery," Mara confessed. She wondered if the woman had any for herself, hidden somewhere in the maze of metal and plastics. "My automated system broke, again, and I can't . . . I need a way to keep it alive. Please."

Mara's voice cracked, and her stomach clenched, because she hated the desperation that squeezed her lungs. She hated the thought of an empty, lifeless pod more; she'd beg, if the woman asked it of her.

"Of course," the woman said. "Just a moment while I look through my records."

She escaped back among the wires and shadows. In the quiet, Mara heard the irregular tip and tap of a keyboard. A tongue clicking, then a murmured voice.

When the woman returned, the soft lines reappeared around

her eyes as well.

"You're in luck," she said. "A patron returned this yesterday. I think it should have what you need."

The hands that extended toward Mara were littered with minuscule cuts and flaking, dry patches, perhaps a result of years spent in the irregular climate tempering of the interior. Mara took the book, tongue between her teeth. The cover showed little painted flowering greenery.

"I'll be here cataloguing if you need anything else," the woman said. "Stay as long as you like."

Then the space only held Mara, the blue-green lighting, the scattered words, and the book on greenery. She crawled closer to a circuit board to better see the book's contents. Inside, each page held print and tiny illustrations. Other, irregular notations in genuine handwriting corrected and added to the otherwise uniform text.

Mara flipped through the pages, slow and savouring. Some of the depicted greenery she'd never seen, might not even exist on the *Gateway*. Might only exist in these pages. Some she'd seen in other pods, other hands, and the need to grow her collection burned within her like a faulty thruster. She wanted a future where she'd proven her worthiness to the gardening unit. Where she could save her maintenance pay and more of these tiny images might fill her pod. Make it whole.

Her own greenery waited near the centre of the book.

Grass.

Notations included information on how often to water it and when and optimal amounts of light and temperature to ensure the greenery remained vibrant and beautiful. Mara photographed the page with her handheld. Paused, then photographed a few more. The drawings made her warmer than any of the automated heaters, than the old pictures of planetary life in her modules. Those drawings grew a sharp spark in her chest for the future, something to be protected and cultivated.

Crouching, Mara tucked the book beneath her arm and crawled over uneven flooring to where the woman had disappeared. She stood there among shadows and scattered paper, glancing between books and a small screen that illuminated her partially covered face. Metal creaked beneath Mara's weight. When the woman turned, multi-coloured wire stretched and flexed around her.

"Finished already?" the woman asked, reaching forward at Mara's nod. The book passed carefully between them. When the woman inspected it, bringing the pages close to her face, she nodded, too.

"It had exactly what I needed," Mara said. "Thank you for your help."

"I'm happy to hear that," the woman said. "Is there anything else I can do for you?"

Mara hesitated, feeling for the handheld in her pocket. Its weight made her feel no better prepared to face the darkness.

"I just need to get home," Mara said.

"Out of the walls?" the woman asked. "Oh, I can help with that."

Mara blinked at her in the dim lighting. The lines around the woman's eyes tightened.

"Some find me here and don't handle our materials well," the woman said. "They lose their privilege to ask questions."

Mara thought of the smooth, sturdy book cover and the shredded paper among the pipes in absolute darkness. She pictured the woman shoving Mara away from her book-strewn alcove, the glow of the circuits slowly shutting off. In the dark, the interior became an impossible, crushing maze.

Reaching behind her screen, the woman wriggled free a small paper and handed it to Mara. On it, a small map sketched a path toward what appeared to be an exit through a ceiling tile. Mara could reconnect to the mainframe from there.

"Is this . . ." Mara's voice faltered until she cleared her throat. "If I had another question, should I re-enter this way?"

"Oh, sure," the woman said. "If you want to. Otherwise, I'm sure you'll find another way in and make your way to me or one of the others."

Mara glanced sideways, only able to see a handful of feet before the view dissolved into dark piping. The thought of others out there deep inside the *Gateway* brought no comfort.

"Come back whenever you need us," the woman said, returning her attention to her screen.

Mara followed the map. Lines scratched out the layout of pipes and gears and incomprehensible electronic components. Through wiring and past tubing and frayed connectors, she crawled. The farther she travelled, the worse the page crumbled in her hand, pressing against coils and tangled wiring. Eventually, her handheld pinged, the full shipmap returning alongside her connection to the ship's systems. She followed the brightened lines on the screen, guiding her back to the exterior, and left her crunched paper behind.

Mara could save her greenery. She could find her way back through the wiring and metal, if needed, to keep her little patch of peace. Mara smiled, straining to pick up the edge of a ceiling tile to free herself, and then dropped down into the light.

WHAT THEY DON'T TELL YOU

Mackensie Baker

There was a patron at the door.

The library door was shut, the metal bar hooked firmly into place. The patron was little more than a dark grey smudge on the camera. Any identifying features they might have had were unclear due to the hoodie they wore under a thick parka, and the black scarf they wore around the lower half of their face almost as a kind of mask. They looked from side to side, lingering on the spot where the camera was fixed to the side of the faux-stone building, and knocked again.

It was eight minutes to closing time.

April hesitated. She didn't have to refer to Database for the correct protocols—she knew she wasn't supposed to open the door to new patrons after 11:45. In fact, she had already told the three patrons she'd had in at that time that the library would be closing soon and all but one of them had left right away. The last was an older, tired-looking Black woman in the indigo coat of the Ministry. She had been in there for some time, poring over some hard-copy materials in the Physical Archives room and brushing off both of April's offers to help narrow down her search.

Now, the woman was approaching her slowly, with a wary gaze, like one might a stray cat to gauge whether they would purr or scratch. April resisted the urge to scowl at her. Sometimes, she got looks like this from young children and other first-time patrons, who had never seen a librarian before. The cybernetic enhancements could be alarming to those who weren't used to seeing them, especially when done so extensively.

Her left eye was the least noticeable of the enhancements: the iris was a silver metal disc that acted as an aperture for the camera mounted into the socket, imperceptible unless someone was looking for it. This was doubly hard to see because of her glasses, which were tinted to hide the smartscreen in the right lens.

More noticeable was the arm prosthetic, which had been upgraded with the usual tech, namely a touchscreen interface that tapped into the East Coast Library's system, Database.

The woman had something in her hands. A manuscript, April noted with alarm. She forgot the person at the door for a moment as she turned her full attention on the woman in front of her.

"Ma'am, you cannot have that out here. All physical materials need to remain in—"

"This is mine," the woman said hurriedly, breaking into an awkward smile. "I . . . I hate to bother you so late, but I'm afraid . . . I'm afraid I may not be able to come back another day."

April considered this. It was possible the woman was speaking to the demands of her job, doubtless a stressful career if she was working for the Ministry. She could also have been thinking of her age and health, as she was, at a guess, in her late sixties. But most terminally ill people did not come to the ECL to peruse the archives for hours at a time.

"Are you in some kind of trouble?" she guessed, speaking in a hushed tone even though they were the only two left in the library. She remembered the figure waiting outside the door then and switched her glasses feed back to the external cameras. They were still there but had moved further down the side of the building, into a corner that was well-shadowed.

Nervous now, April did start an internal review of safety protocols. Since the budget cuts, they hadn't been sent any cybernetic security guards to any of the ECL's branches, and instead merely offered a free upgrade and training videos to each of the librarians. The librarians, though, were often the last to leave the library, and ended up being alone due to those same cuts.

Without answering, the woman proffered the manuscript in her hands. It was not particularly old, April saw. Perhaps from the 1990s or even the beginning of the 21st century. A textbook from the looks of it, the cover still attached: glossy and dented at the corners, with some scratches marring the surface lightly. Overall, it was in relatively good shape. April took it, half out of curiosity and half due to the urgency in the woman's gesture.

April flipped it open and immediately dropped it onto the countertop when she saw it: the large red stamp reading BANNED in large capital letters. Circling that was the name of the Ministry of Information itself.

She extended her arms as she took a step back, fingers flared out, as though the stamp had been a red-hot brand.

"Why? Why do . . . ?" she started to ask, before realizing she did not want an answer. She didn't want to be here anymore at all, in fact. She wanted to be going home on the light-rail, to power down her enhancements and take up her current crochet project, a guilty pleasure she had developed out of an increasing aversion to all of the screens and video feeds and constant noise she had to put up with in her day-to-day life.

But she had already said enough. The woman finished the sentence for her: "Why do I have a banned book?" She looked down at her coat, lifted a corner of the material and dropped it, laughing a short, humourless laugh. This was followed by a sigh and—more disturbingly—a wobble of her lower lip, as though she might cry.

The woman overcame it and jabbed a finger at the stamped manuscript. "This is the last one," she said.

April nodded, slowly. "Yes. Good! That one shouldn't even exist."

"I know that," the woman snapped. She pulled a faded black ID card out of her coat pocket and pressed a button. It lit up with her details, showing her Ministry badge with her name and number.

"June," April murmured. It felt like a joke. "June *Carson*? As in . . . ?"

"Look," the woman, June, said, stabbing the book once more with her wrinkled fingertip.

The author byline read, unmistakably, Dr. Harold M. Carson, Ph.D.

Her left eye had scanned this before she could look away, and Database flickered to life on her arm. April quickly powered it down again, but a cold sweat had broken out on her forehead, and she felt a prickle on the back of her neck. Sometimes, she thought, smart technology could be a little too smart.

June took all of this in silently, with a tenseness to the set of her shoulders. After a beat, she let out a breath and said, "I'm so sorry, but I need your help."

No! April wanted to scream at her. *Take your illegal manuscript with your infamous relative's name far away from here and leave me out of it.*

But she was a librarian. She was supposed to help people. And this woman, though she worked for a government organization that April feared but did not respect, seemed kind, and tired, and afraid.

"What can I do?" she asked. It wasn't in the usual tone she might have said those same words in, but a more pleading, confused one.

June pursed her lips. "First, I need you to take this." She slid the book forward across the counter. "I need you to show me a back door where I can leave without being seen. And I need to you to pretend you never saw me here tonight."

April was already shaking her head. "I don't want to get in any kind of trouble," she said. "And besides, librarians don't choose what material gets allowed or restricted—you know this, you're Ministry, for God's sake!"

"You don't understand, this is important!" June hissed at her. "My grandfather wasn't a criminal, wasn't any of the things they said he was. He wanted to fix this system, the corruption, he wanted to do the right thing! I didn't understand before, but I do now. Please, you must read this. You have to get it into the right hands. *It's the last one.*"

A high-pitched beeping sounded. It was five minutes after close, and April hadn't put in the alarm code. She swore and ducked around the counter to the wall beside the door to punch the code in.

She turned back to see that June had taken several steps towards the fire exit.

"Take it," she said, looking to the book. "Please."

"Wait," April said. She paused. Then she checked the front cameras. The hooded figure was still there. "Out the back. You can follow me."

"The book!" June hissed at her again when she started walking toward the back. April barely hesitated this time as she swiped the textbook from the countertop and marched to the staffroom at the far end of the library. She hadn't done the last of her usual closing duties, but she put them out of her mind and grabbed her coat and bag. June had followed her without another word and was standing in the tiny storeroom they used for breaks and staff meetings and clucked her tongue.

"Maybe you could put a word in for us at the Ministry," April said with a wan smile.

June returned the smile sadly. "Oh honey," she said. "I would if I could."

Outside, the late-February air hit them like a shovel. The metal staircase leading down to the staff parking lot was rusted and rickety, more like a fire escape than a proper set of stairs. The parking lot was little more than a paved roof, and they were immediately exposed to the mixed wind and freezing rain that was common almost year-round in the Territories.

They were on the building's second-level due to a low hill on the west side, which offered them a limited view of the vast lake which, against the snow-covered land, simply looked like a shinier stretch of gleaming white. Across from them, a curve in the lakeside revealed the Factory District, where the mined oils and metals were processed. Here, the endless white and grey of the clouds, buildings, and landscape turned black. They said that the smog itself was not as bad for the environment as it looked, and the official word was that they had cleaner energy here than in the neighbouring provinces.

There were no cars left in the lot, which April assumed meant that they would be walking together towards the light-rail station. She was still logged into the ECL cameras, so she checked the front again just to be safe. She stopped in her tracks and sucked in a cold breath when she saw that the figure had disappeared.

"I think we should hurry," she said, turning to June.

But June, too, was gone.

Damn. April stood still a moment, listening to the rushing wind and the city sounds beyond the low wall and ramp of the parking lot. She let her left eye scan the footprints June had left so stealthily about twenty feet back, the security upgrade telling her that June had clambered over the low wall where her footprints stopped. It was maybe thirty feet to the ground below, but in four feet of snow, even an older woman could make the jump easily.

"Damn." She said it out loud this time, running a gloved hand over her sweaty face. Was she being tested? Was this some kind of sick new way of sniffing out would-be traitors to the Ministry of Information?

Her hand went to the bag at her side, feeling the rectangular shape of the illegal material within. Again, she thought of the author's name and the glaring red ink of the stamp. June had been in the Physical Archives room for hours. And the name on her badge did suggest she really was related to Harry Carson. So then if it wasn't some kind of entrapment scheme, what *had* June been looking for?

April knew better than to look through Database, as convenient as it was. She might as well have had a device called Informant attached to her arm and connected to her other cybernetic enhancements. But there was nothing else that could help her. Even the Physical Archives room would have nothing on early 2000's-era philosophers who had been tried for treason and large-scale arson. She could have told June that.

The only reason anyone knew that much about him was that the Coalition as it had existed at that time (about thirty years after the publication of this particular book) had *wanted* him to go down in history, as an example of what happened to those who opposed the government's regulations on information. From what she could remember, he had been a liberal university professor who had become an anarchist after the Coalition's formation in the 2030s. What had started as peaceful protests and angrily written "anonymous" letters to the country's biggest news sites had escalated into him instigating riots on his university's campus, and when he was inevitably fired from his job in spectacular fashion, he had set fire to the Dean's office. Every librarian was taught about him in their first semester. Even those who felt the regulations were too strict knew you didn't want to ever get onto the Coalition's bad side. You didn't want to become the next Harry Carson.

April got to the light-rail station without incident. If the hooded not-a-patron had been waiting for her, they didn't jump out at her from a dark alley or follow her onto the train. She was mostly certain of that last one.

The light-rail cars were heated, thank God, so she had a little respite from the vicious wet snow that the freezing rain had now become. The flickering fluorescent lights of the car reflected her own weary, pale face back to her, making her look more ghost than human. She clutched her bag to her side and stared blankly between her reflection and the alien shadow-shapes of the drill rigs below her window until she got to her stop.

Another swift march through the snowy streets got April to her apartment complex. She rushed inside and locked the door, then considered—but decided against—shoving a chair up against the handle as an added security measure.

She refused to be paranoid, and she refused to look guilty.

Still. April did go further into her apartment before taking off her coat and setting down her bag. She lived in a standard studio apartment, and her bed was hidden behind a folding screen, which is what she used as cover to both undress and to slide the book out of her bag and onto the bed.

It sat there, staring up at her with its unassuming, glossy cover. She read the title again, this time considering it together with the author's name.

The Ethics of Censorship by Dr. Harold M. Carson, Ph.D.

Censorship. It was a word that had been tossed around in bars with wry criticism when she'd been younger (along with "controversy" and "rights"), and discussed at school in strict, non-nonsense terms. It was the subject of many board meetings and news headlines, and it was among the main talking points for all the politicians hoping to get the Coalition on their side.

As a librarian, April had to deal with censorship every day. There were things she wasn't allowed to know about, and Database would ping her file if she tried to look up too many taboo subjects. But it was a word that used to have a different meaning, she knew. It wasn't always used to mean protection and safety. It used to be spat from the lips of those who wished to push the boundaries of the system. It had been a word that went against freedom and the exchange of ideas.

So, she started to read.

Physical books were dusty, smelly things that tended to yellow over time. Unused to the slippery thinness of the pages, she slit her fingertip open twice in the first chapter. By chapter two, she didn't notice the stinging anymore. The mustiness of the paper started to smell of vanilla and peppercorns. Her eyes didn't ache from the light of a screen.

In the early hours of the morning, close to the end of the book and the glossary she had already flipped to multiple times, there came a knock on her door.

Calmly, she went to it and opened it up to find two Ministry members, a tall woman and a middle-aged man with a stocky build. Both were imposing enough in their deep indigo coats, though they sported a dusting of snow across their shoulders and the woman's hair was damp and frizzy. Behind them stood a younger man in a parka. The hood of the sweater he wore underneath was down, and he no longer wore the scarf.

"Can I help you?" April asked.

The tall woman frowned.

"April Donoghue?" she asked, folding an ID wallet out of her coat and flashing the badge at her, much as June had done just a few hours before. This woman was much sleeker, though, the lights of the display brighter. Her name was Adrienne Lafontaine, and she was a Councillor.

"Yes, that's me."

"May we come in?"

April said *yes* again and stepped aside. The younger man did not look at her; his gaze went past her, roaming about the small apartment and cataloguing each item.

"Are you with the Ministry?" she asked him. In response, he held up a different kind of badge.

"Detective Dixon here has been working a case on behalf of the Ministry for some time now," Councillor Lafontaine stated. She was inspecting April with the same kind of scrutiny the detective was paying to her furniture and personal possessions. "That prosthetic," she said, gesturing to April's arm. "Was it put in before or after your accident?"

"Before," April answered simply.

The Councillor pursed her lips. "April, we know you spoke to a patron earlier today, a woman by the name of June Carson."

April nodded. The Councillor and her fellow Ministry worker exchanged glances.

"So, you know what this is about?"

"Not exactly." This was an extremely honest answer, she felt.

It was the Councillor's turn to nod, like this answer fit better into her neat little narrative. "We have been monitoring your Database for some time, April. It is highly likely that June was too before she was fired. She never turned in her badge and has been fleeing prosecution across the provinces. We believe June has contacted other librarians like you, ones who have shown a potential for . . . rebellious sympathies, let us say. We need to know if she gave you anything."

"Did you find her?"

The older man beside Lafontaine let out a laugh. "Did we find her? She had nowhere else to run or hide. She turned herself in hours ago."

April found it hard to believe that, but she stayed silent.

"April. You need to tell us whether June Carson gave you anything tonight. We have a good idea what she might have said to you, but we need to know about the location of any document or other objects she might have had on her person. Did she ask you to upload anything?"

"No."

"I found it."

This was Detective Dixon. He held up the textbook with both hands, delicately. He wasn't wearing gloves, but that didn't matter in cases like this.

Councillor Lafontaine's heels clicked vigorously against the cement floors of April's studio as she stalked over to the Detective and took the book from him. She opened it, letting out a deep huff of air as she did so.

Her partner was still staring at April. "Why didn't you tell us about the book then?"

April did not reply.

Lafontaine's triumphant grin faltered as she checked the Database on her personal device (it wasn't fixed to her arm like it was to April's prosthetic, but everyone was attached to their devices in a way). Her partner did the same. As did Detective Dixon.

"You *bitch*," Dixon breathed.

"It's everywhere." The note of despair in Lafontaine's voice was oddly satisfying.

The one kind of information the Ministry couldn't stop from spreading was word-of-mouth. And now that Dr. Carson's book was uploaded to the ECL's Database-connected devices . . . Well, April supposed that everyone would soon be learning about the ethics of censorship.

"You're coming with us," the detective said. But April only had one regret: that she hadn't been able to finish reading the textbook's final chapter. At least she had uploaded it first.

Maybe it wouldn't be so bad to go down in history as the next Harry Carson.

LIBRARIAN'S ASSISTANT

Robert Lauderdale

A s the image loaded, the certainty he'd been correct all along washed over him like chill water. This was exactly how he'd always imagined they'd try to deceive him. A woman, average height, indeterminate age, generous in figure and tight in clothing, shoulder-length auburn hair, and a pair of anachronistic spectacles through which he could make out her speculative gaze. An image suggesting his isolation might end, a promise of a return to humanity, a composite image drawn from his computer browsing. Browsing images had become a compulsion, a way to remind himself he'd been part of something before being imprisoned. A feminine voice, half purr, called to him through the speaker. "Tennant?"

Whatever was behind the image knew his name. Not surprising, as he'd told it to them despite their silence. All the countless times he'd rehearsed this conversation, practised this moment, yet now he found himself unable to speak. Overwhelmed. Yes, he'd been correct, yes, he'd been waiting for exactly this, but now it was here, and he'd been waiting so very long. From the moment he'd woken in the remains of his pod, the survival capsule stripped from the small craft and somehow placed in this prison. He'd hauled himself from the capsule, explored the two-level interior, tried to figure why he'd been taken. His captors would surely speak to him, offer an image pleasing to him to keep him calm and obedient. But they hadn't.

Days, months, then years passed without contact, but his mind couldn't dislodge the fantasy of speaking with them. How would it happen? What sort of deception would they attempt? Would they present themselves as human? As someone beautiful, an amalgamation of the images his loneliness demanded he view, nothing. For years . . .

Until now.

The image of a beautiful woman on his screen was calling his name.

He closed his eyes. Breathed deeply. He could feel, in the calm and darkness, the edge of his sanity. He needed to be careful, to speak cautiously, but first he needed to take care of himself.

He covered his camera. Looked around at the dullness of his reality, the pale, blank walls of his prison. He'd flown free once; the lower deck of his two-level cage still held the picked-over carcass of his capsule. Not trusting his captor's technology, he'd scavenged what he could of his pod's remains. Some of it, he'd carted up to the upper level. His office, where he went to work. An attempt at normality, a reflex of the man he'd been. Activity to divide days from nights, a blow struck for interstellar harmony, his work was all he had. He had no idea if he was having any effect but, lately—

Was that why they were contacting him now? Because things were going well? More calming breaths, leaning back in his chair, thinking as rationally as he could. He glanced at the screens. There she was, looking adorable despite the menace she represented. He shuddered but forced himself to focus. She, the image, wasn't real. It was just a likeness designed to manipulate him, a drawing of a carrot to lure a hermit-monk from his cave.

Once he felt calm, ready, he uncovered his camera so whoever was sending the image could see him.

On screen, her seductive features adopted an expression of concern. "Tennant? I lost you there for a minute. Are you okay?"

He would need to adjust the sound, change the tone, that voice was startlingly sexy. Or, more likely, the loneliness they'd cultivated in him for so long made it seem so.

"I'm here," he answered, the rough sound of his voice strange to his own ears. "This is Tennant. Who am I speaking to?"

"A friend," the image answered.

"Where were you captured?" Tennant asked, wondering if he

should mask his sarcasm. How many human mannerisms could they understand? Was sarcasm universal? Something they might comprehend? "I didn't know any other—of my species—had been brought here. No one has spoken with me."

"I'd prefer not to say," the image answered. "I am new here."

"Of course you are," Tennant replied, trying not to roll his eyes. "Well, I've been here for a long, long time. Almost seven years, if the timekeeping onaf my capsule can be trusted. There's no way to calibrate it. In all that time, I've not seen another soul. In person or on screen, just the image files I had in the capsule."

"Sounds lonely," the image sympathized.

"I keep busy. I've not seen or spoken with anyone, but there are other ways to communicate. If my captors, whoever brought me here, wanted to contact me I'd have talked to them, but they haven't. I suspect there are other prisoners here, captured like I was, but they've not reached out. I've tried to get through to them. It's difficult."

On screen, the image frowned. "Why do you believe there are other prisoners here if you've never seen them?"

Tennant chuckled. "There's no way I could see anyone. This cage they've got me in; it doesn't attach to anything."

A quizzical look crossed her face. "How can you know that?"

Tennant leaned into the camera, then stopped himself. He was so eager to talk, it was almost frightening. He took a breath. Calmed himself. "There was a handheld device in my capsule. I used it to measure the thickness of the walls, map the reflected energies to detect structures outside. There's a rim along the floor here, but it extends less than a metre. Thicker up top, and there are cables or pipes tethering my cage to a station. Gravity here is produced by centrifugal force; you'll have noticed the Coriolis effect by now. I calculated the radius of the swing by observing the difference in the time it took falling objects to fall on the upper level compared to the lower. Took me forever to work out how to time the falling objects but, well, I had time to kill. I've no idea where you are but they're spinning me around in a bucket at the end of four long ropes. Visitors are unlikely. I expect I'll die in here, without ever laying eyes on anyone again."

"Sounds horrible." The image's expression appeared sincere. Tennant wasn't surprised by that, it was what she was designed for, but he was surprised by how convincing the image seemed.

Maybe she wasn't sincere; maybe like his sudden urge to talk, it was a reflection of his need.

But damn it all, it felt amazing to talk to her. "It's better if you face your captivity directly. I've no idea how they keep the environment going here. I mean, maybe some of those cables are pipes, maybe supplies fall down the cables. In the end it doesn't matter, it works well enough. I suspect my cage is attached to a larger station but that's just speculation."

"You said there were other prisoners?"

"Probably. When I woke up here, once I got out of my capsule, the first thing I found was a computer on the upper level. Not built by humans but, obviously, designed for use by our species. I tried to use it to communicate with my captors, but they refused to speak with me. Frustrating, as you can imagine. I had some dark days. Finding no way out of my physical prison, I decided to explore my cybernetic environment through the computer. I found there were other distinct nodes, twenty-seven of them. At least one would be my captors but the others . . . I'm not certain. There could be others, captured like I was, imprisoned as I am. It's a working theory anyway. I have no idea why anyone would go to so much effort to collect prisoners and then refuse to communicate with them. But it happened to me, maybe it happened to others. I decided if my captors were silent, I would try to speak to the other prisoners. It's difficult though."

On screen, the image nodded. "It's always difficult to communicate with an alien species."

"More so as a prisoner," Tennant insisted. "As a captive, there are matters you cannot discuss. Having no idea why I've been taken prisoner, I must be concerned about what I reveal of my people. I cannot assume my jailers have good intentions. It's unlikely I've been abducted for any scientific reason, but I can't just assume their motive is military either."

"Why would you say the reason for your capture wasn't scientific?" the image asked, her features arranged in convincing confusion. "I would think science the most obvious motive."

"But totally false," Tennant corrected her. "There was nothing exploratory about my capture. They knew exactly what they were doing. Obviously, there was collusion with the outpost in the system where they grabbed me. Whoever my captors are, they arranged with others of my species to capture someone. Not to brag, but I was a crewmember on an exploration ship. From the locals' perspective, new in town, unloved, expendable."

"That sounds like coincidence." She was cute when she argued.

"No. The outpost reported an anomaly in the planet's ring system on our approach, asked if we could take a look. Five-day mission in a pod. If the readings were correct, it was a potential windfall for the outpost, but they hadn't checked it out. I had some work I wanted to finish, five days alone in a pod sounded good to me, so I volunteered. My pod was loaded up with solid rockets in case we needed to vector the anomaly towards the outpost. As I approached, someone started shooting at me. I figured I'd go up like a nova—I was hauling solid fuel thrusters remember?—but there wasn't any explosion. Instead, my pod was skilfully disabled. I had no choice but to jettison in my capsule. Then the anomaly came to me, swallowed my capsule. It'd been waiting for me to escape. No way they could've known I would do that unless they'd talked to the outpost or someone from my ship. Since no one on the ship would sell me out like that, it was clearly the outpost.

"Understanding the outpost betrayed me, it follows science was not the motive behind my capture. The outpost would've told anyone who asked whatever scientific information they wanted to know. No, my capture is something else. I don't know what, but I need to be guarded about what information I share. So do the other prisoners.

"My first attempt to communicate was our ship's usual contact protocol, in case anyone wanted to talk. They didn't, not my fellow prisoners or my captors. Took me a while to figure out what to try next but I was lucky. Well, relatively lucky, within the context of life forms abducted against their will by unknown aliens. You see, I'm a librarian.

"When I said I volunteered for five days alone, it was because I had a project to work on. I wanted to re-catalogue a mass of literature created before my species' first interstellar flight. I'd hoped to make it more accessible for my crewmates, but I could never find the time to get it done. Always things to do on an exploration ship. When I said I was a librarian, it was just one of my jobs on the ship. I had three others, four if you count pod-pilot. Anyway, as a result, I had a core full of pre-interstellar literature. I figured I could share it all, it wouldn't give away anything. Given how old it is, there's no chance it contains any relevant information regarding our technology or current society. Of course, it had to be prepared for alien consumption. No easy task."

"I cannot imagine how you would do that," the image swooned.

"Oh," Tennant stalled. He'd spoken more this morning than he had in years, but he was proud of the work he'd done. He wanted to talk about it, but he needed to consider if he was giving away any secrets by indulging in the luxury of answering. By design there wasn't anything sensitive in his work, and it had been so long since he'd spoken aloud it was difficult not to answer.

"You need to understand how stories—human stories—are made, break them down into pieces. Convert how characters from my world talk and match it to how other species communicate; break out how the author viewed relationships within our society and match it to how other societies view their similar relationships. If I describe a beautiful woman to an alien lacking gender, or composed of multiple genders, I need to have the woman's description broken down enough to have her role understandable to my theoretical reader. That's the double encryption, why I sent them programs requiring the other prisoners' input in order to make human stories comprehensible to them. It's a challenging process but I have my machines to help. Unfortunately, while they can sort information into distinct classes, it requires a different, biological thought process to refine what they produce. Hardly the machine's fault, they were designed to solve different sorts of problems. And that's just the basic plot. Story atmosphere, narrative tension, the reader's perspective, they all must be broken apart and coded into a form adaptable to the reader. And the discordant elements which make a story unpredictable and engaging, it's a challenging process even for the shortest stories."

Nodding, the image looked directly out of her screen to him. "You take enjoyment from the process."

"Well . . ." It wasn't something he'd considered before. "In a way, I mean, it's not something I would've chosen to do had I not been imprisoned. If I were free, I'd just read whatever I want and simply enjoy the stories. I must admit, I'm proud of the process I've developed. I've enjoyed the work for the simple reason there is nothing else to enjoy in this wretched place. It is satisfying that some of the nodes have requested more stories. It's gratifying to think I could make their captivity somewhat more tolerable."

"What of those nodes who have not responded, who have not asked for more stories?"

"They have my respect. Everything they receive could be our jailers' ploy and they refuse to offer their enemy anything. How can I, a fellow prisoner, not admire such a stance? I can only offer; I can't make anyone take it. Besides, I'm not so arrogant to think my work here will be comprehensible to all civilizations. It's a vast universe, full of unimagined marvels."

"You said if you were freed you would stop your work." The image frowned, concern in the pixels of her unreal eyes. "If you enjoy the challenge and are proud of the process, why not continue it?"

"Because if I were free, I could read whatever I wanted without having to tear it apart, assign values to each sentence. I wouldn't have to limit my reading to stories from before interstellar travel. Free people can read whatever they desire. My process requires a great deal of time and concentration, as well as assistance from my machines. I am proud of it. If I were reunited with my people, I would love to show it to them so they could understand what I've tried to do. They could learn from it, make improvements, employ what I've done so we could share more of our culture with others. Your question is ridiculous though; I know how interstellar travel works. I know how unlikely it is that I will ever be free again. Not only is your question ridiculous, but it's also cruel."

"I apologize," the image offered in unlikely, animated sympathy which nevertheless appeared sincere. "My intent was not to cause harm. If I may, I have one more question I would like to ask."

"Ask away," Tennant replied.

"All of the work you've done, what if your captors are one of the nodes replying to you? If that were true, would you stop your work?"

"I don't know." His admission came at some cost, but Tennant strove to be honest. "Until I understand why they brought me here, I have to consider them an enemy. Perhaps it's a failure of imagination on my part but I can't imagine any reason to justify what they've done to me. Even if they explained it, it's unlikely I could consider them anything but a foe. I've known all along that at least one of the nodes would be them but if, through the stories I share, they can better comprehend my people then I'll considered my efforts rewarded. Understand: I don't do it for my captors; my efforts are to make my fellow prisoners' existence more bearable. They are the community I serve, because I am one of them."

The image nodded, then turned away from the screen. She was going. Tennant couldn't help but lurch closer to the screen, to the camera there. "Are you leaving?"

"Only for a time," the image assured him. "I appreciate you speaking with me. We will speak again."

And she was gone. Against his will, he felt his spirit drop and he followed it down to the floor. He was, he knew, far more vulnerable to manipulation than he'd anticipated. How could he have known? He'd never heard of anyone who lived in solitary conditions for so long. A pretty face, a voice to speak with, he'd bubbled with an urge to talk. Had he betrayed humanity in anything he'd said? He didn't think so but how could he know? He lay on the floor, his eyes sweeping the stark, colourless walls of his prison. He wondered when the image would return, five years or six years from now? Was she an avatar generated by life forms experiencing time differently? He couldn't know. The list of things he had no way of knowing bore down on him, pinning him to the floor as he searched for the will to rise.

Eventually even abject hopelessness becomes boring. Since he was unwilling to end it all, he rose to his feet and tasked one of his computers to review the conversation for possible security lapses. He didn't expect usable results, but it felt like something a responsible person would do, so he did it. With a sigh he looked around at his environment. He didn't feel up to tackling the detective story he was hashing out, nor ready for review of the romance he was close to sending. Since he wasn't just a librarian, but an astronaut, he would do his exercises.

Stretching his exercise out until, exhausted, he collapsed into his chair. He reviewed the computer intelligence report on the conversation. Unhelpful but, somehow, the ill-prepared analysis made him feel better. He finished reviewing his code, ended up sending out both works. Somewhat reckless but, after the morning's conversation, he felt reckless. Weary, falling into his cot, he fell quickly into a deep sleep.

A gentle pressure on his chest woke him. He brushed at it, his hand encountering an arm. Fear shivered him, rolling him out of the cot and sending him scrambling across the deck like a crab.

She was here. Impossible, but standing by his overturned cot. The image, the woman from the screen, exactly as she'd appeared during their conversation. Behind her spectacles her eyes followed him, her expression more bemused than startled by his fright. She looked human but her lack of response to his sudden terror marked her as something else.

Tennant sputtered. Trying to spit out questions but producing only choked and incoherent noises which, even to his own ears, didn't resemble language. She looked down at him, her expression curious but calm. Immune to his terror. Falling to his side, he curled into a ball, his trembling limbs locking together as his chest struggled to contain his racing heart. Curled up, struggling to control his breathing, the fear eventually washed over him. He was left drained, flotsam on the shore after the tide retreated. What was left of him gathered himself, gingerly rising to a sitting position.

"I didn't think you were real." His voice was weak, but she heard him and nodded. "Have you come to kill me?"

"No," she answered.

"You're not human." An edge crept into his voice, a weariness of deception.

"Not exactly," she admitted.

A sigh escaped him. He looked at himself, wasn't pleased by what he saw. Or smelt. Yesterday's workout had been intense. Gingerly, he rose to his feet. He looked at the shower he'd jury-rigged. If he was to receive company he'd need to make some modifications to his lower floor, the first being a shower curtain. He glanced at the toilet he'd fashioned and amended the order of his list. Nothing he could do about it now. He really needed a shower.

"Could you, um"—the question didn't come naturally but it seemed polite. Pointless, but polite—"turn around? I'd prefer to shower without being watched."

She started to speak, but he interrupted before her words emerged. "I know I am always observed but this is different. Privacy between people is a show of respect."

She turned around; eyes turned to the blank wall. He showered. He had to concede he was uncertain if he'd be able to match her chivalry. Drying himself off, he searched for clothes. All he could find was a set of coveralls meant to fit over his flight suit. It didn't fit but wasn't too dirty.

"So," Tennant said, feeling more himself. "Why are you here?"

She turned, fixing her gaze on him. No change in her expression. Whether he was filthy and curled up in terror or dressed in his best, she was focused on and interested in him. It was unnerving. "I have been sent to explain things."

"Well, it sounds like a full conversation. I'll make tea."

His tea left much to be desired, tasting more like licorice and plastic than his memory of tea. His captors duplicated powdered flavours to add to his food; a paste delivered in porridge-like viscosity. He had no idea where they got the flavour, but it hadn't been from anyone human. He'd had time to learn to make do but it required some creativity and low standards. Hosting laid his culinary inadequacies bare. He pulled a metal frame over to serve as a table, and another smaller cylinder to serve as a chair. His guest sat on his bed, which was distracting but not enough to goad him into asking her to move.

Offering her a cup, Tennant spoke first. "Let's start with you. What, exactly, are you? Where are you from? Who sent you? Do you have a name?"

She watched him sip his tea, duplicating the action. If the taste surprised her, she covered it well. "I'm a constructed being. As you said, I was made to appear human, but I am not. Please forgive my inexperience. My construction occurred on the planet we are orbiting, the planet of your captors. I should explain I was not built by your captors but by others of the same species who object to your imprisonment. There is a diversity of opinion regarding your captivity. Those responsible for my construction believe it immoral to keep you imprisoned and are attempting to have you freed. Until such time as they achieve that goal, they hope you will accept me as a companion. I do not have a name yet. It was assumed you would select one for me."

In his head, Tennant groaned. Looking up, seeing the quizzical expression on her face, he realised he'd expressed himself aloud. He'd been alone for a long time. His social skills needed to be sharpened.

"Okay," Tennant said, speaking slowly as he spoke his thoughts. "Can you tell me why I'm here? Why was I captured?"

"I can," she confirmed. "The culture below is, in many ways, like yours. They have a history of conflict. War. Before interstellar travel, there existed a widespread custom of taking prisoners. When one faction wished to declare war, a prisoner of the opposing faction would be publicly executed to announce their intent. This custom and its associated rituals continue to the present day."

"I'm still alive so I assume no war has been declared?"

"That is correct," she agreed, smiling. "Contact was made with your people shortly before you were captured. No hostility was planned but your capture was deemed necessary in the event something unanticipated brought your people and theirs into conflict. Your capture was a precaution."

"And their refusal to explain any of this to me?" Tennant tried to keep the bitterness from his voice but wasn't entirely successful.

"Ritual. As you correctly surmised, your capture had nothing to do with science or diplomacy. Part of their custom of war is to humiliate the enemy before their death. Normally prisoners, particularly those from social cultures, suffer mental trauma and collapse. For the purposes of declaring war such breakdowns are preferred. They demonstrate the enemy is weak and incapable of reason. Your resilience is not helpful to their plans."

"Right." It was a small victory, but he'd take it. "You're here now, offering to help, so has something changed?"

"Yes."

"Look, if we're meant to live together," Tennant explained. "We need to set some guidelines. I know nothing about the culture who constructed you, and clearly, you're designed not to share information about them. It's okay. I don't blame you. I know you were made that way. However, if you have information you believe I need to hear: Please just tell me. Don't wait for me to ask. I understand I'm not in great shape, and you're concerned about my well-being, but waiting for me to ask the right question is not helpful. It's not how humans interact. If you are meant to be a tool for my use, well, I'll adjust to that. If you're meant to be something more, a companion, this caution will be a barrier. Companions are equal, both with their own needs, they help each other. It's not easy but it's honest. Am I making sense?"

Her expression went, for the first time since her image appeared, somewhat flat. Withdrawn. It hurt a little to lose the interest she'd focused on him, but Tennant considered it a positive sign. He waited a moment, was about to ask her to continue, when she spoke without prompting.

"Each captive acts in ways unique to their nature but your captivity has confused your captors more than any other. You asked for information but did not beg. You shared information but not in an attempt to gain advantage. You sought to offer comfort to other prisoners. You risked your safety to provide for those you had never met and would never meet. You acknowledged you were part of a community despite knowing nothing of them save their existence. To the culture below, this represented courage.

"All of which might have been a footnote in an unread record except for a fortunate occurrence. You shared stories, sharing them in a way to be enjoyed by those unlike yourself. Your translation efforts worked beyond all reasonable expectations. Others have enjoyed your efforts. As you hoped, it has provided some of your fellow captives comfort and insight. Your captors also enjoy your work."

"I didn't make them for my captors," Tennant objected.

"They are aware of that, yet they enjoy them. In time those who served as your captors were released from their service and, against their instructions, they brought your stories to more of the population. Your stories have become extremely popular. As a result, your situation has become widely known and many object to your captivity. Those objectors had me constructed. It is part of the old rituals: A prisoner who displays exceptional courage can be elevated to an ambassador. It is a tradition not invoked in ages, but it remains a tradition. It is being considered. While it is, I am permitted to remain here."

"They might take you away?"

"No creature can foretell the future. Based on the knowledge I have been granted, it seems unlikely. However, I cannot assume

I know all of the situation, nor am I likely to learn more of it here. It is a possibility."

Tennant sighed, his face grim. "You understand my fear? They could just be offering you so they can take you away later. You might be a tool to manipulate me. All this talk of my work making a difference outside these walls, it could just be flattery."

She looked at him with no answers. "There are several ways I could assist you. I could list them; however, I sense such information would be premature. I do not wish you to feel I am manipulating you."

Pleased, Tennant nodded. "Your answer seems very self-aware. At this point, I can't know exactly what you are. I really don't know you. Are you an independent, free-thinking, intelligent creature? Or a puppet sent by my captors? There's no way for me to know. Keeping you here is a risk to me."

She nodded, frowned, then spoke. "I understand if you decide to send me away. You have endured much; it is unreasonable to expect you to risk further suffering. It is possible they will allow me to continue to study you from a distance."

"But I would be foolish to disregard help," Tennant argued. "Here's what I'm thinking: Let us both assume you are a fully independent, intelligent life form with free will and opinions. I admit that's what I hope for. I don't know what your studies have shown you about humanity, but I have no need for a servant or a geisha. I need someone to talk to. I need a partner I can trust. I need someone who can sympathize, and I can sympathize with. I want to let you stay, but I need some promises from you first."

"What promises?"

"The first is that you will not tell me which node, or nodes, my captives are listening to. Even if I ask. It will change how I work, so it's better if I don't know. Secondly, I need to know that you're keeping your well-being and long-term goals in mind. If we assume you're more than a puppet, our interests will not always align. You need to be honest. I'll try to do the same. It'll take time. Finally, you will pick your own name. A name that pleases you. We can read stories together, maybe you'll find a name there. Does that sound okay?"

"It is agreeable."

Tennant smiled. "Can you read? I mean, in my language?"

"Yes and no," she admitted. "I understand vocabulary but

often lack context, so I am uncertain if my experience is equivalent to yours. Discovering these differences is one of my objectives."

"Look, I know we've more to talk about, but I'd love to read to you. It's been a long time since I read to anyone. We'll talk more later, unless there's something you feel I need to know right now?"

She shook her head.

"I don't suppose you have any favourite books?"

She shook her head. "I do not. I am sorry."

"Don't be," Tennant assured her. "Every librarian loves a challenge. Come on, this could be fun."

THE REVOLUTION WILL NOT BE FERTILIZED

J. W. Schnarr

It's hard to describe the first time you see a flower.

Not those gene jobs with the glowing petals. Everyone has seen those. A real bloomer. Made naturally, the way environmental pressure forcing advantageous change at the genetic level intended.

Your first time is in an alley near your house. You are walking to work when it happens. There's something sweet in the air, easy to pick out in the industrial oil and wet pavement stink of the city.

An odd splash of colour in the garbage jammed behind a trash bin where the collectors can't reach. A stem of vibrant green. Leaves open and pointed toward the endless grey light and neon above. Petals are a dozen different shades between white and yellow. A dandelion, but you won't find that out until much later.

You climb the bin to get your hand down where you can feel the cold silk petals. It seems wrong to disturb it.

There is a small pile of dirt heaped on paper food cartons. In one of the cartons are the broken remains of a Christmas ornament. A delicate red glass ball with sparkled snowflakes. You can reach it with the tips of your fingers, careful to avoid cutting into your hands.

The inside glass is silver primer and caked with mud. The flower is growing out of it. You pull the broken globe into your freezing, shaking hands. You walk back to your flat, cupping the globe in your hands. Do plants need warmth or light? You won't find that out until much later.

The growth of plants is a highly regulated industry. Unauthorized gardening is a felony.

Something about uncounted plants messing with the operation of the expensive and noisy climate controls for the city. Gardening without the proper licensing fees and permits in place also takes money out of the pockets of the corporations that supply you with such and the government parasite that lives off additional fees and taxes.

Growing a house plant might give you the idea you could grow a potato. And if you grow one, you might grow two. And suddenly you're eating more than your allotted ration like a giant fucking pig. Your allotted rations are just one of the ways they control you. The entire system is about order. Structure. Safety.

This flower in your hands is an asymmetrical wonder. It doesn't glow, and it doesn't appear to contain gene modifications. None of the ones that make it glow, anyway. Do they do that with jellyfish? Or is it something else?

At the bottom of the Christmas ornament is a scrap of paper with an address on it. It is the big public library downtown.

You're sitting in a room with a bunch of strangers. The air is heavy with their smells, earthy colognes, sage, and hash. They are non-descript, for the most part, people from all the poor walks of life. People left behind by the economy. People with axes to grind against all kinds of oppressive authority figures. People like you.

The man at the front of the room is Charlie. He dresses better and talks smarter than the rest of you. Right now, he's talking about delivery systems. What makes a good bomb? The perfect amount of fertilizer and water. Small is ok. Bigger is better.

What are your targets? That's up to you. Charlie jokes about stuffing them down the Prime Minister's throat and a couple people laugh uncomfortably. Others laugh loudly. A challenge, and a flag, letting everyone all know what they think of that guy.

"Don't think of this as terrorism," Charlie says. "It's activism."

You get a feeling those words have been said before, by men in similar rooms, facing similar people. Around the room, these people are nodding in agreement. Similar responses.

Charlie reaches down into a bucket at his feet. "Don't worry about ammunition. I raided my seed library."

Everyone lines up. With cupped hands, you accept Charlie's

sacrament. It's a small paper envelope, not much larger than a soup packet. There is green on the cover, spring green and faded, the colour of new things and old things. The bottom of the package is a photo of ripe tomatoes on a tomato plant. Faded red. Stems of faded green. The seeds inside rattle when you shake the packet, letting you know they are in there.

Charlie holds up a gumball-sized ball of brown earth.

"You're going to mix the fertilizer and soil and clay into a tight ball like this. You'll be able to throw it further with a little weight. Once you have the ball started, make a hole with your thumb and put your seeds in. Just a couple. Use some water to seal it up."

He holds up his hand again, showing a perfect ball. "Don't worry if yours doesn't look like this. I've been making these for a while."

A guerilla gardening class isn't the kind of thing that your local library just broadcasts. You won't find it on their website, listed along with the new releases and children's reading times. You don't see them listed in the monthly events list that comes with your water bill.

These are the kind of events that get taped to light poles outside bars. They are found in bathrooms and left under empty beer glasses at local music venues. Someone might put a poster under the wipers on your car as a joke. They are intentionally cheap looking, using black ink and coloured paper. Amateur layout and design. Maybe spelling mistakes—though not this particular one, because Charlie makes them himself and he is one of the librarians at the big public library downtown.

Charlie knows his shit. He talks a lot about the long and proud history of guerilla gardening going back to the 1600s with Levelers and Diggers. Folks who wanted people to abandon their evil city ways and return to an agrarian lifestyle. They were communists who grew crops in common areas for common people.

Gerrard Winstanley's writings at the time reflected on a relationship between man and nature. People and their surroundings were bound by more than existence. He declared, "true freedom lies where a man receives his nourishment and preservation, and that is in the use of the earth."

You don't know much about communism, but Charlie does.

You know that nourishment and preservation come with a monthly fee and are heavily regulated to the point where you can't do it yourself anymore.

Charlie's lesson wraps up and he asks if anyone has questions. The first one is the big one. Three neo hippies start talking about a tire yard in their neighbourhood. How nice it would be if flowers grew there instead of pollution. How much better off we'd all be.

Charlie smirks and cocks his head. "That's not a question."

Lucy, an old woman with long, blue hair, says there is a pothole on her street that is threatening to take over the road.

"Nobody drives it anymore," she says. "It's all fliers. I think it would make a nice tea garden."

Four people sitting together say they are planning a community garden.

"You don't need seed bombs for that," Charlie says. His voice is a cannon of exuberance. "Think bigger. Be bigger!"

"I want to destroy something," you say, and everyone turns around to look at you.

It's out there now. A sea of disapproval staring back, their gaze a heat lamp of shame. Neo-hippies are uncomfortable with the idea of violence hanging in the air.

Charlie just snaps his fingers. "Show me."

When he talks, people listen. When you are with him, you're not just a bunch of nerdy stack rats spending your free time surrounded by state-approved reading material. You're being moulded and fertilized into something bigger.

"My dandelions!" Charlie isn't just a middle-aged librarian curating state-approved reading material for fascists. "Little seed parachutes floating to your destinies. Fly! Fly!"

The meeting over, your custom is to loiter around, talk, and share the spoils of your efforts. Lucy with blue hair has a handful of little warped tomatoes. One of the neo hippies brought carrots. There is always something to try. Some new flavour you have never tasted before. When you pick up a sliver of tomato, you notice the middle slime holding the seeds has been removed.

The flavour of a tomato is bright, metallic, and grassy in a pleasant way. It's a far cry from the red paste issued at your pay grade.

"We're hoping the next batch will be bigger," Lucy says, beaming. "We're still learning, but we're optimistic."

"Are flowers optimistic?" you ask, licking tomato from your teeth.

"Even better." Charlie grabs a handful of tomato and carrot wedges off the plate. "They're relentless."

The secret to throwing far is isometrics. This is the art of tightening your muscles without moving your joints. It's counterintuitive. You know this because one of Charlie's classes was to teach people who grew up in a world without competitive sports—too individualistic!—and have no idea how to properly throw.

Constant tension in your muscles improves endurance, and it can also build the muscles up to increase dynamism. Plank your way to better health. A glute bridge can be your ticket off the oncoming cliff of heart disease. Dead hang until your Latissimus dorsi is wide enough to make you look like a turtle. It's science, dummy.

Over the next six months, you do a lot of isometrics. Your nails are always black with mud. You give up on water and start using boba for a little added texture. Charlie says tapioca starch is a great binder and fertilizer. Even the fake stuff they pump out of the tea shops.

Your first few weeks are tough ones. You have been shitting the bed with the Fukuoka Method. Your throws barely clear the second floor of any building. As often as not, too much pressure on your hands and not enough moisture results in your seed bombs exploding in the air, and you scrambling away before The Authority tags you.

The Fukuoka Method is also called "do-nothing farming." You know you are bad at it because you run yourself to exhaustion night after night trying to do nothing.

"It's not lack of effort. It's lack of structure," Charlie says. "It's punk rock."

You attend more classes, take more lessons. Sometimes there is food. More often than not, there is only water filled with sweeteners and colours. Charlie turns them into object lessons. Notice how grapes don't taste like grape flavouring. Look at an image of a strawberry. Why is the drink a murky pink but the berries are a shock of red?

You steal a length of rope out of a demo yard and use it to keep your chest tight. You practice maintaining a small box for your shoulders and hips and keeping your arm in an arc directly overhead. Think of the act of throwing as a whip and use your entire body to stay fluid.

Hard work pays off. The first time you throw a seed bomb up onto a second-floor balcony, you're nearly pinched because you cheer instead of run. Eventually, you can hit the fifth floor with a good upwind.

Your lack of effort is starting to show results.

Tomato plants keep showing up on the upper floors of the Peace and Prosperity Building. The big neon sign of the Ministry of Compliance becomes a bed for a dozen white daisies. Sunflowers are taking over the top two floors of the Quantum Node Complex. This is a big deal.

But not without casualties. The neo hippies get pinched throwing seed bombs into the tire yard. Apparently, those tires were more than just an eyesore. In a public trial, the neo hippies are convicted on terrorism charges for contaminating a national energy source. The government was planning to turn the tires back into petroleum.

Terrorism is an automatic life sentence.

After the trial, your classmates start vanishing by ones and twos. Sometimes new people replace them, but mostly they don't.

Charlie is frenetic. "Each of you needs to be more dandelion!"

The new people have no idea what this means. But you do.

You take stacks of intentionally cheap-looking posters of black ink and coloured paper. You tape them to light poles outside bars. You leave them in bathrooms and under empty beer glasses at local music venues. As a joke, you leave them under the wipers on parked cars.

You know your shit. You talk about the long and proud history of guerilla gardening and about Levelers and Diggers. You talk about growing crops in common areas for common people. You still don't know shit about communism, so you switch it out for isometrics and how to keep your body box small and your arm straight over your shoulder when throwing a seed bomb. This information seems more useful.

These new people don't care much about arm strength. And they don't give a shit about whether boba or water is a better binder.

You demonstrate the proper way to throw a seed bomb.

These new people think it's all a big joke. "It looks like you're throwing a ball of shit." Their laughter is hard and cold.

Charlie isn't talking about seed bombs anymore. He has dug up an old shotgun loader from somewhere, and thanks to his private book collection culled from years of skimming library ban piles, he has a host of new lessons.

Your new assignments include shitting in buckets and then filling the buckets with water and your own piss. A pressure cap will keep it from exploding, but it makes your bathroom reek to high hell.

"It's great fertilizer," Charlie says, and some of the other students smile knowingly. The way they talk, the way they act, you are starting to wonder if there are other meetings taking place without you.

You visit vintage-themed restaurants and clean out their match bowls. Sulphur is an excellent fertilizer. You manage to collect a few grams of the yellow powder and are shocked to see your classmates show up with bricks of it.

One of them even pats you on the shoulder. "There's a good lad."

Charcoal is easy to get. In recent months, there have been widespread fires in some of the oldest districts of the city. People have died. It's easy to step under the police tape and pick your way past wet teddy bears and pictures of families. Charcoal, you can get by the pound.

You get used to the hand cramps caused by a mortar and pestle. Your classmates don't seem as interested in doing this so much as they are interested in pushing you to do more. Some classes, you spend all night grinding ingredients. You're too tired at the end of the night to throw seed bombs or work on isometrics. The tomatoes, sunflowers, and daisies are fading from your mind, like an old pack of tomato seeds scrounged from decaying urban neighbourhoods.

One night on your way to see Charlie and his guerilla gardeners, you catch word the old woman who wanted to make a tea garden out of a pothole is dead. Killed by a self-driving transport truck. The impact caused it to malfunction, and it drove for another twenty-two minutes with her trapped between the front bumper and axle. Police followed a three-foot wide blood streak on the road until they ended up in a Truth-mart parking lot. The source of the streak appeared to be about thirty pounds of ground beef with wisps of blue hair running through it.

Charlie is stoic about it. He assures you he is very disturbed. He shows it by giving the class a one-hour presentation on how much potassium nitrate, sulphur, and charcoal goes into a black powder mix, and how much of that mix should go into a shotgun shell. He talks about the best seeds to fill them with.

"Anything sort of round and hard. Use sunflower seeds if you can find 'em. Use apple seeds if that is possible. Hell, fill them with gravel and metal shavings. Point is, you need impact. You need stopping power."

The final straw comes when Charlie makes an announcement. "We're going to the museum. Keep people from their history, and they are easy to control. Pack a lunch."

There are many nods in agreement to this last line. You have no idea who said it. But Charlie pulled it from a book somewhere.

Everyone is carrying identical bags of flower shells. Everyone has identical black children's backpacks. There is little talking. The men in the class stand as one, they fill their pockets with shells as one. The rest are put into their backpacks. There is a flash of gunmetal in the backpack when one of the men nearly spills his seed shells on the floor.

You don't have any shells or backpacks. You feel like you missed another meeting. Sensing disappointment, Charlie puts an arm around your shoulder.

"I have something I really need you to do for me. Can I count on you?"

You're almost indignant in your response. The words are milkweed bitterness poisoning your mouth. Of course he can.

You're to drive a rental van to the Ministry of Compliance and leave it there so Charlie can pick it up later. You're to park in the front so he knows exactly where to find it. You're to do this by 1500 hours and no later than 1530 hours.

"What do I do then?"

Charlie hands you a little red book with no writing on the cover. "To each according to his needs."

You can do this. The truck is a big old gas pig with a heavy load. One of your new classmates tells you not to look in the back.

The road is slick black with rain and full of potholes. The roads of the inner city are filled with trash from vehicles flying above. Robots are supposed to keep these areas clean, but that only happens in the government quadrants. You roll the window down manually and let the wind and wet electrify you.

You pull into a space in front of the Ministry of Compliance. Mission complete. It's only 2:30. You have some time to kill. You grab the little red book and flip through the pages. You don't know much about communism, but you're not going to be able to say that for much longer.

You're neck deep in proletariat struggle when there is a knock on the door. It's Charlie, smiling at your success. His smile grows when he looks down at the book in your hands. "Right on time. I knew you were the perfect man for this job."

"Why am I here?"

"Walk with me," Charlie says, glancing at his watch. "Quickly."

You slide out of the seat into the wet cold of late afternoon. Charlie motions toward a bench across the street.

"Where are the other guys?"

Charlie doesn't look at you. His eyes bounce from the truck to his watch and back to the truck again.

He tells you how the other guys took their seed shells and their prison shotguns and got busy blasting their seed shells anywhere there was a chance a plant might take root.

"The guns sound like real guns," Charlie says. "The Authority converged at the museum. It was a perfect distraction."

You have no idea what is going on. But Charlie isn't looking at you. He is looking at his watch. He is looking at the truck.

"Remember what you said last year when I asked everyone what they wanted to accomplish?"

At first you don't. But then you do.

"Charlie? What's in the truck?"

Charlie looks at his watch. His teeth chatter from excitement more than cold. "That was a brave thing you said."

You put a hand on his shoulder and ask him again.

"A revolution," Charlie says.

Across the street, there is an eruption as the back of the truck peels open.

The boom that follows is swift and terrible. Ten pounds of gunpowder going off in a controlled area, erupting in a ball of fire that belches out of the back of the truck. *Straight up.*

The noise and shock of it knocks you on your ass. Charlie stays on his feet. The look on his face tells you he has been waiting for this moment for a very long time.

The eruption fires hundreds of pounds of seeds, soil, and boba into the air. Fifty stories at least. Farther than you can see.

Charlie's face is a mask of rain and fervent joy.

"*A revolution!*" he screams, his hands balled in fists over his head. Reaching into the sky. Trying to be one with the seed cloud that has just burst out of the back of the truck.

The revolution actually starts a few seconds later, when the rain turns to mud and boba and seeds. The mixture lands everywhere, painting everything brown. Seeds land in cracks on the pavement. They land in potholes filled with mud and water. They land on parked vehicles. They get in people's hair and their eyes. The explosion ruptures glass on several floors of the Ministry of Compliance, and the wind showers the shocked, confused people looking down on the scene in flower seeds, mud, and rain.

It is an act of terror. An act of whimsy. It is the most glorious thing you have ever seen.

"See?" Charlie says. "You weren't just driving a truck. You were planting a future for us."

Sirens have started up. Far away but getting closer. Charlie pulls on your sleeve.

Looking around, there is nothing but filth and wet. People walking around confused, like zombies, clutching their heads and holding shredded umbrellas.

But you don't see that. You see what the place will look like in a couple of weeks, when a massive, verdant carpet has erupted from the grey and neon, and the Ministry of Compliance becomes the biggest, greenest middle finger to The Authority this city has ever seen.

"Come on," Charlie says. "You have nothing to lose but your chains."

"We have a world to win," you say, finishing the line. You take one last look around and then turn to follow Charlie into whatever this new future holds.

THE CARD CATALOGUE

920 : Biographies

Shannon Allen is one of those rare breeds, a third generation Calgarian who recently took the step into the quiet life of small-town Alberta with her husband. Her journalism pieces appeared in Calgary Community Publications before turning to fiction. Her first work, "Confession", was published in *Enigma Front: Now Everything Changes*. Her work has also appeared in *Enigma Front: The Monster Within*, and *By the Light of Camelot*, a double Aurora Award-nominated anthology co-edited with JR Campbell. She has a work of poetry in the 2020 YYC Pop Portraits project run by Calgary Poet Laureate Sheri-D Wilson and Frontenac House. In 2023, *The Astronaut Always Rings Twice*, co-edited with Jeff Campbell, was awarded the 2023 Aurora Award for Best Related Work. Shannon is active in the writing community and the Suzy Vadori Inspired Writing team and is inspired by all the people she meets. Shannon is a member of the Imaginative Fiction Writers Assocaiton, Write On, Take 24, and the Canadian Science Fiction and Fantasy Association.

JR Campbell is a Calgary-based writer and anthologist. With co-editor Charles Prepolec, his anthologies include *Professor Challenger: New Worlds, Lost Places* and five volumes of the Sherlock Holmes *Gaslight* anthologies, thrusting the master rationalist into fantastic, often terrifying adventures. The latest of these is *Gaslight Ghouls: Uneasy Tales of Sherlock Holmes*.

With co-editor Shannon Allen, his anthologies include *By the Light of Camelot* and the Aurora Award-winning *The Astronaut Always Rings Twice*. A collection of his Sherlock Holmes short fiction is available from Weird House Press entitled: *Improbable Remains: The Bizarre and Unconventional Adventures of Sherlock Holmes*.

Mackensie Baker (she/they) grew up in British Columbia, mainly in the aisles of bookstores and libraries, as well as any suitable reading nook she could burrow into. Her writing has been published on Lifted Geek, Reality Skimming Press, Trembling With Fear, and in the 2019 WCSFA anthology *Power*. In addition, their self-published novella *In Her Shadow* can be found wherever ebooks are sold.

E. C. Bell is the author of the award-winning paranormal Marie Jenner Mystery series. She lives in Alberta, Canada, and when she's not writing, she's renovating her round house where she lives with her husband and the three feral cats that have taken up residence in her backyard.

That's right. Her house is round.

C.B. Hingston was born in Bangor, Wales, in the decade when a British Astronomer-Royal stated that the idea of manned spaceflight was "utter bilge". Happily, the guy was not fit-for-purpose.

Hingston moved to northern England, aged four. In his teen years, he became so addicted to science fiction that he had little time for A-level exams, which duly went over a cliff.

Jobs which followed included textile machinist, warehouseman, darkroom technician, and (in Jamaica, for three years in the '80s) librarian, and *ad hoc* teacher. Finally, he bit the bullet, went back to college in Bradford, Yorkshire, and studied engineering, going on to work in medical electronics for the National Health Service. This included a stint in the Falkland Islands' hospital, where make-do-and-mend was a challenge.

He now lives on the south coast, in Hampshire, with Jamaican-born wife Pearline, plus cats Basil and Zulu. Aside from SF, Hingston enjoys playing bass in a classic-rock band, and encouraging Cinnabar moths to flourish in a wild patch of the garden.

Robert Lauderdale calls Western Canada home and enjoys writing Sherlock Holmes and science fiction stories. His previous work has been included in *Gaslight Grotesque: Nightmare Tales of Sherlock Holmes.*

Trisha Jenn Loehr is a romance writer, developmental editor, and Author Accelerator certified book coach. She helps busy women who want to write romance novels without guilt or shame prioritize their writing, develop their craft, and find joy in the journey toward their publishing dreams.

Her writing can be found in places such as JaneFriedman.com, *Business Insider*, the *Calgary Herald*, Wicked Authors, and *Birthing Magazine.* She is currently writing two interconnected novels, a small-town enemies-to-lovers romance, and a reality tv show grumpy/sunshine romance.

With a decade of experience as a communications and events professional, she understands writing, marketing, the importance of identifying your audience, and the necessity of continually learning.

Along with her book coach certification and a whole host of other writing workshops and courses, Trisha holds a Bachelor of Arts in communications and professional writing with a minor in political science, a certificate in leadership and applied public affairs, and a certificate in dance performance preparation. (Yeah, it's a weird mix.) She is also mom to an angel boy in heaven and a sweet rainbow of a little girl who got to stay earthside and is an advocate for infertility and pregnancy loss awareness.

Nico Martinez Nocito (they/them) writes speculative fiction and poetry with a queer, feminist bent. Their work can be found in *Strange Horizons, Utopia Science Fiction*, and Flame Tree Press, and has been nominated for the Rhysling Award. Learn more about Nico and their writing on Bluesky and Instagram @nicowritesbooks, or on their website, nicomartineznocito.com.

Lesley Moody is what happens when a librarian, speculative fiction writer, and tabletop game nerd collide. She's been making up stories since she could talk and turning them into books like *Charred: An Adventure in Wonderland* and contributions to *Enigma Front* (2015). When she's not buried in fiction or library work, you'll find her conquering dungeons, building decks, or rolling for initiative.

Donna J. W. Munro taught high schoolers the slippery truths of government and history for twenty-five years. Her students are her greatest inspiration. She lives with five cats, a cute curly-haired dog, a fur-covered husband, and an encyclopedia son. Her daughter is off saving the world.

Donna's pieces are published in *Corvid Queen, It Calls from the Forest, Apparition Lit, Pseudopod 752, Shakespeare Unleashed, Novus Monstrum, ParABnormal*, and many more. Check out her novels, *Revelation: Poppet Cycle Book 1, Runaway: PCB2*, and *Revolution: PCB3*. Her first collection, *Dark Workings of Wild Women*, came out May 2025. Her website has a complete list of works at https://www.donnajwmunro.net/.

Aggie Novak lives with her wife by the beach in Australia, where she spends most of her time hiding from the sun and heat. She writes around studying for her pharmacy degree and entertaining her two dogs. She loves all kinds of speculative fiction and often draws inspiration from Slavic folklore and mythology. When not writing she can be found drinking tea and reading everything in sight. Her published works can be found in *Hexagon*, Flash Fiction Online, and more! For the full list see http://aggienovak.com

R. Overwater is a longtime Calgary-based author and comic creator. His crime stories and speculative fiction are available in a number of anthologies and novels. His graphic novel, *Futility: Orange Planet Horror* was nominated for a 2019 Aurora Award in the Canadian Science Fiction and Fantasy Association's Best Graphic Novel category. Rick holds a Bachelor's Degree in Broadcast Studies from Gonzaga University and a Master's Degree in Creative Writing from the University of British Columbia. He likes long naps and short sentences.

When she is not tumbling rocks, playing D&D, or cheering on the

Edmonton Oilers, **Rhonda Parrish** is creating shiny new poems and stories. She hoards them, like a magpie dragon, at https://www.patreon.com/RhondaParrish—the only place in the multiverse many of them can be found.

Kara Race-Moore studied history at Simmons College as an excuse to read about the soap opera lives of British royals. She worked in educational publishing, casting the molds for future generations' minds, but has since moved into the more civilized world of litigation. Ms. Race-Moore has written and published several short stories in a number of genres, including Steampunk, Science Fiction, Horror, and Fantasy. She currently lives in Los Angeles, the land where fact and fiction tend to blur. She can be found at: https://kararacemoore.wordpress.com/

Jennifer Rahn is the author of four novels and eleven short stories in the genres of science fiction and fantasy. The novels were originally published by Dragon Moon Press and Bundoran Press, but have since been revised and reissued through her own imprint, Deadeye Bookcraft. The short stories have appeared in the Tesseracts anthologies and the Aurora Award-winning *Blood & Water* anthology. When not writing, she works as a cancer research scientist in Calgary. She enjoys crafting, gardening, gaming, and hiking. Her favourite colours are purple and green, and her favourite authors include Dean Koontz, Joan D. Vinge, and Tanith Lee.

J.W. Schnarr is a former award-winning journalist and photographer from Alberta, Canada. He's the author of two novels, two short story collections, and editor of three anthologies. His fiction has appeared in *Imaginarium: The Best Canadian Speculative Writing* and the Aurora Award–winning *The Astronaut Always Rings Twice.*

He also writes original Dungeons & Dragons 5e adventures, including The Amberblight Quintet, a dark fantasy series exploring ancient elven magic and corruption.

He enjoys reading, music, and collecting guitars. Find more at jwschnarr.com.

Lisa Timpf's work experience has ranged from human resources and corporate communications to farm labor and stints as a sportswriter and an assembly line worker. A graduate of McMaster University's Physical Education program, Lisa also took several English and philosophy courses while attending university. Her work and life experiences, as well as her interest in nature, pets, and science, often find their way into her writing.

Lisa's speculative fiction has been published in a number of anthologies, magazines, and zines, including *This is Your Bike on Plants, To Every Dog His Day, Electric Spec,* and *Home for the Howlidays.* When not writing, Lisa enjoys bird-watching, organic gardening, and walking her cocker spaniel-Jack Russell mix, Chet. You can learn more about Lisa's poetry, fiction, reviews, articles, and artwork at lisatimpf.blogspot.com. Lisa is also on Bluesky at lisatimpf.bsky.social.

Liz Westbrook-Trenholm, a retired federal public servant, has written in a variety of genres and forms over time. Most recently, she has published, republished or been translated in *Neo-Opsis, On Spec, Solaris,* and *Year's Best Canadian Science Fiction and Fantasy, Volume 1.* She won the Prix Aurora Award for short fiction in 2018 and has been nominated three times since. She lives in Ottawa with her husband, Hayden Trenholm.

C.N. Wheaton is lucky enough to live within walking distance of a library, thus fulfilling a lifelong dream. When she isn't playing around in fictional worlds, C.N. Wheaton can often be found teaching science to semi-reluctant teens. Her short fiction has appeared in *The Fairy Tale Magazine,* the *Queens in Wonderland* anthology from No Bad Books Press, and *The Initialization of Briar Rose* anthology from Manawaker Studios among others. You can connect with her on her website: cnwheaton.wordpress.com

Kayla Whittle has previously had short stories published in *Uncharted Magazine* and *The Colored Lens.* She also has stories in several anthologies including *Lesbians in Space* (Space Wizard Science Fantasy), *Beyond the Veil* (Ghost Orchid Press), and *Nightmare Diaries* (Moonstruck Books), as well as *Dangerous Waters, Daughter of Sarpedon,* and *Seers and*

Sibyls, all out with Brigids Gate Press. Her work has been featured on Flash Fiction Podcast. Most often she can be found on Instagram @caughtbetweenthepages.